MY 15 MINUTES

MY 15 MINUTES

Sara Faith Alterman

AVON
TRADE

An Imprint of HarperCollinsPublishers

HarperCollins books may be purchased for educational, business, or sales promotional use. For information please write: Special Markets Department, HarperCollins Publishers Inc., 10 East 53rd Street, New York, NY 10022.

FIRST EDITION

Interior text designed by Elizabeth M. Glover

Library of Congress Cataloging-in-Publication Data

Alterman, Sara Faith.
  My 15 minutes / by Sara Faith Alterman.—1st ed.
    p. cm.
ISBN-13: 978-0-06-075591-1
ISBN-10: 0-06-075591-1
1. Motion picture actors and actresses—Fiction. 2. Apartment houses—Fiction.
3. Celebrities—Fiction. 4. Waitress—Fiction. 5. Fame—Fiction.
I. Title: My fifteen minutes. II. Title.

PS3601.L825M9 2005
813'.6—dc22   2005001803

05 06 07 08 09 JTC/RRD 10 9 8 7 6 5 4 3 2 1

For my girls Becky Girolamo and Julie Jordan

Special thanks to Stacey Glick
for being a terrific agent and invaluable guide.

I am enormously grateful to Lucia Macro and Kelly Harms
for their hard work, endless patience, and fantastically fun attitudes.
Thanks, ladies!

Thanks to my guru, Eugénie Seifer Olson,
and to Sydney Urbach for being excited about this book
since the day I wrote my first page.

Mom and Dad, I can't possibly thank you enough
for your support and encouragement.
I'm on my way, thanks to you. I love you.

Last, but not least, thanks to the bro Dan
for keepin' it real.

MY 15 MINUTES

 **One**

"Grab that leg, Dan!"

"I can't, dude, she's moving it around!"

"Wait . . . watch out! It's slipping!"

"Oh, for Christ's sake, can't you just hold still?"

It was nine-thirty on a sparkling California Tuesday, and I was sweating desperately, anxious to get this over with as quickly as possible.

My couch was being a bitch.

I guess I'd be one, too, if two clueless guys and a frizzy haired woman were trying to shove me up a flight of stairs. Especially if one of the guys smelled as strongly of pastrami as Daniel did.

My name is Julie Jorlamo, and I've just promoted myself from a shelter mooching couch crasher to a status that's a little more comfortable. My new apartment is in Los Angeles. It seems cliché to shack up with friends in L.A. in order to scrape together enough cash for an apartment, but here's the twist: I actually grew up here. No soul searching, westward journey for me. I'm not corn-fed, not an aspiring actress, and certainly not looking to get addicted to smack. I'm simply too lazy to bother starting over in a new place.

To further the stereotype, I do have a large chest and

work as a waitress, but the boobs are real and the job is temporary. I hope. I did go to college; the problem being that I majored in liberal arts and beer. I had imagined a postacademia life of coffeehouses and freelancing, of dancing my pinkie across a keyboard and procuring $10,000 advances on volumes destined to become international classics. Not having earned a degree in sorcery, alchemy, or gold digging, however, I have been unable to realize this dream of instantaneous cash flow. At least my hooters are big enough to warrant some generous tips, which generally accompany a pinch on my ass.

At the moment, that ass was squished against a wall in a narrow stairwell.

"Daaaan!" I whined. "You have to push. You can't just stand there holding the couch and expect me to pull the whole thing up!"

Dan is my mild-mannered brother. He had agreed to help me move if I bought him groceries for a week. He'd brought along his friend, Hoff (real name a mystery), who, thankfully, was built like a linebacker.

"Julie." Dan grunted, straining under the weight of my pink velvet Salvation Army couch. "What number is your place?"

"Um . . ." I flattened myself even closer to the wall and shimmied a hand down my pocket. "It's 4C," I panted, squinting at the tiny scrap of paper fished from the depths of my Levi's.

He dropped his end of the couch.

"*Julie.* We've gone up *five* flights of stairs!"

Oops.

Forty-five minutes and a great deal of wiggling and straining later, we'd managed to backtrack the couch and force it through the front door, into my humble living room.

The whole place was humble, actually, a cookie cutter rental. Minuscule kitchen to the immediate left, with a cutout in the wall that peered into the living/dining area. Oblong bathroom, pink toilet, mustard tile. One bedroom, sliding door closet, beige shag carpet. Waiting for me on the kitchen counter was a parking permit and the bright pink steering wheel club that my landlord, Al, had proudly offered when I signed the lease. ("Pink for the ladies, blue for the men!" he'd crowed. "They're complimentary! I'm the only landlord in town who gives a shit about my tenants' cars!") The apartment itself was sort of grim, but I didn't care. It was mine.

I'd spent the last two months playing houseguest in my best friend Billie's studio apartment, perched unabashedly above the Batik Boutique on Rodeo Drive. It was a cushy place, though a month of rent could have easily taken nine thousand Polynesian orphans off Sally Struthers's hands. It had been fun for a while, strutting amongst celebrity consumers, reveling in the surrounding glamour, but living out of a duffel bag leaves something to be desired. And, as much as I treasure Billie's friendship, I was ready to kill her after six days, when I discovered that her preferred method of housekeeping was to allow filth to accumulate in gigantic proportions until I would finally break down and clean up her mess. She's one of those people who buys new underwear instead of doing laundry. Maddening. Obnoxious. But that's just Billie.

Billie is my dearest friend. We met in eleventh grade, in the woods behind school, after I had sprinted, humiliated, from third period math class. It was April, the season of crowning glory for pollen, and it seems my allergies had planted a booger squarely between my miserable left nostril and my twitching, bloodshot eye. Thanks to Adam

Sharpton for pointing that out to every jock in the third row. Asshole.

So, I bolted. First to the girls' room down the hall, where I scrubbed my face and bombarded my helpless reflection with insults. After I collected myself, I grabbed my Esprit bag from my locker and took off through a fire exit, marching away from that teenage hellhole into the forest, to sit on a log in peace and console myself with a Chunky bar.

I had a mouthful of raisins and chocolate when—

"Are you a fucking narc?" came a scratchy voice from above me. I almost peed myself.

"Jesus . . . Jesus!" I sputtered, trying not to choke on the brick of chocolate in my mouth. "You scared me!"

There in front of me, head cocked and gum cracking, stood the most spectacularly adorned girl I had ever seen. Eat your heart out, Cyndi Lauper; this girl had layered three pairs of colored socks over electric blue fishnets, over which she wore pink denim shorts. Her cropped, off-the-shoulder top was festooned with safety pins, and her electrocuted hair, blond at the roots, was from her ears down dyed a magnificent tomato red. It was as though she had stumbled haplessly into the path of Rainbow Brite's projectile vomit. Keep in mind, it was 1993, charter year for Seattle grunge.

She looked me up and down, smirking at my pegged chinos and rolled socks. Finally, satisfied that I wasn't harboring a badge or cattle prod, she lifted a cigarette to her orange lips and took a deep drag.

"Naw, you look like a pansy who just ran sobbing out of class," she sneered, exhaling an impressive cloud of smoke directly into my face.

I turned away, coughing and choking on carcinogen and tears. I was a pretty shy kid, and normally I didn't protest when the cheerleaders snapped my bra or taped tampons to my locker. Something about the course of events that day, however, had driven me beyond the edge of reason.

"Don't," I sniveled, desperate to summon some courage.

She peered at me and puffed again. "Don't what?" she asked, her lips spewing thick gray clouds with every syllable.

I took a deep breath. "Don't . . ." I stammered. "Don't blow smoke. Don't blow smoke in *my fucking face!!!*" I finished with a bellow.

Ha!

She blinked.

For a second I preened like an Olympian, but my satisfaction faded when I realized that this girl was wearing brass knuckles and had a safety pin shoved through the flesh between her thumb and forefinger.

Shit.

I stared at her for a moment, knees locked, armpits damp enough to breed gators. I was reaching for my backpack when she broke into a grin.

"I'm Billie," she laughed, stomping out her cigarette.

It still surprises me that we ended up as friends, since we were brought up so differently. My parents are about as square as you can get. My dad, Eli, is a Jew who somehow ended up with an Italian last name. He teaches American history at my old private school, coaches Little League on the weekends. Bonnie, my mom, is a recovering Southern Baptist who tries to be Jewish, but she's too afraid of God and my grandma. Instead, she calls me "Bubbie," and wears the same gigantic orange reading glasses owned by half of Long Island.

I look more like my father's side of the family, who all

have thirty pounds of brown curls and round birthing hips. Puberty hit me like a Louisville Slugger when I was thirteen; it took me most of high school to learn how to tame my wild mane and generous chest. Nobody could believe that I was related to Dan, who fell naturally into the role of unattainable heartthrob. He came out blond and tan, a musical genius with soulful eyes.

All in all, we were a typical American family; lived in a decent house on a nondescript cul-de-sac, normal neighbors, no perverts. We took nice vacations together, visited the relatives faithfully. Had I grown up anyplace else, I would probably have been normal, maybe even cute. Mom used to tell me that I should have been an East Coaster, with my raven hair and extra fair skin. It still confuses me that she would choose to root the family in the heart of Los Angeles, a middle-class brunette's worst nightmare.

Blond. Skinny. Rich. Stylish. These were, apparently, the mandatory characteristics for attending Brownstone Academy, a private Beverly Hills high school favored by elitist California parents. Believe me, if Dad hadn't taught there, I would have been just fine struggling to fit in at P.S. 108. At least there I would have had a fighting chance. Instead, I had to skulk around a campus peppered with celebrity offspring and teenage computer moguls.

Since I wasn't allowed to dye my hair or showcase my boobs, I was pretty miserable. Meeting Billie was definitely a turning point. Her parents were loaded, too, and totally exotic in an artsy, airhead kind of way. Before she transferred into Brownstone, Billie had spent the last five years living on a yacht, sailing around the world with her weirdo family.

She was born "Alice Schuster," thusly christened to pay homage to her parents' favorite song by their then-obsession, Jefferson Airplane. However, her name was legally changed to Billie Jean in 1982, when Michael Jackson's "Thriller" assaulted the airways. Her parents were unusual people. Although a penchant for suede monopolized her wardrobe, Billie's mother Janaki had been a strict vegetarian since 1968 ("Before it was the trend, girls!" she would often crow. "I was cutting edge!"). Obsessed with junk food and candy, yet attempting to mask an eating disorder, she took to renaming household objects after her fervent culinary longings. She actually took it one step further and had Billie's last name legally changed to Twix before her husband intervened and dragged her off to therapy. Dad was another story; he weighed in, soaking wet, at 142 pounds, yet insisted that everyone, Billie included, refer to him as "Big Bob."

It's remarkable that Billie didn't rebel by cutting her hair in a pageboy and developing an affinity for sweater vests; instead, she became a ghetto glamazon, often donning Jackie O sunglasses to accompany her vintage rock tank tops and acid-washed camouflage miniskirts.

Billie's like a walking advertisement for any and all trends of the 1980s. Inspired by her namesake, I guess, she seems to feel it's her duty to represent the decade in all manner of dress, culture, and slang. And man, does she drive it home, staying true to her school of dated pop culture.

She smoked enough to rival four inmates; incredibly, she was an all-star tennis player in high school, and actually convinced the coach to let her smoke while playing. She argued that the heat from the game counteracted the searing nicotine to produce a euphoric buzz, thusly encouraging her to push herself to the limit and seize the game. If you ask me, it was emphysema battling heatstroke for the win.

Really, the only thing about Billie that has changed since high school is her brand of cigarettes. No longer Lucky Strikes, she has fortified her nicotine diet with a filter. Needless to say, her lips have harbored more tobacco than the state of North Carolina.

After we graduated, I took the traditional route (four year college, failed endeavors in human resources, general discontentment), while she opted for pottery classes, a brief affair with a tai chi instructor, and the occasional gig as a nude model for local art classes. As for permanent work, she tells everyone that she works in film production, but only I know the truth; that she's a boom operator for a municipal cable station in Pacific Palisades.

We've remained close, but her absence from my morning routine will definitely make my heart grow fonder. I guess I enjoyed living with her, but there's only so many times a girl can wake up at seven A.M. to ear-shattering Oingo Boingo before she's ready to close the window on her head.

I finally managed to save up enough for two months' rent, working endless shifts at Junebugs, a nondescript chain restaurant of the "suspenders and flair" variety. It pays the bills. I packed my shit.

I have even inherited a dog. Dan rescued a tiny yapper from a Dumpster a year or so back. He was thrilled about his new buddy, until proper nutrition set the pup on its natural growth track. The vet estimated it to be half pit bull, half rottweiler. Fast approaching 120 pounds, with paws the size of T-bones, Riley can best be described as a barking moose that can do tricks.

Dan managed to hide the dog from the landlord for almost a year, until Riley took a tremendous shit in the living room on a scorching August day. Unfortunately, at the time, Dan was out playing congas at an all day emo punk festival. Neighbors complained, suspicions arose. Faced with eviction from the only rent-controlled apartment within a three-hundred-mile radius, Dan made a desperate phone call to a weak-willed sucker. It's nice having a four-legged bodyguard, but the dog eats more in a day than I do in a week.

By seven o'clock my new roommate was gnawing happily on the remote control, while Dan, Hoff, and I hauled the remainder of my haphazardly packed boxes up those horrible stairs. By the time the sun was drooping, we were all starving. I sent the guys down the street to pick up takeout while I dragged my last box out of the sagging rental truck.

Apparently, Scotch tape doesn't work so well as a packing accessory, because I didn't get five paces from the truck before the bottom gave out and miscellaneous trinkets exploded onto the sidewalk.

"Damnit!" I cried. "Damnit, damnit, shit, shit, damnit!" There was crap everywhere. Not being terribly organized, I had used a sort of "wad and stuff" method when I packed. Therefore, the sidewalk was littered with scrabble tiles, pot holders, two ashtrays, thong panties, a stapler, oregano, teabags, DVDs, a potato masher, tampons, and two and a half pounds of chocolate-covered peanuts.

I tipped my head back and groaned, then dropped to my knees to collect the hodgepodge. I had a handful of cotton butt floss when a shadow loomed before me.

"Can you believe this, Dan?" I whined. "Help me so I can eat my cheese fries before they're cold."

"Wow." A fluid baritone coated my ears with honey. "I hope you didn't actually pay someone to move you."

It was clearly not my brother. I swiveled to see who the voice belonged to. A gorgeous neighbor, perhaps? A lonely studio dweller looking for a playmate?

His face was partially obscured by the citrus dregs of sunlight, but when I shielded my eyes I could tell he was, in fact, adorable. The silhouette of his face was nicely chiseled, and his hair was short and messy. No wedding ring. No worries. I flipped my hair, dropping my ragged underthings behind me in an attempt to be smooth. All cool was lost when I got a good look at him.

Two

"Chad Downing!?" Billie crowed. "Chad *Downing* was outside your new building?"

Her voice pierced my ear like a jewelry store sales clerk. I pulled the phone away until the shrill yelps of incredulity tapered off into mumbled "Wowwwws!" Not that my reaction had been any different at first.

As I crouched over the mess on the sidewalk, and realized who the handsome stranger was, I was completely helpless, rendered mute by my awe and desire. The sun had slipped behind a cloud, offering me an unhampered view of the man who loomed above me. Only then did I recognize him. His face had launched a thousand premieres, websites and tabloids were stuffed with his likeness in the manner of a Thanksgiving turkey; yummy little bits and pieces spilling out all over the place. He was every woman's wet dream, every frat boy's hero, and he was frowning at my belongings like a sack of grubs had spilled onto his Gucci loafers.

Chad Downing, it was.

"I couldn't even say anything!" I gushed into the phone. "It was like—like he cast a spell on me, and all I could do was nod my head. It was awesome! . . . It was terrible."

Chad Downing is a big movie star, the sexiest man on the silver screen since James Dean bit the dust. A celebrity with staying power, he'd been a child commercial star before bursting out of puberty like Bavarian crème from a Sunday cruller. Women adored him, dedicating songs and children and panties to his essence in cultlike fashion. And here I was, schlumped on the pavement, Crouching Loser, Hidden Dignity.

"Need a hand?" he'd asked, smirking at the handful of peanuts wedged beneath his shoes.

"Oh," I stuttered, "oh, uh, yeah. Yeah, that would be great. I'm such a klutz. I'm, um, wow. Wow. You're, uh, you're . . ."

"Late, unfortunately," he finished, casually checking his Rolex and flipping a cigarette into his gorgeous lips. "Or I'd help you out. But you can probably handle this. You look pretty, uh, tough."

Yeah, I guess shabby black overalls and a toothpick hanging from your mouth does radiate "tough." Or, at the very least, rabid man-hating bulldog.

"No, that's okay." I breathed. "I'm okay. You go. I'm okay. Okay?"

Aaaaaand, I'd blown it. But could you blame me for crumbling in the presence of such splendor?

"Greeeat." He raised his eyebrows at me. "Well . . . you must be new in town. Let me guess. Aspiring actress? No, probably . . . screenwriter. Working as a production assistant? Wait, are you a tour guide at Universal?"

"No, no." I shook my head, still clutching a renegade pair of skivvies that wouldn't release itself from my grasp. "I'm Julie. I'm a waitress."

"Of course you are, sweetheart." He smiled. "Well, gotta dash. Welcome to the big time, honey. Ciao."

He spun on his heel and left me panting on the sidewalk.

His head bobbed in time to a personal soundtrack as he made his way to an orange Hummer loitering in a fire lane. I sat back on my heels and farted.

"So that's it?" Billie shrieked. "No autograph, no lock of hair? No abandoned tissue, or cigarette butt?"

"Billie," I groaned into the receiver, "he's not a Beatle. Besides, I had no pen, my scissors landed in the gutter, he was still smoking it, and he wasn't sniffling."

"Well, what in the fuck was he doing in your crummy-ass neighborhood? Was he lost? Maybe you should have offered to escort him back to his mansion. Maybe he saw you on the street and thought he'd make his move on a damsel in distress. Why didn't you throw yourself at him, you dumb cow?"

"Hmmm, let's see . . . why didn't I throw myself at the hottest man on the planet? Probably because I'm not a coked-up super blonde. Probably because my hairstyle didn't cost as much as my handbag. Probably because I would have been *rejected*. But not only would I have been rejected, but then I would have had to relive said rejection when Chad Downing giggled about it on late night TV next week. 'And *then* McTubby tried to pull down a strap of her overalls and make me grab her tetherball boobs! Can you believe the gall of some of these hood rats?' Really Billie, I don't know what I was thinking."

I could hear her taking a deep drag off her cigarette as she mulled my stupidity.

"We need a rehash session," she sighed. "I'm on my way."

When she showed up, I had already killed a pint of Mocha Moocow ice cream and all hopes for fulfilling a celebrity relationship fantasy.

I knew Billie had arrived when I caught a whiff of the sweet raisin odor of freshly packed Marlboros.

"Jesus," she wheezed when I opened the door, "could you—*caaaaannnch*—live any higher up? *Caaaaaaaaaaaauuunch*—I need to catch my—*caaaaunnch*—breath."

"Billie, I only live on the fourth floor. Maybe it's time to quit when you start to cough like a goose in heat?"

Death glare.

"Fuck you—*wheeeeze*—bitch. Now tell me about Chad."

"Not here. I need to booze for this one."

"Fine. *Caaaaaauuunch*. Let's go to Murphy's. It's right—*cccaaaunch*—up the street."

"Do you want to catch your breath first?"

"Yeah—*caaaaaauuunch*—that'd be good. Do you have any—*caaaaaauuunch*—food?"

"Billie, I just moved in a few hours ago. Besides, I doubt I would have anything you'd eat, anyway."

"*Caaaaaauuuunnnch*—that's true."

Billie's eating habits are just as quirky as her personality, as unabashed as her wardrobe. Maybe they developed as a result of being raised by a junk food junkie, maybe it was the vegan thing. But she's very . . . picky. Is picky the right word? Normally, picky people only eat grilled cheese and pancakes; you know, uncomplicated kid foods like that.

Naturally, Billie struts to the whirl of her own food processor.

Her diet consists of a strict hodgepodge of culinary "delights," mostly limited to stinky vegetables and processed food items that, in their natural state, should really be refrigerated. Her favorite combo? Brussels sprouts and cheese in a can. That's right. As a meal. No butter, no salt and pepper, no crackers or toast or extraneous items to gussy anything up. Cheese in a can gets squirted directly into the mouth, brussels sprouts get boiled until they smell like feet, strained, then tossed into the air and gobbled in the manner of movie popcorn.

She was a hellish high school sleepover guest, let me tell ya.

I, of course, will eat anything you put in front of me (or anyone else, for that matter. I'm pretty sneaky), but that's not a big deal. We had other things in common.

Such as lusting after pretty boys on the television.

I think I was seven when my monster crush sprouted, while Dan and I were watching *Gimme a Break* after dinner. During a commercial, I was dyeing my Barbie's hair with a Magic Marker when I heard a familiar tinkling noise. I looked up at the TV, and lo and behold, it was that little fairy from Peter Pan! She perched her cartoon self on the shoulder of a little boy hawking toilet paper, and my heart stopped. It was Chad, fresh as a cute little daisy with a shiny bowl haircut and enormous Play-Doh eyes. You could say we came of age together; he enjoyed a phenomenal run as Tinkerbell toilet tissue's spokesman for almost ten years, fuel for the obsessive teenage fire. His commercials sparked a consumer phenomenon when sales hit the roof in the thirteen-to-nineteen age bracket. Little girls from Tuscaloosa to Beaverton were desperate to wipe their asses with a little piece of Chad. At sixteen he graduated to the silver screen, and I was a total sucker. I gobbled up every scrap of information I could get my fat little hands on. *Tiger Beat, Sixteen, Bop, Big Bopper, Wap-bap-a-loo-Bop*; his beautiful face was everywhere.

Unfortunately, my mom was a recovering Baptist Bible thumper ("Worship God, not a boy! Boys are the devil! Have a graham cracker!"), so I wasn't allowed to keep the monster Trapper Keeper scrapbooks that my friends pulled out at sleepovers. Instead, I pulled some drastic girl crimes, smuggling my beloved magazines into the house via math books, keeping tiny cutouts of my darling taped to the back of posters that Mom ordered from the library. You know the ones: milk-whiskered kitties sliding down yardsticks and sleeping in teacups.

It was a girlhood crush that stuck around, and still doggie paddles to the surface whenever I see him in a movie. It's so stupid, but I can't help it, he's the perfect man. He's hot, he's charming, and I can mute him whenever I want.

"Christ, I don't believe this!" Billie yowled, jolting me from my thoughts.

I shook my head. "What? What? What's the problem?"

"Some asshole is parked in the street and I'm fucking blocked in! Shit, I don't belieeeeve this! Do you know how long it took me to parallel park?"

Her beat up Volkswagen Rabbit was squeezed in between two Chevys. And she was right, someone had decided to bypass the hassle of scouring for parking and had simply parked *next* to her, blocking a lane of traffic and keeping us from making the tail end of happy hour.

Someone who drove an orange Hummer.

"Oh my . . . ohmigod, Billie! Billie! That's him, that's his car!"

"What? Who? Whose car?"

"Billie, that's the car that Chad Downing got into today. That Hummer! Ohmigod, he's here. He's here! Where is he?"

I primped frantically while Billie artfully reached into her Punky Brewster halter top and adjusted her boobs. She sucked on her cigarette and pursed her lips.

"Okay, Julie, just play it cool, low-key, you dig?"

"Listen, Sammy Davis," I hissed, "I can barely breathe,

much less play your Rat Pack charades. Stop trying to act like a fucking beatnik and just figure out how we can find him!"

She glanced at me, then at the Hummer.

"Well," she mused, "I'll need to know his license plate number if I want to report him for parking violations."

"Billie," I warned, "what are you doing?"

Billie smiled, and casually wandered over to the Hummer.

"Nice wheels," she said. "How many Oscar winners do you think he's porked in this backseat?"

She circled the car slowly, pausing to flip off a Mexican passerby who yelled something about her chi-chis.

"Maybe he's here looking for you?" she continued. "Maybe he felt so bad about ditching you before that he came back, and he's wandering your building trying to find you and apologize!"

"He didn't look like he felt too bad. Maybe he dropped something while he was here? Maybe he's really a perv, and he's hoping I left some panties on the sidewalk? Maybe his grandmother lives around here?"

Billie suddenly broke into a grin. "Or maybe," she chuckled slyly, "*he* does."

"Billie, that makes absolutely no sense whatsoever. We're talking about Cha—"

"*Shhhhhh!!!* Dude! He could be listening! He could be right around the corner, *right now*! Don't say his name! *Never say his name!*"

"Fine, sorry. We're talking about, er, someone rich and famous, here. Someone who can clearly afford to live in a better neighborhood than I can. Someone who could *buy* my neighborhood. There's no way, no mothafucking way, that he lives around here!"

Billie's grin widened.

"*Au contraire*, my little potato. Look at this, Jule," she yelped, pointing to the Hummer's back window. "Would you fucking look at this? He's got the same parking sticker that the landlord gave you today. The same resident parking sticker. He lives in your neighborhood."

It was my turn to make weird animal noises. I tried to speak, but it came out sounding like a monkey fighting for the last banana.

"Holy shit, Julie! Come here, you *have* to come here! I don't fucking believe this!"

"What? What?"

She pointed to the front seat. I made sure nobody was watching, crept over to the Hummer and peered in. The steering wheel was locked with a baby blue club.

"He lives in your building." Billie smiled.

Caaaauuunnnnggghhh!

 # Three

I woke up this morning with a head full of grapes, the breath of Joe Camel, and a rekindled, teenlike obsession with my famous neighbor.

Billie and I ended up walking to the bar last night and stayed out way too late, rehashing my unbelievable luck over bottles of merlot and endless cigarettes.

"It's fuckin' destiny," Billie had slurred, pointing dangerously close to my face with her cigarette. "A fucking Hollywood star fucking lives in your fucking building, dude. I say, show up at the door naked."

I glanced down at the two fat rolls stacked like inner tubes above my waistband.

"Dude," she nodded conspiratorially, "just bring a six pack, too."

I was impressed with myself when I awoke to my alarm, until I realized that I had been hitting snooze in my sleep for half an hour. Late again. Shocker. Not that I care, anyway.

Waiting tables is definitely not my dream career; it's more like a nightmare, actually. My feet hurt, my nails are broken, I constantly reek of marinara sauce, and I have to pay for everything with dollar bills. I get a lot of accusatory "Oooh, ho-bag stripper" glares. Especially from my mom.

I waitressed my way through college, tolerating ass grabbing and lousy tips with the hopes of a better future for my troubles. It's a thankless labor, a lesson in human relations proctored by the devil in a lecture hall deep within the bowels of hell.

Try as I might, however, I've been unsuccessful in getting the fuck away from it.

There's an aura to the restaurant business that functions as magnetic force. It's like those invisible dog fences: you spend days running around in circles, waiting for someone to throw you the bone that's never big enough to satisfy. You soon tire of the monotony, and sprint full force for the hills, only to get zapped the instant you cross into free terrain. It's Pavlovian torture; eventually you're psychologically conditioned. You stop trying to get away, and face your fate, tail dangling between your legs.

I have more in common with Riley than I care to admit. Let's face it: I basically play fetch for two dollars an hour.

The restaurant of late is called Junebugs, a corporate monstrosity of the "flare" variety. My uniform is a green and white striped shirt with insects dancing across my breasts, worn over green elflike leggings. Add the sparkly headband with bobbly bug antennae, and I look like a dance recital gone horribly wrong. My boss is a pervert, my coworkers are bitter lifers, and yet I continue to show up every morning.

I took the job out of desperation. After college, I spent nearly two years "living" (i.e., surviving) in Boston, holed up in a crappy studio in Central Square. Let me tell you, nineteen months of temping and starving are about all a girl can handle. I couldn't afford food, I couldn't afford beer, I couldn't afford to get laid because even cheapo roulette condoms were three bucks a pack. To boot, I was terribly lonely. Bostonians are reluctant to accept outsiders. They're a tough breed of people, having spent years developing a protective spiny shell to shelter them from urban hardship. Unfortunately, as I came to discover, underneath the shell of most lies a core made of iron spikes. My only regular conversation was with Veteran Joe, a homeless man who collected soda cans from the Dumpster outside my building. Got any change today, pretty girlie? Not today, Veteran Joe. Well, shit, when you win the lottery, you know where to find me, sugar buns. I sure do, Veteran Joe.

I guess Billie was sick of my maudlin phone calls (free long distance access when I temped at Arthur Andersen, until they traced $300 to my cubicle and fired me on the spot), because one Saturday morning she showed up on my doorstep with a roll of packing tape and a first class plane ticket to LAX. We gave my air mattress to Veteran Joe and drank Bloody Marys until the stewardess ran out of vodka.

Living on her couch was great at first, but Billie is one of those people that's like your favorite food. Take quesadillas, for example. For a little while you can't get enough of the quesadilla, you're eating it at every meal, you exclude all other options in favor of consuming delightfully crispy, cheesy wedges. Then, abruptly, the passion fades into overkill. Suddenly, you're desperate for variety, kicking yourself for filling your refrigerator with tortillas and pico de gallo. You move on for a while, relinquishing the quesadilla to a food which bores your palate and turns your stomach. But you never completely wean yourself from the quesadilla. The allure is too enticing. You start to order it in restaurants again. The partnership is renewed.

That about sums it up with Billie. I adore her friendship, spend every waking second with her while I'm on the kick.

And then I need to get away, just to remind myself why I'm so drawn to her in the first place.

Moving into my own place seemed like a logical option, and I needed the cash, fast. The one good thing about waiting tables is that you can put the green stuff in your pocket at the end of each shift, without having to wait two weeks for one lump sum paycheck. And any asshole can do it, which was basically my motivation.

Since I'm not a peroxide twig with chicken legs and Bambi eyes, Spago, The Ivy, and Planet Hollywood (!) laughed in my face when I tried to fill out applications. Junebugs was the first place that called, so I took it, completely oblivious to what lay in store.

The repugnance of my job is enhanced by the creatures that lurk about, posing as coworkers. Leading the freak parade is Stuart Simpkins, the general manager with a superior smirk, an effeminate lisp, and a raging case of penis envy. He slimes about the restaurant at a towering five-foot-four, his beer gut bouncing in time to the comb-over flapping gently against his flaky scalp. He talks to the staff like we're zoo exhibits, but it's hard to take him seriously when he tells you you're "puthing it."

Flunky to the troll is Kylie, Grand High Priestess of the Junebugs franchise. Kylie has been a waitress since she was old enough to count change, and she'll be with this restaurant until the world is usurped by robots, rendering food obsolete. She's a loud-mouthed, bitter know-it-all, one of those people who'll yap in your face about restaurant policy and food presentation. I started to actively hate her the time she grabbed me by the elbow when I was taking food to a table and bitched at me for garnishing my plate incorrectly. She moved the kale to "three o'clock" and moved me to a new level of passive-aggressive hatred.

You can't even sneak into the place a few minutes late, because the damned time clock won't let you punch in unless you're on the nose. Usually, I have to skulk into Stuart's office and offer some half-baked excuse about traffic or car trouble before I'm on the clock and ready to start my shift. Today was no exception.

This time Stuart was waiting by the staff entrance, the back door of the kitchen, probably to head me off before I snuck into the bathroom and pretended to have been in there getting changed.

"Nith try, Mith Jorlamo," he smirked, "but we all know you haven't been in the bathroom for twenty minuteth.

"Why tho ditheveled?" he continued, looking me up and down with the eyes of a vulture. "Get a pieth latht night?"

Anytime a man talks to me about sex, I can't help briefly imagining what they'd be like in bed. It usually influences my response; launch into flirt mode, or act disgusted and sexually harassed. Stuart is a shorter, more irritating George Costanza. He wears tiny glasses that are too small for his piggy face, and he's constantly pulling at the tighties that creep up his bulbous ass. I picture him as a grunter and a squealer, pumping away like porno Porky.

"None of your business, Thtuart," I snarled, pushing my way past him into the kitchen.

On second thought, that lisp mock probably wasn't a great idea.

"Well," he gurgled, lips twisting into ugly snarls, "what *ith* my buthineth, Jorlamo, ith that you're late *again*. It'th the third time thith week. You're puthing it. Ath the manager of thith thtore, I'm warning you, you'd better get your thit together or you'll be out of a job!"

"Assistant manager," I spat under my breath as I walked away.

Of course, the next person I ran into was Kylie, who smiled a little too sweetly.

"Good morning, Julie," she chirped. "I don't usually say that this late in the day, but you look like you just dragged yourself out of bed. Is that last night's eyeliner?"

Bitch bitch bitch bitch bitch.

"We've left plenty of sidework for you." She pointed behind her to the dishwashing line, which was piled with nasty, crusty dishes, probably from yesterday's dinner. "Ronaldo had to leave early last night, so he didn't get to finish up the dish line. I think that's a good job for you today."

Bitch bitch bitch bitch *bitch*.

What most people don't know about waitressing is that you're not just serving people. You also vacuum, wash dishes, scrape under tables for gum and ketchup crust, scour the walls behind trash cans, polish woodwork with lemon oil, dust lamps and other such wall decor, clean the bathrooms, mop, sweep, scrub, and seethe. This is a labor tactic employed by restaurant managers everywhere. Trick people into thinking they're hired to wait tables, and employ them in the manner of illegal alien housekeepers for less than three dollars an hour. And then wonder why the restaurant never passes health inspection.

I attacked the dishes with a vengeance and plotted an elaborate fantasy in which the restaurant burns to the ground on my night off, damning Stuart and Kylie to a fiery death, appendages sizzling like little sausage links.

When I finished I felt much better.

I finally started taking tables around twelve-thirty. Nothing spectacular; a few families with young kids, a jaded looking group of teens, a couple so old they could barely pick up their forks without spilling. Customers in this place are never any fun. We don't get celebrities in here, or tourists, or even halfway attractive people, for that matter. Certainly nobody like Chad Downing.

Sigh.

I wonder what he's doing right now. Maybe he's thinking about the adorable woman he met outside his building yesterday, and kicking himself for not crouching on the peanuts beside her? Maybe he's planning our first date, or naming our children? I bet he's great in bed. His hands looked so strong and capable, and his eyes . . . wow. I could stare into them for hours, especially if they were two inches away and he were lying on top of me. Mmmmm. His feet were big, too, and wide, so I bet he has an incredible—

My horny daydream was interrupted by the jangling of the front door. Damn, just when I was getting to the money shot. I looked up from filling a salt shaker to see what pennypincher the hostess would stick me with next. Instead, my jaw dropped.

He was tall and slim, with spiky black hair and killer green eyes, evident to me even from across the restaurant. A tribal tattoo snaked around the curl of his toned forearm, which clutched a *New York Times*.

Why, helloooooooo!

He caught my eye and smiled, and then, as I googled like a teenage boy in an adult video store, he raised his eyebrows at me. I licked my lips and was about to raise mine back—a coy little invitation to go shag in the meat cooler—when I realized that he was trying to get me to come over and seat him.

Duh, Julie.

Dixie, the sixty-five-year old hostess, cut me off as I stepped toward the door.

"Well, hey there, cutie!" she drawled (a transplant from

Greenville, South Carolina. I guess it was a bad divorce).
"Are you all by yourself today? That's a damned shame."

The Adonis cleared his throat. "One for lunch, please.
Smoking."

Be still my blackened lungs.

Men that attractive make me nervous, which Dixie gets a
kick out of. I watched, helpless, as she led him over to a
table in the corner. In my section.

Dixie winked on her way back to the front. "Good luck,
honey," she hissed. "No ring!"

He's also, alas, no movie star. Oh well. Maybe I'll flirt a
little and take my mind off of Chad.

Sometimes I think it's really nice and cute the way Dixie
looks out for my romantic interests. Then again, we're talking about a divorcée who subscribes to a string of Internet
S&M dating services.

I smoothed my hair as best I could under the sparkly antennae and headed over.

"Hi, my name is Julie, and I'll be taking care of you
today."

He looked up from his paper.

"Oh yeah?" He grinned, amused.

"Um," I paused, "yeah."

"No offense," he chuckled softly, "but you look like you
can barely take care of yourself. Here," he offered, plucking
a beer bottle cap that was, apparently, tangled in my leftover hairstyle. "I take it you had fun last night?"

Jesus, I'm a perpetual jackass. At least this time I'm not
starstruck.

"Oh, um, yeah," I stumbled, pulling a pen out of my
apron and immediately dropping it on the floor. "Oops,
oops. Hold on, let me just get my—" Of course, I banged
my head on the table on the way back up. I hope Kylie and

Stuart are enjoying this from the kitchen doorway. I hear their giggling. They sure seemed to find something funny.

The man leaned back against the booth and laughed. "You're really having a rough morning, aren't you? Poor thing. You need some strong, nasty coffee and greasy food, I think."

I tried to recover my composure. "Well, at least I'm in the right place for that. Shit. I mean, shoot. I mean, not that our food is that greasy. It's not. But it's not dry. It's good. Good food. Good food."

"What are you, a caveman?" he teased. "Good food, good food. Me want woman bring me food." He beat his chest and then poked my arm. "Come on, that's funny. Have a laugh with me, Julie the hungover waitress."

I grinned in spite of my humiliation and throbbing noggin.

"That's better. I'm Tyler, by the way, Julie, and so far you're the best thing about my day. How about some of that strong, nasty coffee?"

I managed to be a relatively normal person for the rest of Tyler's meal. His kindness and sense of humor put me completely at ease, so I could almost forget that I was talking to a fox way out of my league. He asked me a lot about myself, and, in turn, I discovered that he was twenty-six, from San Diego, and worked as a grant writer for a national nonprofit organization. He also played the bass, couldn't cook, and was entirely fed up with women. Damn.

"I just can't figure you ladies out." He shook his head, dashing salt on his fries, "You want one thing but say another. You're ecstatic one minute, and then you're screaming about dirty laundry and rings on the coffee table. Oh, and holidays are the best. 'No, no, honey, I don't want anything.' Do you know how long it took me to figure out that

'No honey, I don't want anything' actually means 'You'd damned well better buy me the shiniest jewelry you can afford'? It's useless. I give up."

"Well, you guys aren't exactly treasures, either." I rolled my eyes as I filled his coffee cup. "You don't get excited about anything except sports and cars, your feet smell, you drink your paycheck and then need to borrow gas money, and most of you are completely clueless about a woman's anatomy."

"Most of us," Tyler said with a wink. Yuuuum. In contrast to Stuart, Tyler was first rate in my fictional bedroom. I envisioned candles and chocolate and neighbors banging on their ceiling.

"Anyway, Julie," he said, pulling out his wallet and throwing some bills on the table, "you've been so great. I don't eat alone very often, and I was afraid you'd think I was a big geek."

"Oh, I do think you're a big geek," I smiled, "but I'm a bigger geek, so it's okay."

"Well, then I guess it's a good thing I got you as a waitress. Otherwise, I might have been thrown out for not being cool enough."

"I think Junebugs is just happy to have customers, geeky as they may be."

"In that case . . ." He slid out of the booth and stood close to me. He towered over my five feet and seven inches, and his cologne was subtle, sexy. "I'll have to come back and give you some more business. Only when you're working, of course. I need someone else who's geeky around here so I can blend in. When's your next shift?"

I gave myself away and blushed. "Tuesday night."

"It's a date." Tyler smiled, winked again, and strolled out.

My 15 Minutes

Fortune works in mysterious ways. Why has my s͙
magnetism suddenly launched into full gear after lurki͙
in the shadows since I first got boobs? This is terrible tim-
ing. I'm busy obsessing unhealthily over an unattainable
demigod, damnit. Why all of a sudden the unusually promising distraction?

On second thought, flirting with Tyler would probably
be excellent practice for planning my attack on Mr. Hollywood. I needed to work out the kinks in my wooing strategy, and I was sick of using my reflection as a guinea pig.
This would be much more effective. And maybe I'd get
some sex, or at least some dinner, out of the deal? Besides,
with those arms, Tyler was almost man enough to make me
forget about Chad.

Almost.

 Four

Whatever it is that I've been hoping for hasn't happened. I don't know what I expected to get out of moving back to L.A., but so far I've come up empty-handed. No impressive career, no new glamorous friends, no titillating romance. I'm back to working the same job that I had in college, hanging out with the same girl from high school, lusting after the same man who decorated my teenage bedroom. Sad, so very sad.

At least the rest of my neighbors are keeping it interesting. After only three weeks of residence, I determined that my building seems to serve as a dormitory for a coalition of the awkward and bizarre. I am awakened each morning by Yan, the hairy Russian giant who lives next door to me. Yan is practicing religiously for Who's Yodel-a-he-Who, an international yodeling festival held each year in Geneva. The one thing worse than a man who yodels at six A.M.? A man who yodels badly at six A.M.

Next to Yan lives the Gonzales family. Four children, three grandparents, one mother, two bedrooms, no English. They pay the rent by busking on the street corner, hassling bystanders into tossing a few bucks into little Esperanza's tambourine. It's sort of the Telemundo version of the Par-

tridge Family. Across from them are Kit and Cory, two mor-
bidly obese drag queens who run a phone sex line out of
their apartment. I've seen their ad in the phone book, and
let me tell you, false eyelashes and some packing tape can
work wonders.

Aside from my floor, I only know the people who live directly above me, the Gilmores, and that's because they're so
fucking loud that I can't help but eavesdrop. He's a mort-
gage broker, and she thinks she's a housewife. I'd call her a
"lady of the evening," but it's usually the afternoon, if you
catch my drift. I don't think the two of them actually have
sex together, unless he's been out drinking and she's had a
slow day.

While doing laundry this morning, I bumped into my
other next-door neighbor, Leila, one half of a May-
December marriage driven to the brink by her seventy-two-
year old husband and their six young children. The poor
woman's only escape was to submerge herself in local gossip, so an encounter with her inevitably leads to a conversation about old Mrs. Norris and her secret double life as a
dominatrix for the local senior's scene.

Ick.

Imagine my surprise when she started pumping me for
tidbits while I tried to stuff my T-shirts into a shopping bag.

"Come on, Julie, you must have some dirt on him. You're
in the prime position! Everyone's dying to know what he
does in there!"

Shit. Pink undies again. Must have put a red sock in the
whites again. Do I own red socks? Does anyone own red
socks?

". . . Julie?"

". . . Um . . . what? I'm sorry, Leila, who are we talking
about?"

She blinked at me.

"Honey! Chad Downing, of course! God, he's so cute. Did you see the movie where he fucked that blond girl while they were suspended in a sleeping bag on the side of a mountain?"

Cliffbanger. Mmmmm. Sure did. Not for the academy crowd, but that video and a pint of Chocolate Fudge Chip are enough to coast me through even my Saharaesque dry spells. But wait . . .

"Leila, why would I have gossip on Chad?"

"Well, honey, you're in 4C, right? You live right above him! You've got to have heard something! Come on, all the women in this building have been dying to talk to him, but nobody has the nerve. You've got the prime location for eavesdropping! Does he get a lot of ass? Is he a groaner? I've been trying to find out from the lady in 2C, but she's deaf as a doornail, and barely speaks English."

Did she say I live right above him?

I mumbled a quick good-bye and raced back to my apartment, where I spent the next twenty minutes pacing (though careful not to tread too heavily for fear of sounding obese and oafish).

On the one hand, the thought of eavesdropping liberally on a man whose children I intend to bear is unnervingly arousing. However, the prospect unfortunately puts into perspective a sad truth, which, until now, I had stuffed into the recesses of my subconscious . . .

"Sex." I sighed, slamming my shot glass onto the bar. "Lack thereof."

"What are you talking about, retardo?" Billie asked, cocking an eyebrow and lighting up the latest in an unbreakable chain of Marlboros. She had rushed over from her Sensual Sushi class at the Spiritual Healing Center and ushered me to her favorite bar, the Red Toad. It was kind of a dive, but the bartender knew Billie's drink and her home address, handy for those helpless fifteen minutes after last call.

"Nobody cares that you're not doing it!" she screeched. "Except you, of course. But I thought that the catalogue I gave you last year had fixed that problem?"

Giggle. "Oh no, that aspect is, uh, well taken care of."

"Then what's the problem?"

Then, "Oooooh!!" She finally got it, thank God, because although I was thinking it, I didn't want to actually say it out loud.

I cleared my throat. "He can probably hear everything I do! Every time I walk to the kitchen, every time I dance around in the bathroom, every time I sing in the shower. Oh my God, he can probably hear me peeing! Billie, he could hear if I'm having sex. God knows, I can hear the Gilmores upstairs after she's hit the chardonnay and he's come home from the Itty-Bitty-Tittie bar."

"Ew, really?" Billie scrunched up her nose. "I knew that guy was a perv. The mullet/handlebar mustache combo is a dead giveaway."

"Billie," I whispered, slightly annoyed that she wasn't humoring my neurosis, "if he could hear me doing it, then he can hear that I'm not doing it. Which means, he probably thinks I'm a total loser! A dork who can't get laid, and sits home every night watching late night talk shows and Nick at Nite reruns!"

At this, the bartender muffled a snicker.

"Oh fuck off!" Billie snarled. "Go pull me a beer, you schlep."

She turned back to me. "But that's so easy! So easy to fix! All you have to do is make him think you're wildly popular."

"What?" I sputtered. "How?"

I shouldn't have asked.

Billie insisted on coming back to my apartment with me a few pints later. I had barely wiggled my keys out of the dead bolt when she charged past me and into the bedroom.

"Billie, shhhhhhh!" I giggled, and followed her in. "What the fuck are you doing?"

"Checking shit out," she tossed back at me. She stopped at the foot of the bed and placed her hands on the mattress.

"Let's see what this baby's got." She pushed a few times. "Not a bad squeak, Jule, but you'll need to make a little more noise than that. Here, help me move the bed so the headboard's against the wall. . . . There, that's much better!"

She shook the bed again, so it struck the wall with each push.

"See, listen, the mattress makes a lot of noise if you push right here. . . ."

Uuuurrr urrrrr. Urrrr urrrrr. Thud. Urrrrrr urrrrr. Urrrrrr urrrrrr. Thud.

"And just gradually push it faster until you stop suddenly! See!" She turned triumphantly to me. "That sounds just like sex!"

I was in awe.

"Billie, this is so lame!"

"No it's not, Jule! All you have to do is shake the bed a few times a week, and presto! You've got a sex life. Now the question is, how often, and for how long?"

I love how scientific her mind is.

"Well," she began, "you can't shake it too early on Friday or Saturday nights, because then he'll think you're in a long-term relationship and would rather stay at home cooped up on the weekends. And you can't do it early Sunday morning, because then he'll think you're a kinky religious freak who gets off by doing it before church. *And* you can't do it between nine and five on the weekdays, because then he'll know you don't have a normal job and he'll think you're a loser."

I pondered this.

"And you can't do it too often or he'll think you're a slut," she continued, "but if you do it too little then you're desperate and boring. Soooo, okay. You need to pick a few optimal days and times, but not the same ones every week, because then he'll think you're stuck in a routine. Okaaaaay." She lit a cigarette and paused. "How about Tuesdays and Thursdays at six, so he'll think it's the first thing you do to rejuvenate from work, and late late Fridays or Saturdays, say, three or four in the morning, so he wonders if you've brought some guy home with you from the bar."

Ultimately, we decided that late Fridays and Saturdays would be good, plus alternating Mondays and Thursdays. Not too much thumping and screaming, Billie warned, or he might think I'm a faker. And no man wants to sleep with a faker. Best to make him wonder who I'm up here with, and if it's the same guy every time.

Perfect.

Mom called the next morning at the height of Yan's big finish.

"Julie? Julie? What is that? Are you watching the *Sound of Music*?"

"Hi, Mom," I croaked, pulling a pillow over my head. "That's just Yan."

"Who the hell is Yan? Did you get a boyfriend? Oh my God, Julie, are you having sex?"

I yawned. "You mean right now? Or in general?"

"That's not funny, young lady. Jesus H, I know you're not

waiting for marriage, but you could at least have the courtesy to put the brakes on to take a phone call from your mother!"

As if on cue, Yan's voice broke on the final strain of his yodel, and he was silent.

"What do you want, Mom?"

"I want you to get out of bed, lazy bones! You promised to come to my class today!"

Ohhhh noooooooo.

Having spent the last twenty-five years of her life as a maid/nanny/short order cook/crisis counselor, my mother has spun uncontrollably into an official mid-life crisis. Dad warned me it was coming; she's been driving herself crazy, fluttering around the empty nest. I tried talking her into taking up a hobby, like a pottery class or a walking group, but she couldn't get into it. "Too many yuppies," she'd complain, "and they're all so young! I have the saggiest boobs in class!"

Apparently, the boob thing struck a chord, because she joined a class, all right.

"Kickboxing! But, Ma," I'd pleaded, "you're fragile! You weigh ninety-five pounds! You're a tiny little person!"

Six weeks later, and my fifty-six-year-old mother has the muscle tone of a pop princess. Suddenly, men are doing double takes.

"What the hell is happening?" my poor dad whispered into the phone one night, "Everything was fine, and all of a sudden I can't take my wife out to dinner without some putz trying to pick her up when I go to the bathroom! And she thinks it's funny! She actually told me that if I don't lighten up, she'll kick my ass! I didn't even know your mother had 'ass' in her vocabulary!"

Like a sucker, I'd agreed to try the class out, but truthfully, I'm not what one would call "in shape."

"Ooooh. Is that today, Mom? Are you sure? It's not tomorrow?"

"Julie, I go to class every day."

"Oh."

"Get up."

Sigh. Maybe kickboxing wasn't such a bad idea. After all, I do have a celebrity to impress. "Okay, Ma." I glanced up at my headboard, "There's just something I need to do first."

That night was a killer at the restaurant. I could barely walk because I got my butt handed to me by the kickboxing instructor, a tiny little German man named Timmy.

"Vun, two, vun, two!" he would screech. "Keeck, keeck, keeck! Bonnie, looking gud! Your daughter, though, she ees a mess. Keeck tovards ceiling, not tovards my crotch! Vun, two, vun . . . oh, you are terrible. You come to class six times a veek vith your mother. I vhip you into shape!"

"Isn't he great?" my mother huffed. "Timmy's"—kick, punch—"the best in Los Angeles. I hear he's got"—kick, kick—"quite a celebrity following!"

"Mom"—kick, pant—"so does liposuction." Huff, puff, punch. "And the knife is looking pretty"—*wheeeeeeeze*—"good right now."

"Don't let Timmy hear you say that!" Punch, block. "Extra crunches for"—kick, kick—"pessimists!"

By the end of class I was drenched in sticky sweat and running late for work. No time for a shower, so I spritzed my whole body with deodorant. Eh, good enough.

I could barely keep up with Dixie tonight, who was seating tables at lightning speed in order to cram in as many smoke breaks for herself as possible. I didn't even have time to plan my aural sexual attack on Chad; I was too busy expediting mozzarella sticks and fried Snickers bars.

Tyler actually came in tonight. Figures, when my hair looks like seaweed. He sparkled at me from my only empty table, a huge, round booth that seats ten.

"Hey!" He grinned when I walked up. "No bottlecaps today? Must have spent a boring night in last night."

The table made him look tiny and vulnerable. It was adorable.

"I'm sure there are, um, smaller tables that you could sit at. Do you want me to ask the hostess to move you?"

"What, and miss out on the opportunity to look this popular? It's all part of my strategy, baby. Everyone in this joint will take one look at me sitting at this table, and think, 'Hey, that guy has nine people on their way to see him. He must be cooool.' I swear, it'll be good for my image."

"Or," I chuckled, "everyone will take one look at you sitting at this table and think, 'Aw, poor guy. He's such a loser that none of his friends actually showed up to have dinner with him. But he's so pathetic that he's convinced himself to just keep waiting, and someone will eventually show up.' And then instead of thinking you're cooool, people will pity you and think you're either really obnoxious and boring, or have Tourette's syndrome."

"Hmm. I didn't think about that."

"So . . . do you want me to find you another table?"

"Is there another one in your section?"

I gave the room a once-over. Junebugs was crammed. At table 84 six goth kids were smoking cloves and picking parmesean artichoke dip out of their lip piercings. At 63, a harried-looking woman spoon-fed her toddler triplets while her husband swilled Manhattans. The four old ladies at 71 were sharing one club sandwich. No open tables.

"Looks like you got the last table in here," I told him.

"Well," Tyler said, flipping open his menu and lighting a cigarette, "then I guess you're stuck with me."

I can't understand why a man this attractive would make an effort to befriend a chick in a googly eye headband. Maybe he's a serial killer with a fetish for women who work in subservient professions, like waitresses and prostitutes. Hmmm. Tricky.

"Julie!" crowed a voice from across the restaurant. I spun around, to find Kylie glaring at me from behind an enormous tray of purple Doodlebug cocktails.

"Wow, she looks pissed." Tyler grinned at me.

"Shit, those are my drinks for the bachelorette party," I moaned.

"You mean some poor broad chose to spend her last unattached evening in a G-rated chain restaurant? That's kind of . . . sad."

"Are you kidding? They've been here since brunch. The bride is so fucking trashed she hasn't been out of her seat since two this afternoon."

"Aren't you supposed to stop serving them when that happens?"

"Her fiancé is my manager's brother. If I had to marry into a family of midget Yetis, I'd drink myself into a coma, too. Her last three rounds have been on me."

Tyler laughed. "Just trying to help her out?"

"Julie! I do not have time to babysit your tables!"

Arg.

"Gotta go. I'll be back in a few."

Kylie was rapping her fist on the bar when I caught up to her.

"Um, thanks for dropping my drinks at that table."

"Julie, this is *not* social hour," she snarled at me. *"Some* of us are trying to make a living, here. If you can't handle the dinner rush, then take fewer tables, and let the *experts* earn some more money."

She flipped her stringy hair out of her face and stalked into the kitchen.

I'm pretty sure she hates me.

A few minutes later my suspicions were confirmed.

Although the restaurant was crammed full of customers, I wasn't too busy. The bachelorettes were taking up four of my five tables, and they were too drunk to notice if I disappeared for large chunks of time. I had split most of my evening between smoking cigarettes and chatting with Tyler, whom the bachelorettes were eyeing hungrily. I was feeling pretty relaxed, when—

"Julie," Dixie drawled, "since you're not doin' nothin', would you pick up one of Toni's tables? She's swamped."

Easy enough. Table of two, husband and wife. Two iced teas, one Marshmallow Meatloaf, one dinner salad. I rushed their drinks and returned to Tyler.

"Julie! I need you to take table nine for Kylie."

Okay, four diet sodas, a few burgers, and some chicken thumbs.

"Julie! Mark just got double sat. Take fifty-eight for him!"

Okay four diet sodas, three beers, a chocolate malt, six chicken thumbs, four curly fries, three taco salads, two beehive mashed potatoes, and some ribs.

"Julie!"

"What?" I turned to Dixie in exasperation.

"Your big party is ready for their check."

The bachelorettes were slumped in their chairs, the bride facedown in her Honeycomb Pudding Cake.

I gritted my teeth and walked over.

"Well, ladies, I guess we're ready to call it a night?"

"We need sssssepparate checksssss," slurred a redheaded mess.

Yikes. "Um, all of you? Can you remember what each of you had?"

She looked at me like I'd just asked her to present a dissertation on Descartes while giving an alien a blowjob.

"Right. Okay, just give me a minute."

The computer system that waitresses use to order at Junebugs is archaic. Not only is it slow, but if you want to separate checks, you'd damn well better be organized from the get-go. Of course, I'm not.

Twenty minutes later I had finally sorted out who had what, and I began printing out the seventeen separate checks. Unfortunately, the printer is older than the computers. A monkey with a chisel would have been more efficient.

In the meantime:

"Miss? I need honey mustard!"

"Hey, this burger is supposed to be Medium *well!*"

"Excuse me, can I have more water?"

"Another round over here, lady!"

"Yeah, yeah, *yeah*," I muttered under my breath as I raced around to shut everyone up.

I finally got the bachelorettes out of there, and the rest of my tables were munching quietly. Tyler was still sitting at the giant table, lingering over his steak. I headed over.

I was intercepted by Kylie.

"I'll check on him, Julie."

"Um, thanks Kylie, but I got it."

"No, I don't think you do."

I blinked. "Excuse me?"

She grinned at me wickedly. "Turn around."

In a flash, Dixie had seated *all four* of my newly emptied tables. It was a waitressing nightmare: *quadruple sat,* with three other tables and a fourth that I was dying to flirt with?! What the *fuck* was she thinking?

I barged up to the hostess desk.

"Dixie!" I boomed, then noticed the lobby full of customers. I lowered my voice to a threatening whisper. "Dixie. Are you trying to kill me? What the hell are you doing?"

"What do you mean, honey? Kylie said you were dying to get some more tables. She told me to fill your section right back up!"

That little bitch.

"Dixie, I can't possibly take all of these tables!"

"Well, darlin', I don't know what to tell you! Toni's up to her ears, Mark's got two big parties, Donna just slipped in the kitchen, and Kylie's over there trying to get laid."

I spun around. Sure enough, Kylie had plopped herself into one of Tyler's empty chairs and was batting her eyes faster than a coked-up hummingbird. And he didn't look like he minded one bit.

"Well, better hurry, honey, you just got a whole mess of tables!" Dixie trilled.

The rest of my night went something like this:

"Miss! I need ketchup!"

"Where's my milk shake?"

"This is *not* what I ordered!"

"What is this crap you're trying to serve me?"

"Hey lady, we need the check! Now!"

"Miss? Miss? *Miss?*"

"How much longer for our food?"

"Daaaadddy, why is the lady taking so looooong?"

"This steak is *pink* in the middle!"

"We've been waiting for a half hour!"

"My fries are cold!"

"You call this chili?"

"Can you get the manager?"

"I want your manager!"

"We'd like the manager."

"Get the fucking manager!! Now!!"

Ooooooh, is Stuart pissed at me.

In total, he comped $150 worth of meals from my tables, gave away thirteen free desserts, nine free beers, and had to pick up the dry cleaning tabs for a party of six very angry vegetarians. I mixed up their gardenburgers in the kitchen, and one of them ended up with a Meatmonger's Pig Burger. Which ended up on the rest of them, in a less solid form.

To ice the rancid cake, I was so busy that I didn't get to talk to Tyler anymore, which I suspect was Kylie's brilliant idea. She was all over him like pleather on a drag queen for the rest of the night. In fact, she completely took over, bringing him free dessert and taking care of his check when he finally left.

And didn't say good-bye to me.

 **Five**

Daaaaargh. Bright. Sun. Hurts. Eyes. Burning.
Damned dog.

Riley charged into my room at 6:03 this morning, full of boundless canine energy and doggie pee. He gnawed at my socks, whining and begging for me to take him outside, to his infinite toilet.

"Riiiiiley," I croaked, stuffing my head under a pillow, "can't you wait? Pleeeeeease?"

He cocked his head at me, pondering my groggy appeal, then . . .

"Mmmmmmmmmnnngggghhh?" A subtle, urgent growl gathered deep within his throat.

Goddamnit. Riley didn't care that I was stuck at Junebugs until two o'clock that morning.

Stuart pulled me into the office after the dinner rush last night to scream at me. I've never seen anyone actually turn purple before. All I could really make out was something like, "Thould fire you! Tho many thimple, thupid mithtaketh! Thit, you thtupid thlacker!" He was yelling so fast, he sounded like a cobra about to strike. I can't believe he didn't fire me. But as punishment, I had to stay until we closed, and vacuum the entire restaurant. The little weasel even gave the rest of the staff free shots after he locked the doors, probably to guarantee a fucking peanut gallery, I'm sure.

Kylie kept stuffing her goony pumpkin face with crackers and spraying little crumbs all over the place when she cackled. It took me damn near an hour to do the entire restaurant, and by the time I finished, the bar floor was littered with staff trash.

"Hey, Julie," Toni snickered, pointing to a pile of lime rinds on the floor, "you missed a spot!"

"Oopth, and here'th another one!" Stuart nearly choked on his own fucking laughter as he tossed a crumpled napkin on the floor.

They were all killing themselves laughing, the air ripe with the donkey sweat odor of cheap white tequila.

"Well, come on!" Stuart hooted, "it'th your own fault that you're on clean-up duty, mithy. Awwww, are you getting pithy?" He swallowed a hiccup and grinned at the rest of the boozy vermin. "Hahahahaha, Pithy Mithy! That'th her new nickname! Pithy Mithy! Hahahahahaha!"

I gritted my teeth and snatched up their trash with a vengeance.

"Maybe you should lay off the shots, Stuart." I said, "I noticed you have your hand on Kylie's knee, and you've got to be closing in on alcohol poisoning if she's starting to look tasty."

Either Kylie didn't really hear me or she was too drunk to stand up, because instead of coming after me, spitting and swearing, she just muttered into her drink. Although, she could have been casting a Wicca death spell on me, for all I know. She's creepy like that.

"You're a bitch," Stuart spat darkly.

"Yeah? Well, you're short. Now, if you'll excuse me, if I'm

not fired, of course, I have work to finish, and then I'm leaving. If I am fired, Stuart, tell me now, because if you can me after I finish cleaning this joint I'm going to be *really* pissed."

"Why fire you, Pithy Mithy, when I know how much you hate thith plathe? I'd rather thee you thuffer."

"I know you would, Thtuart," I said sweetly, "and that's because you're a bitter little man. Now, if you'll excuse me, I have better places to be than this shithole." I spun on my heel with a huff and headed for the door.

It would have been a very dramatic exit if I hadn't slipped on a stray cocktail onion on the way out. My only consolation was that Kylie laughed so hard she choked on an oyster cracker. Stuart was still trying to give her the Heimlich as I dimmed the lights and left. Oh well; if she's dead tomorrow, it's her own fault. Karma's a raving, pissy bitch.

I was so tired when I got home that I forgot to walk Riley, just plopped on my bed and passed out in my uniform. Guess that explains why he was hopping up and down on three legs when I woke up. Faced with the option of dragging myself out of bed or spending the day scrubbing the carpets with vinegar, I threw back the covers.

"Down, Riley! Just let me change my . . . No . . . No!!! No, drop it!!! Drop the sock!! No . . . Ow! *No!!!*"

Last year I spent an estimated $6,000 on doggie chew toys. The little bastard still prefers my socks.

Realizing that he would finally get to relieve himself, Riley was ecstatic beyond explanation. He nearly knocked me over as I grabbed his leash. I clipped it to his collar and hung on for dear life as he bounded toward the front door, skidding and clawing his way desperately over the slick kitchen linoleum.

Outside, the fucking birds were chirping at the rising sun as I struggled to rub dream crust out of my eyes. A jogger bumped my shoulder as she sprinted past me at the speed of light. Then another. Then another. Riley looked up at me in disgust, as if to say, "Would you look at that? All these people exercising and having fun, and the dog gets stuck with the fatty who never moves faster than the vacuum cleaner. Damnit."

I'll admit it—the most I've run in the past three years is eleven feet across an office to beat another temp to the last sprinkle doughnut. But short, frenetic bursts of energy are great for the metabolism, so I hear.

Riley is unusually territorial; he seems to be overwhelmed by an urge to pee on everything. Therefore, a walk with him is more of a walk-and-stop. Every two feet he's marking anything that's rooted in the ground; trees, bushes, mailboxes, even those little reflectors at the end of driveways. Apparently, he feels the need to overpower the scent of his competitors. Kind of reminds me of cheesy bachelors with Drakkar Noir, actually.

I let Riley drag me along for a few blocks and turned around. I felt sort of guilty for shortchanging the pooch, but I knew he'd make up for it by running around the living room in circles for about forty-five minutes when we got home.

My building was in sight when Riley engaged in stage two of the walking routine. I always try to give him a little privacy when he squats and gives me that sheepish wince, that "Do you really need to supervise?" plea. So, I turned my head, shuffled my feet, whistled a bar or two while he finished up. And then my turn to be humiliated.

I reached into my pocket and brought forth a plastic shopping bag.

A scoop and a few gags later, Riley was traipsing happily toward home. I followed, disgusted, the putrid bag swinging at my side. This is by far the worst part of the walk, even more painful than the initial act of wrenching myself out of bed. Have you noticed how you could be in the most unlikely place, doing the most out of character, unbelievably repulsive thing, and you'll run into the last person in the world that you would expect to see? I mean, I could be in a shanty town in Bulgaria, surrounded by nothing but the breeze and a few roasting chickens, and wouldn't you know it, my archenemy from high school would round the bend just as I was reaching down my pants to dig my thong out of my ass.

I'm always a little afraid when I walk the dog, because a stinky plastic shopping bag isn't exactly a glamorous accessory. I mean, I know everybody does it, but *not* everybody has to clean it up and tote it around like precious cargo.

Thankfully, it's daybreak and no one I know is awake at this hour, because after last night's emotional expenditure, I don't think I could handle the potential chagrin of being caught with a bag of—

Shit! Oh my God, oh God. What is he doing up?

Chad Downing, Chad *Downing*, was headed straight for me.

Of *course* he was!

I was doomed. I looked quickly around for a trash can. No such luck, not even a mailbox where I could stow the offending evidence. Shit. Shit. Shit. Shouldn't he be doing Pilates, or dropping off a hooker somewhere?

I took a deep breath, picking up the pace while I tried to calm down. It's okay, I tell myself, he won't even recognize me. I'm just going to keep my head down and stroll right past. . . .

"What a great dog!"

No, no!

Sure enough, Chad had spotted us and was headed straight over, beaming like a virgin at a nudie bar.

"He's beautiful!" he said, stooping to scratch Riley, who was being unusually and disloyally benevolent. Damnit, dog, don't wag your tail, bare your teeth! Growl, snap, anything! Make him flee in terror before he notices the bag of poo!

Apparently, my telepathic skills are rusty, because Riley interpreted my frantic mental plea as "Sit on Chad's feet and lick his hand like it's a chicken-flavored Popsicle." Traitor.

Chad looked up. "Oh, hey, you're the girl who just moved in, right? Jennifer?"

"Yeah," I stammered. "Yeah, it's Julie, actually. Julie. Chad? Chad! It's Chad, right? How are ya? How's it going?"

Oh God, you asshole.

He looked amazing. Messy bed hair, enormous sunglasses, form-fitting black T-shirt eased into a pair of low-riding Calvins. I bit my lip and realized that my breath smelled like fertilizer.

"Did you get everything moved in okay?"

"Yeah, uh, took me, you know, a few days to get unpacked. Had to figure out the whole feng shui of the place. Hard to do with no one to help me out. I mean, I know plenty of people, it's not like I'm a complete loser, or anything! Hahahahaha. But I don't know anyone who can really help me balance my stuff in accordance with my personal karmic needs. That's what the book says to do. You know, the feng shui book. I have a feng shui book."

You *asshole*!!!

Not surprisingly, I got a weird look for that tangent.

"Uh, yeah, cool. My ex was really into martial arts, too."

Huh? Oh, he must be dumb. Well, that's good. Maybe he has trouble stringing together simple facts, rendering him unable to infer the contents of the bag.

The bag. I'm still holding the bag! The poo bag! Okay, Jule, just end the conversation. Just say something witty, and sprint back to the apartment. Come on. Come ooooooooon!

"Well, uh, Chad, it was nice to see you, but I need to get home and—put my groceries away."

No, no, you idiot! Don't draw attention to the bag! Divert! *DIVERT!!*

He looked at me quizzically, then let his eyes drop to the beacon of distaste dangling by my side.

"Oh," he said, "you've been . . . ? There's a store around here that's open this early?"

He knows.

"Uh . . . a store? Yeah, there's a store. It's miles away. Miles. Riley and I went for a jog, and I stopped at this teeny little store for some . . . stuff."

Please don't look at my feet, Chad Downing. We both know I couldn't jog anywhere in these lion slippers.

"Oh." He stood up, brushing his hands on his jeans, "Well, that's good to know. Do they have grass?"

Huh?

"Grass. You mean, like outside? Like, grass outside the store? Or like, um, weed? You know, pot? Do you mean pot? That I'm not really sure about, I mean, I'm kind of square about that stuff, and I honestly didn't even really know that you could just ask at the store! I mean, usually my friend Billie gets it for us, when we smoke it, which really isn't a lot anymore, unless you're into it, which is cool, and if that's the case, you should totally come and smoke with us sometime because she's a lot of fun, and, well, I myself get kind of stupid, but—"

"Wheatgrass. I'm talking about wheatgrass."

"Wheatgrass?"

"It's an organic supplement. Comes frozen. Really good for your skin. Notice how my face gives off a warm glow? That's from two shots of wheatgrass a day. I don't even ex-foliate anymore!" He peered at my oily, gritty, scaly snake face. "You know, no offense, but you could probably benefit from some wheatgrass. And maybe some Plum-Drum Wal-nut Exfoliating Facial Rub. They sell it at Barneys now. You said you waitress, right? Get a small jar. It's all you really need. Well," he glanced at the cell phone clipped to his alli-gator belt, "I'm off to a meeting with my publicist. You know how it goes with the bigwigs . . . or maybe you don't. Anyway, got to dash. Fine line between fashionably late and pompous asshole, you know. Nice to see you.'Bye, Riley."

I stood there, agape, as he spun on his heel and headed toward his tangerine Hummer.

What the *fuck* just happened?

What is the matter with me? *What is the matter with me?* Weed? Come up and *smoke* with us sometime? Plum-Drum Exfoliating Scrub?

Oh holy bejeesus.

As if I had a chance with the untouchable Chad Downing to begin with, but at least before this morning I had the "mysterious new neighbor" vibe going for me. I may not be a Playmate, but to him I could very well have been cute and vulnerable, or independent and worldly, or sexily unkempt. But now—now I've totally blown it. Mystery solved: I'm a poo scooper super loser who smells like an ashtray, has the social habits of a frat boy, and keeps four-legged company.

Riley whined in time with the rev of an engine, and we both stared forlornly at the trunk of Chad's ride as he disappeared into the sunrise.

Left in the dust with a bag of poo and a heart full of shattered hopes.

"Well, Riley," I sighed to the pooch, "there's only one thing to do now."

 Six

My mother could give Martha Stewart a run for her money.

In the kitchen, I mean, not on the trading room floor.

Since they always treat me like a helplessly beautiful fairy princess, I retreat to my parents' house when I'm feeling blue. And after this morning's dog walking disaster, I definitely need a boost.

The house I grew up in is a creamy yellow colonial, nestled amongst a sea of terra-cotta villas and palm trees. Mom's English gardens broke the California orange grove mold, bursting with lilacs, clematis, and four types of roses. The house screams "transplanted from New England by a gigantic tornado," and quite possibly set the stage for my lifetime of not quite fitting in.

Mom herself is one of those people that just makes you blink in amazement. She's constantly got a project in the works. For the normal person, a "project" might be painting the bathroom or matting some photos; for my mother, it's weaving baskets out of dried sea grasses, or making wine from the raspberries cultivated in the backyard. And the holidays! When I was a kid, she made her own Halloween candy to give out to trick-or-treaters; colorful lollipops shaped like bats and pumpkins, tiny (hand sewn) bags of sugared pumpkin seeds and chocolate drops.

And Jewish fascination or not, the woman will never, ever, *ever* give up the baby Jesus.

She begins her Christmas preparations in August, collecting antique glass bottles that she'll fill with homemade coffee liquor. In September the house fills with sweet fragrance, as she steeps vanilla beans in vodka to make her own extract. The cookie recipes begin to cumulate around late November, as she launches into a baking frenzy to rival a French confectioner. Hand-frosted Santa cookies, chocolate peanut butter kisses, snowy almond balls dusted with powdered sugar, Italian biscotti sweetened with anise, delicate stained-glass butter cookies, cinnamon pinwheels, coconut puffs topped with maraschino cherries, cookie after cookie after motherfucking cookie. And we couldn't eat a *single* one.

"Stop that!" she'd screech playfully as we'd grab for a cookie like starving street urchins, "Those are for my Christmas baskets!"

"But Mommmmm, it *is* Christmas!"

"Not for *your* Christmas, dear, these are for friends and neighbors. Dan, put that almond puff *down*, those are for the Normans."

"But Mommmmm, you don't even *like* them!"

"Daniel, do you like swimming in their pool? Because if they don't get an annual Christmas basket, you can darned well kiss their diving board good-bye. Selfish animals. Remember the year I forgot to include home-roasted espresso beans in their basket? And remember the birthday party that Amanda had, with the ponies and the Ferris wheel? Of course you don't, you weren't invited. That's what happens when you piss off the Normans. Goddamned coffee beans. They wouldn't have even known about them if Patty Gorman hadn't been running her fat mouth about my Christmas baskets."

Mom's superachievement in the domestic realm is hard to live up to. Ironic, actually, that I can't even scramble an egg.

When I pulled into the driveway, she was waving from the wraparound porch, dwarfed by a ruffly blue apron.

"Is that my little granddoggie? It *is!* It's my little pookie bear!!"

Most of my mother's friends have grandchildren. She's had to suck it up and spoil the dog.

Riley was woofing happily in the backseat of my Taurus, showering the half-opened window with drool. He loves my mother. She makes him omelets.

"Oh there he is!!" Mom cooed, shuffling out to the car and holding her face up to Riley for a kiss. She was rewarded with a tongue bath.

"Oooh, you have dragon breath. Julie Jorlamo, have you been brushing his teeth? Has Mummy been bwushing your teefy-weefies? Mummy is a bad mummy. You come with me, Riley, and we'll go find you some dinner. I bought some nice lamb chops at Nature's Farm today. Does Wiley wike lamb chops? Yes he does! Yes he does!"

She opened the door and they scurried into the house, leaving me agape, my seat belt still on.

So much for the royal treatment.

"Hi, Mom," I muttered, and threw my door open, "nice to see you, too."

"Nice, huh?" My dad had appeared on the porch, shaking his head at the screen door, really just a frame now that Riley had plowed through it on his way to the kitchen. "Last time you were here, I found your mother in the kitchen cooking breakfast. Steak and eggs! My favorites! I was so touched, until she slapped my hand away from the goddamned pan. 'That's for the dog,' she says. The goddamned dog! 'There's cereal in the pantry,' she says. Unbelievable! Thirty years in the same bed and she makes steak and eggs for the goddamned dog!"

Dad gets a little worked up sometimes. He's an angry Jew. Funny. But angry.

"Hi, Dad," I chuckled, pecking him on the cheek.

"Hi, beaner. Come inside and talk."

Thirty minutes later we were clustered around a feast of roasted rosemary chicken, garlic mashed potatoes, braised summer vegetables with dill sauce ("From my garden, Jule!"), and Caesar salad. Riley snored under the table at Mom's feet, yelping softly the way he does when he dreams about finally catching a squirrel.

"How's the apartment, beaner?" Dad asked. Well, asked the sports section, technically. He prefers to toss out his absentminded dinner conversation from behind the newspaper. He used to take it so personally when kids ignored him in class that he had to fight back by ignoring *them*. I think he meant it to be reverse psychology. Over the years it developed into a perverse talent of multitasking, so he really only talks to you when he's got his nose in some reading material. Mom loves it, though. She can talk him into anything when he's lost in the *Beacon*. But he's started to pay a little more attention since he inadvertently financed a Caribbean cruise for her entire Rotary club.

"Oh, um," I threw back some chardonnay, "it's okay, I guess."

"And the job?"

"Oh, Dad, it's a nightmare."

He finally looked up from his paper.

"Of course it is, beaner, you're waiting tables! People are all idiots, all assholes. They think you're supposed to be their slave for two bucks an hour, and then they tip you a dollar for your troubles. I waited tables in college, and man, I'll tell you, if ever I had homicidal tendencies, it was after a goddamned double shift."

"Did you have to do it after college, Dad?" I asked hopefully.

"Well, no, I was in graduate school. I had grants."

Oh.

"Julie honey, did you see my dahlias? I just planted some last week. My goodness, they love the sunshine!"

"No, Mom, I haven't been in the backyard tonight. Are they by the fish pond?"

"Dahlias by the fish pond? No, silly, by the gazebo! Oooh, and my new antique apple trees, Jule. Your father and I are starting our own backyard orchard!"

"Your father's money, anyway." Dad hid behind the paper again.

"Oh, hush up, Eli!" She turned to me. "He loves to garden as much as I do! He just likes to complain, crazy old fart. Besides, honey, they're a *good investment*!" she yelled. "Here, dear, have some strawberries. I just picked them this afternoon! Organic, you know. Look gorgeous next to my roses."

My shorts were already unbuttoned to accommodate half a chicken and a bellyful of homemade popovers.

"Maybe later, Mom."

"Well, are you staying the night? Do I get the whole night with my granddoggie? Do I? Do I? Oh yes, Mummy, pwease!?" She grabbed Riley's lips and smushed them together like a puppet. "Pweeease let me stay at nana's house? *Pweeeassse*?"

Dad *threw* down the paper this time. "Jesus, God, Julie, just say okay!" he urged. "Otherwise she'll be talking in that voice for the rest of the goddamned night!"

"*Pweeeeeeease?* Mummy, I wike wamb chops in the morning! Pweeeease? Pweeeeeee—"

"All right, all right!" I shouted. "Just stop making the dog talk like a baby!"

"Oh goodie!" Mom clapped her hands, "What shall we do? Want to see a movie? There's a new chick flick out; Eli, what's it called? That one with Katarina what's-her-name, you know, that Jappy looking girl."

"Katarina Conrad?" I was interested now. Katarina Conrad was Chad Downing's girlfriend, and America's ethnic sweetheart. You know the type: too exotic looking to play the girl next door, but generic enough to pass for Italian, Mexican, Jewish, Latina, or Greek. She's got flawless olive skin, enormous chocolate Bambi eyes, a teeny little waist, and enough gadonkadonk to go around the locker room.

"Yes! That's the one. Oh, you know, I just *loved* her in *It Takes Jew*. She's so sassy! Okay, her new movie is called . . .

I'm thinking, I'm thinking . . . *Fancy Pants*! Ooh, that was driving me crazy! Yes, *Fancy Pants*, it's all about some hot-shot fashion designer. It's got that guy in it, too. They dated. What's his name?"

"Chad Downing?" I practically barked, "Chad's in it, too?"

"Oh, he's such a handsome young man! Yes, I read that it was the last movie they made together before they broke up."

They broke up?

"They broke up?"

"Well sure, honey, it's all over the papers!"

Dad snorted. "You read the paper, Bonnie?"

Mom sat up straighter and peered at him down her nose. "I most certainly do, Eli!" she said, looking offended. "I have read the Home and Garden section of the *Beacon* faithfully for the last fifteen years, thank you very much. And every now and again, I've been known to *peruse* the Travel section and the Arts and Entertainment pages. And of course, I see the front page at dinner every night. Covers your face, you know. Anyhow," she turned back to me, "it caught my attention the other day. She dumped him for a cameraman. Don't think I could forget that face, you had enough pictures of him hidden around your bedroom."

"You knew about those?"

"Every last one, Jesus help you. Age fourteen and keeping a man's likeness in your underwear drawer. I damned near dragged you to the convent."

"Mom, you're not Catholic."

"Lucky for you, missy."

I could see that my impure thoughts and idolatry were still a sore subject.

"What time is the movie, Mom?"

"Ooh, goodie, I knew you'd want to go! There's a show-ing at eight. Let's go right after we walk the baaaaaaby."

When I was a kid I used to be embarrassed when I went to the movies with my parents. Now that I'm an adult, of course . . . well, to tell you the truth, I'm still embarrassed. Mom is one of those people who regards going to the movies as an interactive experience. You know the type. She'll talk to the screen, advise the characters in a con-cerned and motherly fashion. Romantic comedies are bad enough. "Kiss him!" she'll scream, while the rest of the the-ater tries to shush her. "What are you, nutso? He loves you! *He loves you!* When are you going to see how perfect he is for you?" And then she'll turn to whoever she's with and try to get them to side with her. "Oh, she's such a dumb cow! Isn't she? Don't you think she's being dumb? Unbelievable."

Not surprisingly, horror movies are worse.

Dad is the opposite, yet inadvertently equally noisy. Maybe it's just been twenty years since anyone's made a movie that he enjoys, maybe he's just narcoleptic. But ever since I was a little kid, every time the man has taken me to a movie, he's fallen asleep halfway through. We're talking cartoons, action flicks, comedies, intense epic dramas. And to call his septum deviated would really be a gross understatement; I'm willing to bet his nasal cartilage looks like Swiss cheese. He snores so damned loudly, you'd think you were being stalked by a mutant woodpecker if you couldn't tell where the noise was coming from. We've been kicked out of many a movie theater by ushers sum-moned by angry audiences. Poor Dad. Just trying to get some shut-eye.

Of course, this outing was no exception, but since it's been half a century since I've been taken out anywhere, I wasn't going to complain, even if my "dates" for the evening were a yappy lady in a yellow pantsuit and a snorting, snoring grump-tater.

The movie was fluffy and forgettable, but Chad melted the audience anyway with his usual charisma. I didn't really catch the plot; I was too busy gaping at my pretty neighbor and trying not to kick my own ass. I think it was something about Katarina being a poor little rich girl from Alabama, whose daddy made his money by inadvertently stumbling upon oil while digging a latrine hole on a camping trip. Something, something, she wins her father's love by becoming a fashion designer, something something, she gets to make sweet sweet love to Chad Downing in slow motion with good lighting and lots of delicious looking foreplay. Hate her.

As predicted, my mother tried to engage me in banter. ("Look at her *hair*, Jule! You could do your hair like that! Wait . . . no, she's a lot thinner than you.") But I managed to ignore her by staring at Chad blankly, drifting into gooey daydreams. Aaaaaaaah. Not twelve hours ago I had been in the presence of the gorgeous man on the screen in front of me. I could have reached out and touched him! He pet my dog! He *loved* my dog! I had a conversation with him! In my slippers! With a bag of poo! (Those last two thoughts snuck in there like the pink elephant on roller skates.)

So Katarina broke up with Chad, eh? That *could* explain his new apartment. Maybe he was tired of the glitz and the glamour, and yearned for something more? Maybe his heart was shattered, and he was hiding from his pain, from the shame of a public breakup? Maybe he spends his nights curled in the fetal position, racked with sobs and soaking his pillow?

Maybe I have an in? A teeny-weeny, fat-chance in, but an

in nonetheless? He's hurting, he's healing, he's *rebounding*. Even the homeliest, plainest, most cynical nondescripts have a chance with a rebounder. Must act fast. Time heals all wounds. I need to jump him while his heart's still bleeding and his romantic standards are bottomed out.

 Seven

I like to deal with stress by going out and getting completely blitzed.

Don't get me wrong—I don't have a problem. This is not alcoholism, or some sort of gateway into freebasing cocaine, or selling my teeth and nails for smack. I simply enjoy going out every once in a while and putting myself in an environment where people are out to have a good time. It's harmless; in fact, I think it's liberating. Especially, you know, when I don't remember anything the next morning. It's actually sort of like a whimsical magic trick. Poof! I didn't really dance topless on the bar! Shazam! I didn't really make out with two Mexican tourists! Bazoom! I didn't really give forty bucks and my cell phone number to the hobo by the late night snack shack!

And let's talk about stress, for a second. I work for a greasy, mediocre chain restaurant with a bunch of people I'd like to stuff a turkey with, make less money than a panhandler, live in a shit box, am infatuated with a fantasy, and haven't had my teeth cleaned in two years.

After successively making an ass of myself in front of Chad (Twice! Twice!), discovering he lives a condom's throw away from me, and learning of his recent departure from the ways of the romantically attached, I needed to relax.

Lucky for me, my best friend is wilder than a poker joker.

"Oooh, a girl's night on the town. I just bought the most fabulous ice-skater skirt, too."

Oh lordy; that meant sequins.

"I've got just the club," she continued. "Get yourself hoed out. I'll swing by around nine-thirty."

That night, when my doorbell rang, I was one sizzling vixen, baby. Hair teased out like a Cosmo cover model, boobs squeezed into a blue pleather tube top, enough mascara to rival a televangelist. I patted Riley on the head and strutted to the door.

One thing about Billie: there's nothing subtle about the way she looks. She never wears a plain or conservative article to make up for another that's flashy or loud. That being said, her ice skater's skirt was indeed a flouncy, twinkly teal, complete with spangles that swooshed in time with her sashaying hips. I personally might have complemented the skirt with a plain top, maybe black, or white, or even the same shade of teal; but something that really made the skirt stand out.

But why make one piece of clothing stand out when you yourself could stand out in a crowd of circus carnies wardrobed by Pucci?

Rounding out the skirt were grape-colored fishnet tights, a sleeveless mesh shirt that revealed a studded bra, white heart-shaped sunglasses pushing back her hair like a headband, and pink sneakers with pockets. That's right, shoes with pockets. To compensate for the lack of storage space, she had her cigarettes crammed under her bra strap.

To boot, she pulled out a cigarette and it was the same shade of teal as her skirt.

"Aren't they fab?" She jabbed excitedly with her nicotine accessory. "They're the latest thing. I had to go to four smoke shops and pay out the ass to get a pack of these. I hear Katarina Conrad will only smoke cigarettes that match her couture!"

"Let's not talk about Katarina Conrad," I groaned. "It just makes me think about Chad, and what a total loser I am."

"Please. You're not a loser, you just . . . um . . . get a little nervous around men. Come on, you can practice talking to guys we meet tonight."

Swell.

When we got to the club (Chez Naw-T, the venue lovechild of Martha Stewart and P. Diddy), the line stretched down the block. I took a closer look. The crowd was comprised of beautiful sparkly giraffe women, none of whom were, apparently, fabulous enough to get in. I took a quick look at us; I had blubber creeping out of each end of the tube top, and Billie was dressed like an abstract painting.

Yeah. We'd be stuck in line until Christmas.

I was ready to shrug it off and jump back in the car, but Billie was nonplussed. She charged the line, hopping up and down on her tiptoes to get a better look at the club door.

"Hey!" she shouted, while she waved at the bald, behemoth bouncer. "Hey, you!"

"Shhhhh!!!" I hissed, frantically snatching at her elbow. "Don't make a scene! We'll just get in line. It's moving pretty fast."

"Fuck that, I think it's . . . it totally is! Awesome, we're in!"

"It's who, Billie?"

"It's Denny!"

"Who?"

"Just this guy. I let him poke me a few weeks ago after a glass-blowing class."

Did I mention that Billie's also kind of a slut?

Maybe "free spirit" is a better description. She meets a lot of men in her new agey endeavors, and, frankly, the girl likes to get down. Usually these poor saps fall hard for her eccentricity, so they bend over backward for her. The last man she got involved with was the lead singer of an indie goth-rock band, and after Billie refused to be his girlfriend, he wrote eighty-two songs about her and ended up with a record deal.

Once Denny spotted her, you'd think we were some kind of royalty.

"Everybody move!" he bellowed to the incredulous crowd. "VIPs coming through!"

"Hey there, kitten," Denny growled to Billie when we'd finally pushed our way through the sea of silicone to the velvet ropes.

Oh Jesus, he had a tattoo on his face. On his eyelids, in fact. A tattoo of . . . eyes.

"Came in handy in school!" he chuckled when he caught me staring. "I could sleep through class and didn't nobody know the damned difference!"

I see.

"So what are you doing in my neck of the woods, kitten?" he continued.

I was about to giggle at the pet name, when I noticed that Billie was practically purring, rubbing her head against Denny's chest like a tabby in heat.

"Oh, you know," she cooed, "just having a girl's night out. My friend needs some cheering up."

"That true, babe?" Denny fixed his gaze on me for a second. Or maybe he was still looking down at Billie. Who knows? The tattoos were creeping me out.

"Um, I guess . . . yeah."

"You've come to the right man, ladies."

He pushed the door open and half bowed, sweeping us into the club with a bulging Franken-bouncer arm.

"Enjoy yourself, mama." He winked at me, patting Billie on the ass as she scooted through the door.

"Wow," I whispered as Billie giggled and blushed, "you actually like this one, huh?"

"Well . . ." She glanced back at him and smoothed her hair back. "He pushed all the right buttons. And he's got a dragon tattooed on his gigantic—"

"Drink? Let's get a drink!" I cut in. Some things are just not meant for my ears, thank you very much.

The bar was filled with disenchanted society chicks and the children of foreign dignities (made obvious by their Eastern European accents and excessive tawny lip liner). Clearly P. Diddy had more influence over the decor; otherwise, I suspect the bar would have been constructed from leftover foam packing peanuts, spray-painted bronze, and littered with napkins hand woven from sea grass. Instead it resembled a genie bottle; jewel colored scarves draping lazily from the rafters, lush velvet pillows scattered everywhere. And oh, how the place sparkled. The tables and chairs were embedded with tear-shaped rhinestones (or maybe actual diamonds; the man does love his bling-bling), the walls flecked with gold.

I was pushing past the tannest white chick I've ever seen when I felt a tap on my shoulder.

"Julie? Julie, I thought it was you!"

Huh?

I turned around.

Oh God.

Brian Colson.

The ex-boyfriend.

I swallowed a mouthful of bile and tried to smile like a normal person.

"Hi, Brian."

"Jule! You look great! Wow, I mean, what are you doing here? I thought you moved to Boston?"

Brian and I dated for a couple of years in college, and I guess I had assumed we'd get married. He seemed like the perfect guy, at first; polite and considerate, showering me with flowers for no reason.

Unfortunately, underneath the poised exterior lurked a freaky little man with an obsessive-compulsive disorder.

He had a thing about colors; Mondays were red, Tuesdays green, and so on. Shirts had to be a specific color, underwear, towels, foods. Do you know how difficult it is to find purple food? God, he would fucking *starve* himself on Thursdays, because all he could find were clusters of grapes.

If his towels didn't match his bath mats, hand towels, and washcloths, he would pitch an elaborate hissy fit, refusing to shower until the situation could be remedied.

I put up with it for a while, until I walked into his bedroom unannounced one day and discovered him holding a picture of my grandmother and jerking off into a towel.

A green one.

And it wasn't even Tuesday.

That pretty much did it for me.

He hates to dance, so I couldn't imagine why he'd be at a club, especially one this trendy.

"Hey, Jule, this is great, because you'll be the first to know!"

"Know . . . ?"

He looped his arm around the impossibly tan girl, who spun around gracefully.

"This is Naomi. We just got engaged a few hours ago!"

Naomi was about eleven feet tall and ninety-five pounds, at least twenty of which could be chalked up to the perfect blond curls cascading down her back. I ran a hand through my own frizzy ringlets self-consciously and tried to suck in my gut.

She was clad all in pink, clutching a purse trimmed with that frou-frou feathery stuff. Upon closer inspection, I noticed a Pomeranian peering out from the bag, its hair coiffed with tiny pink ribbons.

"Pleased," she yawned, extending a perfectly French-manicured hand resentfully.

Errrrr . . .

"Oh my God, Brian? Is that you?" Saved by the Billie, who swooped in from behind me and grabbed for his hand overzealously. "Good to see you. Nice towel. Come on, Jule, I ordered us a Scorpion bowl."

I let her drag me away, waving feebly at my ex, who ignored me and fused into a sloppy kiss with his mannequin.

"Why were you even talking to him?" she asked, leading me toward the bar by my elbow.

"Because . . . I don't know."

She narrowed her eyes at me. "You're not feeling all weepy over him, are you? Here, drink this. Maaaaan," she whistled, scanning the dance floor, "would you take a look at all the anorexic models? You know, maybe we should ship them off to Ethiopia, work out some kind of switcheroo with people who actually *want* to eat."

"Did you see the boulder on her finger? Do you think she knows about the towels?"

"Honey, why do you give a shit?"

I took a long sip of the Scorpion bowl, which, I have to say, was going down very smoothly.

"I don't know. Probably because the only boyfriend I've ever had has found someone . . . else. Someone blonde and spindly. Who accessorizes with teacup puppies."

"Man, fuck them. Things will start to happen for you, you just need some self-confidence."

Still, I couldn't help glaring at the strumpet who had her clutches around my ex's heart (and checking account).

"Do you think I'd attract more men if I started taking Riley around with me?"

"Don't be fucking ridiculous, Julie; you'd need a back brace and a duffel bag if you wanted to tote that beast along with you. Believe me, the hunchback/tri-athlete look won't work out too well for you. Come on, cheer up, let's talk about good stuff. How are things with Chad?"

I snorted, "What things?"

"Well, the sex bed thing, for one. Any response? Has he come a-knockin' yet?"

"What do you think?"

"Hmmm," she mused, "have another drink."

I went to sip the Scorpion bowl again, but oops, it was all gone. Must have sucked that thing down. Oh well, let's have another one.

All the people at dih bar are my besht friendshz! But Billie, loooorve Billie, but this man nicey, too.

Briansss szho dumb stupid monkey boy. Chad is right man for me.

"Zhjule! Have annnother shot. Tekeeeeeela! Buh na na na na na na na. Tekeeeeeeela!"

Chad gotssa love me, I'm sooo pretty. Fuck Chad, shtupid monkey shtupid boy. I doneed them, I doneed anyone.

Maybe I need thish nicey man. He'sh call cab.

 **Eight**

"**S**till here?"

I was wrapping up another spiritually fulfilling night shift at my dream job, scraping the tabletops free of kid crust and "marrying" the ketchups in my condiment caddies. I was closing the restaurant *again*, which means vacuuming, wiping, polishing, toiling, and resenting. Who wouldn't love my life?

I thought Junebugs was empty, except for Kylie, drinking draft beer with the busboy, and Stuart, who had retreated to his office after a particularly grueling batch of dinner customers. When he gets stressed he likes to smoke a joint and stare at the picture of Betty Page he keeps locked in his desk. (Don't ask; it was a serendipitous, traumatic discovery that I prefer not to relive, thank you very much.)

So was I surprised (aroused, elated, motherfucking ecstatic) to discover that Tyler was still lounging in the booth where I had served him dinner an hour ago.

"Looks that way." He half smiled, smoke slithering from his lips like a parade of scarves from a magician's throat.

I abandoned my sidework and wiped my hands on my apron, making sure Kylie was distracted before I made my way over to Tyler.

He was drinking booze tonight, different from his standard iced tea with extra lemons. He had two days' worth of stubble and was alternately chain-smoking and gnawing on a toothpick.

Meeeeeow. Rough around the edges.

"What is that, whiskey?"

He downed the rest of his shot, and grimaced. "Bourbon."

"Jesus, I can smell you from here."

"That bad, huh?"

Actually, his scent was sweet and musky, like vanilla tobacco harvested in the hills of Kentucky. It was mysterious. It was overwhelmingly sexy.

"Not too bad," I managed, careful not to blush or drool as I slid into the empty booth across from him. Good God he was hot.

We stared at each other.

"Ahem. A-hem! So . . . why the sauce tonight, cowboy? Long day on the range?"

Really, someone should stop me. Just reach down my throat and yank out my larynx, for God's sake. I am *such* a dork.

Fortunately for me, Tyler seems to be amused by my social ineptitude. He laughed and lit up a fresh smoke, offering me the pack. Naturally, I accepted.

"Long day, you ask? You could say that. Actually—nah, never mind."

Huh?

"Never mind? No, what? What, you can tell me!"

"Nah, it's—it's stupid. You're fun, let's talk about something fun."

Goddamnit, he's on the brink of a heartfelt confession, here!

"Tyler, every time you see me, I'm wearing googly bug antennae. Of course you think I'm fun. But I can be serious, too."

"Serious," he scoffed. "I don't need to be serious. I need to be . . ." He sighed, "Jesus."

"You need to be Jesus? Well preach on, brotha, there's an Episcopal church three blocks from here."

Well, goddamn, I *am* a funny lady. He didn't stop laughing until tears coursed through his stubble.

"Oh . . . oh man, I needed that. You're good, Julie."

"Hey, I try."

I sneaked a glance at the bar. Kylie and the busboy were now trading body shots of tequila. I shuddered as the shameless shrew licked salt from his neck and giggled. I wondered if she knew he was only nineteen?

"Are you going to get in trouble for sitting with me?"

"Trouble?" I scoffed. "Pshaw."

"I've seen Kylie bust your chops. She's pretty brutal."

"Eh, I can take her. She talks a good game, but between you and me, I can kick some serious ass."

He raised his eyebrows at me. "Oh yeah? I'd like to see that sometime."

Yeah you would, Marlboro man.

"So," he sighed again. "Okay. This is really lame, and I probably have no business talking to you about this, but . . . well . . ."

"Tyler, what?"

"Oh Jesus, this is stupid. I ran into my ex yesterday, and even though it's completely over and I have absolutely no desire to ever date her again *ever*, it was kind of . . . upsetting. Actually, really upsetting. But I don't know why."

"That's funny, I ran into my ex yesterday, too."

"Really?" He looked interested. "How long did you two go out?"

"Ummmm, two years or so."

"Yeah? Us, too. Anyway, I haven't seen her in a while, but she was with this . . . guy, this total, cheeseball preppy guy, with that awful trendy mussed-up hair, and capped teeth, and a fucking manicure! So I said hello, just polite, or shocked, I guess, and she tells me he's an actor. A fucking wannabe Hollywood actor. God," he looked disgusted by now, "how cheesy can you get? She's dating a fucking cliché! I just don't understand how she went from *me* to . . . *that*. I mean, can you explain that to me?"

"Actually, I can't. She had a teacup."

Tyler blinked. "Excuse me? A teacup? Who's she?"

"The new girlfriend. Fiancée, actually."

"Oh Jesus, he's getting married? I'm so sorry. What do you mean, a teacup? Were you at lunch or something?"

I snaked another cigarette from his near-empty pack.

"No, one of those little tiny accessory dogs. The rat dogs. With the foofy hair, the ones that you tote around in your purse because they complement your outfit?"

"A dog? Who the fuck does that?"

"Tacky society bitches, that's who. Tall, blond, spindly women with plastic boobs and one percent body fat and more money in their change purse than I'll make in the next two years."

"Wow," he whistled, "and that's who your ex is marrying?"

"Apparently."

He looked at me for a minute, wheels clearly turning.

"So . . . you have no idea, either? How he went from you to her?"

"Not a fucking clue."

"You still love him?"

"Don't think I ever did."

"Me, neither."

Hmph.

"It's just . . . unnerving," he continued. "Maybe I'm looking at this the wrong way, or being overanalytical, or something. But I feel like . . ."

Ah, hold up. I feel a moment of clarity coming on.

"You feel like you must have done something really wrong to have pushed her that far in the other direction?" I offered.

"Exactly! That's exactly how I feel."

"Well," I looked down at my hands, caked with ash and mustard, "I know the feeling, myself."

For the first time since we'd met, Tyler wasn't looking at me with an amused grin on his face, watching me perform like a trained circus seal. Instead, he seemed curious, affected, like my feminine wisdom had piqued his interest.

"Did he look happy?" he finally asked, after staring into my eyes for an unnecessary length of time.

"Who wouldn't look happy, with a mucus-membraned mannequin hanging off their fucking arm? God, she was like . . . this blonde . . . bored . . . sex toy!"

"Eh," Tyler scoffed, "girls like that are just masturbatory fantasy. It won't last."

"Ha. Hahahahahaha!" I snorted, producing a stream of smoke that burned the hell out of my nose hairs on the way out. "I don't think Brian likes to walk Willie the one-eyed wonder worm when he's thinking about Barbie."

"Excuse me?"

Sigh.

"Oh, Tyler. There's so much to learn about me. Soooo much."

Now he definitely looked interested.

So, I dove in, head first, and didn't stop until the icky, blue-haired, Jewish punch line.

"*Oh my God,* your *grandmother?*"

"Yep. Nana Anna. That's what we call her."

"Holy . . . and you *only* broke up with him? You didn't set the hounds on him? Take out a scathing personal ad in the *Beacon*? Put up flyers around campus with his face and crimes of humanity listed below?"

"Damn, you sound vindictive. Remind me never to date you!"

"Well that's just plain fucked up, Julie. You're better off without him, believe me. Perv."

I took a look at the bar to make sure Kylie was still planted in front of the Cuervo.

"You know what's really fucked up?" I whispered.

He leaned toward me. "What?" he whispered back. His face was gentle underneath the stubble, lean and angular, softened by his emerald eyes. They were gorgeous, framed by velvety lashes, which I was close enough to count. . . .

"What?" he asked again, jolting me from my delusion that we were about to make out. Focus, Julie. This is not a movie.

"Uh," I shook my head, "what's fucked up is that I didn't even break up with him right away."

"What? Why?"

"I was afraid, I guess. Of not finding anyone else. I mean, I broke it off eventually, just not . . . that minute."

"Jesus." Tyler shook his head. "The towel thing would have done it for me."

"Yeah, well, it wasn't that easy. Men have this annoying thing where they make you think they're normal until you're completely hooked. Then they unleash all of their nasty little flaws. Usually around the same time they stop bringing you flowers for no reason."

"No, uh-uh, not true. Women do the same shit. You act so cool and unaffected, but really, there's a jealous harpy clawing at your fucking rib cage, dying to bust loose at a totally inappropriate time. Mind-boggling. Every time I think I've found one . . ." He trailed off and stared into the bottom of his rocks glass.

Does he mean . . . me?

"Um, well, why did *you* break up with your girlfriend? She didn't have a towel thing, too, did she?"

"No, no. No, nothing like that. She was um . . . well . . ."

Come on, what? Whaaaaat?

"She just wasn't the one for me," he finished.

"That's it? I open up about the towel thing and that's all you give me? Come on, Tyler, I could be wiping down mustard bottles right now. Give me the good stuff!"

He laughed. There I go, trained seal again. Arf.

"She was a little nuts, too, okay?"

"Yeah? Go on . . ."

"She had this . . . teddy bear. But it wasn't a bear, it was a dog. A teddy dog? Anyway, she had to sleep with it, all the time, even when I was there. And she used to . . . talk to it. In this creepy, unaffected baby voice, like something from *The X-Files*."

"Tyler, a lot of women have stuffed animals."

"No, but this was *weird*, Julie. She used to make *me* talk to it. Its name was Mister Squiggles. And she'd say shit like, 'Do you *wuv* Mister Squiggles, Tywer?' And I'd play along, but it would get worse. 'Would you *wuv* Mister Squiggles if I wasn't around anymore? Like, if I died? If I *died*, would you still *wuv* Mister Squiggles? Would you have *wuved* Mister Squiggles if I hadn't existed, but he still did, and someone else's mommy had found him in the toy store?' Dude. It was *so* creepy. I couldn't take it! I couldn't take having to have a relationship with a fucking stuffed animal. It was too . . . much."

Wow.

"Wow," I said, "wow, I don't even know what to say, Tyler. That sounds pretty . . . unhealthy."

"Ha. That's putting it mildly."

"Well, it could be worse, you know. You could have spent the rest of your life having to brace yourself through endless ménage-a-trois with Mister Squiggles. At least you got out of it before she did any real damage."

He peered at me for another long moment, finally raising an eyebrow (which he's *really* good at. It's super sexy. Mmmrrrrgggh).

"Are you almost done?" he asked. "I mean, what time do you finish here?"

I opened my mouth to answer, but was trumped by a stuttering snap from above.

"Well, thee'd be finithed already if thee would actually do thome work."

Uh-oh.

I looked up guiltily. Stuart was standing over me (as best he could, for a midget, anyway), arms crossed and combover fluttering against his shaking head. He looked pissed. What else is new?

"Uh . . . I thought you were in the office, Stuart? You know, end of the night meeting with Betty?"

"Excuthe me? Betty who?"

"Uh . . . never mind."

"You've got thome nerve, mithy, abandoning your thidework tho you can thlack off. Were you planning on keeping the retht of uth all night?"

"The rest of *who*, Stuart? The only other people here are Kylie and Jailbait over there, and they look pretty happy to be skimming off the top of the bar stock!"

Stuart glanced behind him at the bar area, where Kylie was now trying to hop up and down on one foot while balancing a spoon on her nose. Pitiful.

"That'th not your problem, Mith Jorlamo. *Your* problem ith that there'th work to be done, and it'th *your* rethponthibility ath tonight'th clothing therver to *get your thit done*."

I felt a kick under the table, and my eyes darted to Tyler. He looked like he was torn between cracking up in hysterics or cracking Stuart in the teeth.

"Julie—" he began.

"No, it's fine." I nodded resolutely and turned back to the evil corporate slave driver.

"Okay, Stuart," I said sweetly, "I'll just finish up now, and then you can go home. I know how anxious you are to sit in your mother's armchair and watch scrambled skin flicks on the basic cable."

Ha! Take that, monkey man.

I stood.

"Tyler, it's been good to talk to you. Thank you for your patronage, and have a pleasant evening. Good night."

I purposely nudged Stuart with my elbow as I made my way back to the ketchup scraper. He sniffed, and started to bitch at me, but I ignored him and threw myself into my cleaning.

So mad. Sooooo mad. Stupid boss and his fucked-up favoritism bullshit. Come on, ketchup, come ooooonnnnnn. Jesus, it's just tomato, you'd think it'd be easy to get up. Come ooooonnnnnnnn. Grunt, scrape, scrub, sweat.

I was so involved with my cleaning that I didn't notice

Tyler slip away. Figures. I wouldn't want to sit around watching me sulk, either.

But still, he could have said good-bye.

It always happens like this, doesn't it? You pour your fucking heart and guts and kneecaps out to a man, and just when you think they're into it, they sneak away, unnoticed.

Fuck it. I don't need him. I don't need any more of this man bullshit. All I need is to swipe the rest of that tequila, buy a bag of corn chips, and fall asleep to the dramatic sounds of a *Law and Order* marathon.

So, I did. Sad. So sad.

 **Nine**

L eave it to a four-legged creature with minimal commu-
nication skills to set the ball rolling.

It's become a weekend ritual; once again I awoke to Riley
frantically whining, poking his wet little nose in my ear and
begging me to take him out. This time, however, I was in
the midst of an alcohol-saturated dream, the sort that seizes
your sense of reality. No idea what may have inspired it,
but I dreamt I was a farmer, residing in a barn in the middle of acres and acres of lush fields. My husband spent his
time with the horsies, but I—I bided my time milking cows
and tending hens that lay black eggs. (I think this may be a
subconscious warning that my ovaries are drying up and
it's time to get on with the babymaking.)

Somehow this dream kept a hold on me, even as I sensed
Riley sniffing at me and began to stir. Half awake, I led him
to the door so I could let him out into the backyard and he
could roam in the fields until it was time to make breakfast
for the farmhands.

An hour later I woke up for real, and realized, horrified,
that I had let my dog out into the hallway of my building,
where he had almost certainly peed on someone's door and
garnered a call to Animal Control Services.

Shit!

I pulled on the closest clothes (my pink, terry-cloth sheep bathrobe) and sprinted out the door, stage-whispering his name as I made my way to the stairwell.

Five doors later, old Mrs. Norris hadn't seen him, neither had the Rodriguez family, the Russians who speak no English, the drag queens in 3B, or Sheldon the trash man.

Oh God, he's at the glue factory for sure. I'm an idiot; how hard is it to keep track of an eighty-two-pound animal? Mental note: goldfish breathe, eat, pee, and procreate in the same space. Maybe I'll look into that.

Dejected, I was making my way to the elevator when I heard it—the faintest of barks followed by spirited laughter and the sound of a ball bouncing.

Riley?

I crept down the hall, stopping at each apartment and pressing my ear to the door. No, not in there . . . no, not in this one . . . not 3A . . . maybe . . . aha!! *Knock knock knock.*

If only I had looked at the number on the door before I knocked. I probably would have run upstairs and thrown on some makeup and an evening dress. But I was hasty, thinking only of my dog's welfare and not the sabotage of a potential sexual relationship.

Footsteps, and then Chad Downing opened the door.

I froze, unable to think of anything to say. Unable to think of anything at all, actually, except my morning death breath and the snarled ponytail atop my head. Christ. Why do I always run into him when I look like Medusa?

"Hey there!" he sparkled, widening the door, yet unable to hide a disapproving glance at my terry-cloth getup. "I think I know why you're here!"

To jump your bones, sexy movie star? Can't you read my mind?

He beckoned me inside. *Inside* his apartment. It's every American woman's wet dream, and I'm sporting sheep and half a tube of zit cream.

I don't know why, but I expected his apartment to be an alternate, glamorous universe, a portal into Hollywood luxury. Disappointingly, it was the standard one-bedroom layout, even more sparsely furnished than mine. The living room featured just a couch and a TV on a card table. The carpet was the same icky puked-up oatmeal color, the kitchen home to the same creaky refrigerator and two burner gas stove. The only decor was a series of black and white pictures, hung like ducks in a row around the perimeter of the living room. I leaned closer, and saw that they were all pictures of . . . Chad.

What the fuck? This was not a movie star's apartment! Where was the velvet love seat? The Oriental rug? The eighty-five-inch TV, the pool table, the gilded fountain spurting champagne into crystal goblets?

I was jolted from my dismay as Riley, ecstatic that I hadn't abandoned him, charged toward me and pounced, nearly knocking me over in his desperation for reconciliation.

"*Oof* . . . I see you, um, found my, um, my dog."

"Yeah, I stepped outside to grab the paper and he was wandering down the hall, whining. What happened? How did he get outside?"

Should I tell him about the black eggs? Maybe he will then want to fertilize me. On second thought, maybe he'll think I'm a Freudian nightmare. My heart pounded.

"He's so smart he probably figured out how to open the door, didn't you, fella?" Chad answered for me, stooping down to pet Riley. The dog, practically swooning at the prospect of attention, promptly rolled onto his back, paws flailing, tongue hanging out of the mouth. Frankly, I would have done the same thing if I thought I had a chance in hell of having my tummy rubbed by this beautiful, beautiful man.

"Well, I'm glad your mommy found you." He gazed adoringly at my lucky bastard dog, whose eyes had now rolled in the back of his head. Unbelievable, this was a totally different Chad from the man who sneered down at me a few weeks ago! Apparently he's fond of doggies. Sweet. I'm in.

"We had fun, though, didn't we? Didn't we?" Chad cooed, his gruff baritone melting into a baby voice. "I wish I had time for a dog," he sighed, looking up at me and grinning.

"Oh, well, anytime, you know, anytime," I stammered, palms sweating like a preteen girl at her first middle school dance, "feel free to stop by. He seems to like you, to really like you! That's weird. He doesn't usually like strange men. Not that I'm around a lot of strange men, but, you know, he's picky. Like me. Picky about men."

I seriously need to consider having my larynx surgically removed.

In a last ditch effort not to appear as a lunatic wildebeest, I summoned my inner bookworm. "I'm sorry, it's early, and I was so panicked about losing Riley. What I mean is that it's unusual that he's so taken with you because he's normally very protective. You should stop up sometimes, if you'd like to see him again. We live in 4C."

Finally, he stopped looking at me like I had tentacles bobbing from my chin.

"I'd love to come play with Riley again. It must be so tough for him to be cooped up in an apartment all day!"

I began to relax. "I don't know if cooped up is the word

for it. He gets a little cranky if he doesn't sleep for at least nineteen hours, so when I'm at work there's no chance of him being distracted from taking six naps."

He grinned, the skin around his eyes crinkling adorably into dozens of tiny puckers. I clenched my clammy fists to avoid hyperventilating, and took a deep breath.

"So, not to be rude, but why do you live *here*? I would think that an, um, actor who has done so many films could afford someplace a little more, um . . ."

"Glamorous?" He chuckled. "Actually, I'm researching a role."

I must have looked at him strangely, because he squirmed.

"Researching . . . ?"

"My next movie is called *John Dough,* and it's about a guy whose life goes from completely ordinary to absolutely wild when he discovers that his dad left him a diamond mine in his last will and testament."

He got this weird glaze on his face just then, like he was reciting a memorized textbook passage. Completely ordinary to absolutely wild, huh? Hm. Didn't sound like Oscar material, but let's face it, I'll probably go see it three times and then reserve a copy of the DVD two months before its release.

"My life isn't exactly ordinary," he continued, snapping out of his promotional trance and shrugging his muscular shoulders unapologetically, "so I rented this apartment so I can see how the little people live. You know, see what it's like to have normal digs. My publicist thinks it'll be fantastic press."

Little people?

"Oh," I stammered, nervous again and painfully conscious of my ranking among the plain folk, "interesting.

Yeah, it must be hard to be so, um, out of touch. Well, not out of touch, but successful. Well, I guess it's not hard to be successful, it must be nice! Hahahahaha. But, surely, you, um, remember what it was like before you were famous?"

He stared at me quizzically, and then I remembered. Tinkerbell Tissue Tzar. He had never been normal.

"Right," I said pointedly. "Right, of course. This is all pretty new to you. Well," I tried to smile, "if you ever need advice from a woman who's been nothing but hopelessly normal her entire life, just stop by. I'll be happy to tell you all about what it's like to live on Wonder bread and canned potatoes."

"Aw, thanks!" he gushed. "Canned potatoes? They really make those?"

Are you kidding? I buy those suckers in bulk. Fifty cents a can, and oh, so tasty. Just like you, Chad Downing. Yum.

He shook his head. "The apartment is going pretty well so far, I guess, but . . . I don't know. It's really hard to get into a role that's so financially inconvenient! My rent," he continued, "well, it's so easy to pay! Check this place out; it's barren! It's practically a mental ward!"

Yeah, never mind that it was pretty much, you know, identical to my hole in the wall.

"I mean," he continued, "how am I supposed to identify with a man who struggles to make ends meet when I receive weekly royalty checks for three times my monthly expenses? Honestly," he seemed disgusted, "it's just impossible to make the transformation."

My lust was instantly mutinied by eye-rolling incredulity. Poor, poor movie star. His life *is* difficult.

Suddenly, I couldn't wait to get out of that apartment. Who am I kidding? The last time I pulled in three times my monthly expenses, I was sleeping in pink bunk beds and hauling in a cool six dollars a week for watering my mom's plants.

And when he referred to the little people, he meant me, too, didn't he?

Celebrity scum.

I'm too fat for him, anyway. He'd be squashed like a little bug.

And I'm staring blankly into space. Come back, Julie. Just pull a good-bye together and grab the dog.

"Uh, yeah," I blinked, "it must be difficult to make that adjustment." I grabbed a whining Riley by the collar and stepped back toward the door. "Thanks again for entertaining Riley for a few hours. We'll see you again, I'm sure."

"No problem," he sparkled, "take care, you two!"

I couldn't grab the doorknob fast enough. What a pompous idiot! Researching a role as a little person by living in *my* apartment building. Either this asshole had no tact or no clue. I suspected it was a little of both.

Shaking my head and sighing, I pulled the door open.

Flash!! Snap!!!

What the . . .

Dazed by a blinding explosion of white light, I stumbled back, knocking my butt against the doorframe. Speechless, I winced as a man with a camera darted away, snickering.

 Ten

I thought Chad would have a heart attack when he yanked me back into his apartment, cursing and spitting like a vengeful llama.

"Son of a bitch. Son of a motherfucking big-tittied bitch. That asshole. Nobody is supposed to know I'm here! How the fuck did he find me? Oh Christ. Shit shit motherfucking dog shit!"

Yikes.

"Um . . ." I felt like a total idiot, but I had to ask. "What just happened?"

"What just happened?" He looked at me like I was a science experiment gone awry.

"Um, yeah."

"What just *happened* is that a photographer shot *you* leaving *my* apartment first thing in the morning. What's going to happen *now* is that you'll be all over the papers, and suddenly I have a mysterious girlfriend that the whole fucking world is going to want to know about. Oh God. Oh God, Phil. I need to call Phil."

"Who's Phil?"

"My publicist. Oh shit, he's going to have a heart attack."

He pulled out a tiny cell phone and dialed furiously.

"Hello? Yeah, it's me. You won't believe this." He lit up a cigarette and began pacing the room frantically. Finally, he disappeared into his bedroom.

Great. My fantasies about Chad's apartment never involved panic or desperation. I sunk into the scratchy brown couch and tried to be invisible.

After fifteen minutes of drumming my fingers, I got up the nerve to lean forward and peer into the bedroom. Chad was still waving his hands around maniacally, but he seemed to have calmed down a little. Eventually, he shut up completely, and just nodded for what seemed like ten minutes. Finally, he smiled, and hung up his phone.

I pretended not to pay attention as he strolled back into the living room, whistling.

"It's all okay." He grinned.

"Oh yeah?"

"Yeah. Come here."

Who, me?

"Uh . . . what?"

He waved me over.

"Come here!"

I got up, confused, and he folded me into a gigantic bear hug.

Omigod.

Chad spent the next several minutes embracing and soothing me like an old friend. He even apologized for being rude earlier, citing stress and blaming early morning crankiness.

This was the stuff of solo session fantasies, and on any other occasion I probably would have needed to change my pants.

I couldn't help but be distracted, however, by what he'd said earlier. Papers? The whole fucking world? By mid-afternoon, would I be on the cover of a dozen tabloids?

Would gossip gurus be savoring my name like German chocolate? Oh God, I could join the ranks of trophy wives, women whose faces stay fresh in your mind even though you can't quite think of who they are or why they've made the social pages! Women who lounge under the grasp of actors, who hang on the muscles of athletes. Women who marry Kennedys. Famous for doing nothing. Was I about to become one of them? In my goddamned sheep bathrobe?

I could feel my pores clogging. Suddenly, I needed to exfoliate.

"So, um, Chad, what exactly do you mean, it's all okay?"

He laughed, and patted me on the head like a lapdog.

"Phil's on his way. He'll explain everything."

Phil Goldbergsteinman, Chad's dedicated publicist, was coming over in an hour. Apparently, he had a manicure he just couldn't get out of. After checking the hallway for photographers, Chad agreed to let me go home and pull myself together, on the condition that I leave him Riley to play with. They were licking peanut butter from the same spoon when I left.

I called for double cheese and pepperoni reinforcements and took a steamy shower, scrubbing at my leftover eyeliner with a vengeance. I was staring dumbfoundedly at a new zit on the end of my nose when the doorbell rang.

Whoever stood there was obnoxiously impatient, because he jabbed at the doorbell three more times in the thirteen seconds it took me to emerge from the bathroom. Fucking impatient delivery guys. I threw open the door, a snarl on my lips and a retort curdling at the back of my throat. I was stopped dead in my tracks at the sight of the creature in front of me.

Remember that saying, "Those who can, do. Those who can't, teach"? I was staring at the physical embodiment.

Only, in his case, it was, "Those who can, walk about freely in the daylight. Those who can't, become publicists." Clearly the man's mother had an illicit affair with a side-show attraction. He was comically short, but wiry, lanky like a miniature version of a middle school boy after a summer growth spurt. His arms, seeming to have outgrown the rest of him (except his nose, natch), hung past his thighs and swung primally, almost to his knees. And his skin was the color of skim milk; pasty, but bluish. But the pièce de résistance, the greatest, strangest attribute, were his eyes. As he stood before me, foot tapping impatiently upon the welcome mat, he flipped his combed-over Brillo curls out of his face and revealed glazed, wintry eyes of the palest, iciest blue. I couldn't stop staring at them; they shimmered like glass. In fact, the left one *was* glass. He glanced up at my boobs and only the right eye moved. I shuddered.

Without an introduction, or even a greeting, he brushed right past me in a frenzy, hopped up on lattes and yanking pointedly on a Virginia Slim.

"Good, just out of the shower," he wheezed, his baritone dripping with Long Island nicotine. "I like to work with a fresh palate."

"So . . . I guess you're Phil?" I tried desperately not to look him in the . . . eye. I was afraid I'd start snickering.

"You got it, sweets. I'm the magic maker. I hear you had your first encounter with the vultures today. Please tell me you had makeup on."

"Um, actually, I was . . . in my bathrobe."

He raised a well-plucked eyebrow in my direction.

"Caught on film emerging from an A-list's apartment in your negligee? Now there's something!" He rubbed his shrimpy hands together gleefully. "That's a little more to work with!"

"Actually, I didn't say negligee." Hell, do I even own a negligee? "I said bathrobe."

He paused, flicking tiny ashes on my recliner. "Are we talking terry cloth, here?"

I nodded.

"Shit." He grimaced.

"With sheep," I offered, humiliated at my definitive unsexiness.

"Sheep?"

"Sheep."

He was silent for a moment, and then his cell phone/pager/heart monitor bleeped.

"Time for insulin?" I asked halfheartedly.

He gave me the eye, and picked up.

"Yeah? . . . Yeah . . . Yeah . . . Yeah . . . Yeah, yeah . . . Beautiful . . . Yeah . . . 'Bye.

"Well," he grinned, "it's on."

Apparently, terry cloth was okay. The caller had been Chad's agent, phoning to report the buzz. My picture had already been posted on Grapevine.com, a website dedicated to celebrity gossip, and although no one knew my name, there was a blurb about Chad Downing and his mystery maiden. The site had received fourteen thousand hits in the past forty-five minutes.

Chad showed up, grinning so enormously I could practically see yellow feathers fluttering in his wake. Good lord, I could eat that smile for breakfast. Now that the shock had worn off, my lust had returned. He's just so pretty.

"Where's Riley?" I asked shyly.

He fixed his baby blues on me. "Sleeping on my couch. We were playing Prefontaine with a paper towel tube as the baton. I think I wore him out!"

"Chad-babe." Phil reached up with his monkey limbs

and threw an arm around Chad's shoulders. "I have had the idea of ideas. The greatest, freshest hook of hooks. You're gonna be bigger than Mel, babe, bigger than Leo. And it's all," he turned his eye on me, "because of this . . . er . . . special lady."

Phil's "hook" did sound promising. Instead of disputing this morning's photo, he explained, we were going to run with it. Chad would pretend that I was, in fact, his girlfriend. His normal, down-to-earth, nonfamous girlfriend. His humble choice in women would make him seem accessible, Phil continued, and would be great press for his upcoming feature.

"After all," Chad agreed, "*John Dough* is about a normal guy with a normal job and a normal relationship."

We would go to premieres and benefits together, and stage romantic dinners at every trendy bistro in town.

"The stuff of Tinseltown," Phil called it. "Dashing screen god sweeps nondescript nobody off her callused tootsies."

He pulled a newspaper from his alligator briefcase and held it up for us to see.

THE DAILY BEACON

WHO'S THAT GIRL?

Chad Downing is definitely up to something. Or is it someone? Seems Mr. Downing has a mystery woman, a vixen in sheep's clothing—literally. Snapped tiptoeing out of Downing's apartment early this morning, the bewildered babe looks like she's been caught with a hand in the cookie jar. Maybe Chad is finally moving on from ex-flame and co-star Katarina Conrad? Only time (and The Beacon!) will tell.

Right above the headline was a gigantic picture of me, googly-eyed like a deer facing down a Hummer.

Why, oh why, didn't I wash my face this morning?

"Holy shit," I whispered. "This is terrible."

Phil chuckled. "No, my dear. This is fabulous."

Good eye twitching like a mad scientist, he began to pace the room and wave his arms wildly.

"Dumpling," he warbled, "this is better publicity than a presidential sex scandal. You're totally normal! Ordinary, average, just totally fucking run of the mill! It's brilliant."

"Gosh, Phil, you sure know how to make a girl feel special."

He motioned to Chad.

"Do *you* want to explain it to her?"

Chad cleared his throat, but remained silent.

Phil rolled his eye.

"You're a fairy tale to these people, kiddo. You were one of them, and now you're one of us. Who wouldn't be fascinated? Think of the appeal! Think of the fan base!"

He went on to explain that since my "normalcy" would appeal to a huge range of people, he wouldn't dispute the rumors. Instead, he was going to fuel them, by pretending that I was Chad's new girlfriend.

Uuuuunnnnnnggggggghhhhhhhhhhh!

"Girlfriend?" I cracked like a thirteen-year-old boy.

"Joined at the fucking hip, Plumpkin."

Probably any self-respecting woman would be pissed off that a man would so eagerly use her as a tool to enhance his image.

I, however, was at the brink of climax.

Not only would I be famous and glamorous, but I would be spending oodles of time fused to the most edible man in the country. I was to be, for all intents and purposes, his woman. His laaaaady. His mamacita. The only crappy part about it was that I wasn't allowed to quit my job.

"A waitress!" Phil practically trilled. "That's fantastic! You're a blue-collar magnet, Plumpkin! We'll nail the working stiffs and the graveyard shifters! Terrific stuff, terrific stuff!"

It would all come to head the following Wednesday. Chad was attending the third annual charity ball to benefit Cukes Not Nukes, a grassroots organization which used recycled military equipment to parachute canned vegetables into Africa. This year, they were raising money to buy can openers.

Luckily, Chad didn't have a date lined up yet ("Still reeling from the breakup," Phil hissed in my ear) so it was perfect. I would accompany him down the red carpet, grinning like a plastic doll and keeping him grounded amidst the glittery bullshit. Maybe we would even make out for the cameras. If he slipped me the tongue, I'd be a goner.

Phil choreographed my debut with a fervor reminiscent of Spartacus plotting the attack on the Roman Empire.

"Something with the hair!" he barked, pulling at my face under a six thousand watt bulb so he could scrutinize every pore. "But not too fancy! Can't look too done up, missy, or we'll lose 'em right off the bat. And your clothes," he continued breathlessly, "what size are you?"

Indignant, I mumbled a response.

He rolled his eye. (He has to stop doing that! It's freaking me out.) "I'm sorry, I don't speak Stammering Loser. Could you reword?"

Oooh, you little fucker.

I cleared my throat. "A twelve." I enunciated the hell out of that one.

"Really?" He looked me up and down. "You hide it well.

Anyway, that's great, too, because you're not skinny. People love to hate the twiggy ones. You're closer to the average size. Brilliant. In fact, if you were thinner I'd probably make you eat blintzes all week."

Finally, a man who appreciated some junk in the trunk. I was beginning to like the little twerp.

"Of course," he continued, "you can't wear designer stuff with those dinner rolls, but, again, it works for you."

I crossed my arms self-consciously over my tummy. Dinner rolls?

Phil studied me for a minute, then placed his hands on my shoulders.

"Honey," he said, "it's going to be great."

And it honestly was.

Chad's studio sent a purple limo for us on Wednesday night, after Phil delivered my ball gown, a hand-stitched gauzy number that he'd called in a favor for. It was amazing; sheer blue silk that rippled softly across my shoulders and plunged into a breezy neckline. Tiny glass beads were sprinkled across the bodice, glittering each time I moved, or even breathed. It took a minute to shimmy into, I was so afraid of ripping a seam or yanking off a bead, but I'd never felt so glamorous. I emerged from my bedroom a vision of poise, glowing as I spun around to show off my newfound elegance to Phil.

He stared for a minute. Clearly, I looked stunning, a bright, shining star ready to cast her exuberant light upon an adoring public. He looked lost for words, lost in the sea of my beauty. Finally, he spoke.

"Try to stick to protein tonight, okay? Don't want you to pop out of that thing. It's on loan."

He spun on his heel and took off.

I blinked.

"Yeah? Well, uh, uh, try not to let the door hit you in the *eye*!" I screamed. "Ass!"

Not my wittiest, by far, but I think the dress was cutting off the circulation to my brain. Good thing I'd be hanging out with actors tonight.

Billie showed up an hour before I was supposed to leave, yielding a bottle of gas station "champagne" and an economy size aerosol of hair spray. I'd been kind of reluctant to tell her about the whole thing, afraid she'd be jealous, or think I was ridiculous. I should have known better.

"Holy fuck!" she'd screamed when I called her. "Are you kidding? Are you drunk? You must be drunk. You can't honestly expect me to believe that you . . . you . . . holy shit. Is that? . . ."

"What? What?"

". . . How did your picture get in the *Daily Beacon*? . . . Are those sheep?"

Needless to say, she was thrilled for me. I felt a teeny bit guilty for ratting us out, because Phil made me swear within an inch of my life that I was *not to tell anyone*! He didn't want anyone blowing the door in on his precious publicity stunt. I figured that since Billie was a borderline pathological liar, this kind of thing would be right up her alley. I'm definitely not telling my mother, however. She's never liked any of my boyfriends, so this might be a great way to rub her face in it for once.

It took almost an hour to sculpt my hair into a pile half recognizable as a "style," but in the end I was pretty satisfied with Billie's creation. And I was half drunk, since we'd pounded the bubbly, so I was just impressed that she could still open the bobby pins.

"You look hot!" Billie crowed as she watched me put the

finishing touches on my makeup. "He won't be able to keep his fucking hands off of you!"

"This is *pretend*, Billie, okay? *Pretend*. I'm having a tough enough time with this without convincing myself that Chad Downing actually wants to be my boyfriend."

"You never know!" she sang, lighting up a smoke. "Regular girlfriends are trendy right now."

"Anyway, I don't think I told you, but I met this guy at work who I think is really—"

"Julie, are you out of your damned mind? Are you thinking about some restaurant schlub when you have the chance to sleep with the hottest thing on earth?"

"*Pretend.*"

At six-thirty the doorbell rang, and my stomach lurched. Billie answered it, while I tried not to throw up boneless skinless chicken breast and four egg-white omelet.

"Yes, of course!" she was saying. "She just finished."

It was Chad!

"She looks fabulous. Come on, Jule."

I swiped one last time with the mascara wand and took a deep breath, grabbing my tiny beaded clutch purse as I glided into the living room.

My stomach nearly ate itself.

Chad was wearing a dusky gray suit, accented by a tie the exact shade of blue as my dress. His hair was rumpled into lazy waves, his chiseled face dusted with five o'clock shadow. The suit fit him like a second skin, and the hair and stubble were just enough to hint that, underneath the polished exterior, he was a total badass. He always looked hot in pictures, but five feet away from me, he was positively edible. I could hardly breathe.

"Ready, Freddie?" He grinned, stooping to ruffle Riley behind the ears.

Not exactly the reaction I had fantasized about. I tried to reply, but it came out as a sort of grunt.

Billie waved maniacally from my window as we made our way down the sidewalk, snickering over the staring bystanders. I climbed into the limo and turned to my dashing companion. Chad grinned, but he didn't relax, as I expected. Instead, he launched into a whirlwind of fidgeting, primping, and preening.

I tried to think of something to say, but he was busy plucking his eyebrows with a tiny set of tweezers. I turned my attention to the minibar.

"Help yourself," he offered absentmindedly. "But don't touch the low carb microbrew, okay?"

Sure.

I comforted myself with an enormous vodka tonic. He yanked a few stray hairs and turned to me.

"Soooo . . . did Phil go over the junket routine with you?"

Before he dropped off my dress, Phil had called to prep me for the chaos.

"I don't want you to know too much about what you're facing tonight," he had said. "You need to look natural, like you don't understand why anyone would want to take your picture. You need to look a little wet behind the ears."

I was actually feeling a little wet between the legs from all the excitement.

"Yes," I said, "but he didn't tell me too much. Wants me to look . . . fresh."

Finally, Chad looked at me, letting his eyes trail up and down. It was about time, goddamnit. It's not often that I put on lipstick and let my boobs hang out.

"Well," he said huskily, "you've certainly accomplished that."

He ran his finger down the nape of my neck and gave my shoulder a squeeze. I tried not to have an orgasm.

"It's just," he began, and leaned closer, peering into my eyes.

Breathe, Julie, breathe. Omigod omigod he's getting closer.

"You have . . ."

Omigod. "Yes?" I cooed hornily, my eyelashes thrust into overdrive. I leaned in slightly, prepping myself for explosive vehicular carnage.

He reached up a hand to graze my face, and . . .

Ow!

He leaned back, triumphant.

"You had this one stray hair. I was going to use my tweezers, but it was so long I got it with just my fingers!" Satisfied with my grooming, he leaned back in his seat and let out a belch.

Jesus, it's a wonder he didn't rummage my scalp for fleas and other snacks.

Fifteen minutes later we'd pulled up in front of the venue. I peered out the window but couldn't see anything but a sea of faces and flashbulbs. The place was mobbed! And everyone was staring at our limo.

"Let's do it!" Chad exclaimed, rapping on the privacy screen to let the chauffeur know we were ready. I took a deep breath.

The door opened, and I was hit with a wave of unbearable noise.

Everywhere we looked, people were screaming their heads off. Photographers were shoving at each other behind a thick velvet rope, screaming at the top of their lungs.

"Chad! Chad, over here!"

"Chad, is this the mystery woman we saw in the paper?"

"Mr. Downing, tell us about your new lady friend!"

"Chad! Mr. Downing, look this way! What's her name?"

I gulped. Chad nudged me gently with his elbow.

"Come on!" he hissed through a beaming smile. "Don't let me down!"

Nodding, I slipped my hand through his arm and summoned a huge grin. He slid his hand over mine and squeezed. We approached the velvet rope.

"One at a time!" Chad laughed. "One at a time. I know you're all eager," the noise dulled, and he gazed at me, "to meet my special friend. Ladies and gentlemen of the press, meet the lovely Julie Jor . . . Jorlamo."

"Jorlamo? Jorlamo, Mr. Downing?"

"How do you spell that?"

"With a J?"

"How did you meet each other, Chad?"

"Ms. Jorlamo, how does it feel to be on the arm of the most eligible man in America?"

"Ms. Jorlamo? Ms. Jorlamo!"

I was completely bewildered. I looked at Chad helplessly for a cue and just kept smiling.

"Julie," Chad continued, "is an incredible woman. We met not so long ago, when she waited on me one rainy afternoon. I took one look at her, and, well . . . she's just so different from women in the business!" He sighed. "It's so refreshing!"

"Waitress?" the crowd mumbled. "She's a waitress?"

"She's a waitress!"

"Not an actress!?"

"How refreshing!"

"How refreshing. A waitress!"

"That's really all we have time for!" Chad spoke over the

wondrous murmuring. "But I'm sure we'll see each other again, at the premiere of my new motion picture, *John Dough*. We go into production next month. Solstein's directing, it's going to be magical."

"Mr. Downing! Mr., Downing, wait! Wait!"

"Terrific job!" Chad whispered, leading me down the red carpet and through an enormous set of gilded, mahogany doors. "They loved you!"

The rest of the night was an endless routine of dancing, schmoozing, and smiling. Chad was a vision of photo ops, leading me shyly onto the dance floor, kissing my forehead, dabbing baked brie from my chin. Everyone wanted to know who I was, and who designed my dress ("And your rack!" one platinum blonde whispered knowingly). I kept the charm flowing as best I could, and was starting to really get into it when I felt a tap on my shoulder. I spun around with a smile, and came face-to-face with the one person at tonight's ball who definitely did not love me.

Katarina Conrad.

Chad's ex-girlfriend and Hollywood megastar.

She was taller and thinner than she looked onscreen, interesting because she had a long running stint as an anorexic mafia wife on the movie channel series Fuhgeddaboutit. Her hair was chocolate, thicker than a Dickens novel and cascading over her ivory shoulders. She was menacing in a midnight gown of taffeta, throat dripping with millions of tiny diamonds. Her black eyes flashed as she took a fold of my dress between two immaculately manicured talons.

"So this is Chad's new work in progress? Nice dress. I wore the same one to the T-Shirts for Toddlers Benefit Roller Derby last autumn. Of course," she sneered, "the de-tail is much easier to see on yours. That happens when they have to use more beads."

My jaw dropped. A half-chewed baby carrot tumbled out.

"Hello, Kat." Chad slid in between us and offered the Dark Princess an obligatory peck on the cheek. "I see you've met my new muse. Enchanting, isn't she?"

"Rubenesque," she spat coldly, tossing me one last red flag stare and retreating to the ladies' room, probably to throw up.

Livid, I watched her sail away, my fists clenched in heat-seeking hammers of rage. I wanted to beat her perfect face in, to yank out her horsehair weave and stuff it up her expensive little nose.

"Take it easy," Chad soothed, plucking orange specks from my décolletage, "she's just pissed because you're getting more press than her. Oh, waiter, can you get my lady friend a glass of white zinfandel?

"On the other hand," he cocked his head, "a catfight would draw a lot of attention. How's your left hook?

"Kidding, kidding!" he protested when I threw him an icy glare. "Her publicist would throttle you. And where would that leave me?"

THE DAILY BEACON

THE LADY IS A . . . WAITRESS?

The stars shone brightly on the red carpet last night, showering the annual Cukes Not Nukes charity ball with glamorous, glittering light. From Tom to Mel, Demi to Arnold, it seemed everyone who's anyone showed up to raise money for the fashionable organization. But it seems invitations extended themselves beyond the usual crowd; brace yourselves, last night's pack leader was a doozy.

The delectable Chad Downing was on hand, per usual method of partying madness, but on his arm? Why none other than . . . Julie Jorlamo. All together now: "Who?" You're not alone, dear readers. Mr. Downing's mystery date brought that very question to the lips of, well, EVERYONE. The skinny? Well, she isn't, but that doesn't seem to matter; the delectable (and usually discerning!) Downing looked like one smitten kitten. Seems the mystery maiden is a waitress, but no word on how the lovebirds hooked up. But trust us, we'll keep you posted.

 Eleven

"The dailies are in; you're a hit! Have another spring roll. Got to keep your weight up, Plumpkin!"

It was two o'clock, the afternoon following my big night out, and I was seated across from Phil on the patio at a swanky Beverly Hills lunch spot. I was the only one eating, however; he just kept taking food from his plate and slipping it onto mine, apparently trying to stuff me like a taxidermied striper bass.

"Phil, I can't eat another bite. Why don't *you* eat something, instead of just eyeing me throughout the whole—sorry, you know what I meant. I hope you don't expect me to puke after this; bulimia's definitely not my Hollywood diet of choice."

He chuckled, "Oh, no, my darling, just the opposite. We need to keep you nice and round so that the whole world will just keep on loving you!"

I leaned back in my velvet-swathed chair and glanced around, hoping no one would notice if I released the button on my khakis. I like to eat, but this lunch had been ridiculous; course after course of goodies like sundried tomato brie tartlets, spicy peanut noodles with seafood, beef saté, Mediterranean spring rolls in a sea of creamy hummus, plates of soft cheeses, strawberries bathed in dark choco-late. Since I'm used to existing on cheese in a can and the occasional screw-up potpourri entrée at Junebugs, I was practically drooling at my dumb culinary luck. I inhaled that meal like it was a cheap Mexican doobie.

I accepted the spring roll, daintily, and crammed the whole thing into my gaping pie hole. Mmmmmmmmm. So crispy and delicious

"What do you mean," I sprayed around the enormous mouthful, "keep my weight *up*?"

"You seem to have a pretty good idea of what I mean, Plumpkin. Napkin? Trust me, take it."

He waved his grubby little paw at me with urgency, clearly reluctant to be seen dining with a hippopotamus. I took it and dabbed at the corners of my mouth.

"Happy?"

"Because you wiped your mouth off? Considerably less disgusted."

This from a carnie with a steel wool comb-over, and a cocktail onion in his eye socket.

"So, now that you're not encrusted, let's talk shop, kid. I'm thinking *Vogue*, I'm thinking MTV. Maybe your own daytime talk show, or even a line of handbags. No? Accessories? What's your take on knee socks?"

"What? Knee socks—what?"

"You know, tubelike cotton things, go on your feet, come up to your knees? I thought you went to college, Miss Smarty Pants?"

"I know what fucking knee socks are," I snapped, "what I mean is, what the hell are you talking about? MTV? My own talk show? You're acting like I'm the celebrity, here."

Phil blinked. Or winked, I should say. Only the good eye closed. Creepy.

"You will be, when I'm done with you. Jesus Christ, toots, after your big night out last night, everyone's going to know your name. The whole world is your Cheers, Norm."

"I don't want everyone to know my name!"

He snorted. "Too late for that, isn't it? You'll like it, trust me. You just need to get used to the hoopla. And believe me, where there's Chad, there's hoopla."

"Well, of course there is. He's so . . . you know . . ."

"Dreamy?" Phil rolled his eye, "Charming and handsome and special? Blah, blah, blah, I've heard it all. It's not exactly true, you know."

Are you trashing my boyfriend, ba-itch?

"What do you mean?"

"It's the business, toots, it's make-believe. He's playing a part every time he goes out there. They all do. You will, too. That's why I'm trying to help you; you don't want to be playing the quiet little wifey for too long."

"I thought you worked for Chad? You don't sound like you're too fond of him."

"I'm fond of his bankroll, babe. I'm fond of his weaknesses, his utter naiveté when it comes to controlling his image. That's where I come in. If he were a self-sufficient brainiac, I wouldn't have a goddamned job."

"He can't be that clueless."

"You haven't spent that much time with him. Just do yourself a favor, snickerdoodle, and don't go getting all emotionally involved. That's the first rule of thumb in this business: don't shit where you eat."

"Ew!"

"I know, I'm a regular fucking Wordsworth. The point, much less eloquently, is don't fuck around with the clients. Too messy."

"He's your client, not mine. Besides, I think he's a wonderful guy."

Phil looked amused. "And you think you're his type, do you?"

"I think"—you son of a smelly bitch—"that Chad and I have a lot in common. I think we make a great team."

"Yeah? The dream team, are you? Just don't forget that that's exactly what this is, okay? Not a reality. Made up. Pretend. Chaddy is not your daddy."

Whatever.

"Let's get back on track here." Phil pulled a pad of paper from his briefcase and began scribbling notes. "Julie Jorlamo; superstar."

I snickered.

"What, that's funny to you? Listen, muffin, I'm going to put you in the spotlight, and you're going to keep yourself there, if it kills you. You have great potential, kid, don't blow this for yourself."

"But Phil, I can't *do* anything!"

"What do you mean?"

"I can't act, I can't sing, I'm not sucking dick in the Oval Office, I'm not skinny and glamorous and gorgeous. I'm just . . . normal. I haven't done anything that would interest anyone!"

"Oh my God, Plumpkin, are you fucking kidding me? Do you watch TV? Do you read the magazines? Who *has* done anything interesting lately? These people aren't Shakespearean thespians, for Christ's sake. They're not Wagnerian lyrical super divas. They're all factory assembled, plain and simple. Plastic and fucking veneer. Nobody *deserves* to be famous; it's all about promotion, butterball! It's about marketing, and placement, and keeping up with the trends. And you, my little gold mine, you can be the new trend!"

"What makes you think that?"

"You're one of them."

"I keep hearing that. It's making me feel like an alien."

"I don't mean that in a bad way. I mean . . . you're plucked from the masses. Everything about you screams everyday American."

"Thanks."

"What are you getting all defensive for? It's not a bad thing! In fact, it's a very, very good thing. Everybody dreams about making it big, but practically nobody has the look. That's what's so great about you—you don't have the look, either. But you're there, you're doing it. A celebrity, a larger-than-life fucking deity, sees something special in you. In someone ordinary. And that, my dear, gives people hope. And magazine subscriptions. It's brilliant. You're going to make me a ton of money."

"I knew there was something in it for you."

"And why shouldn't there be?"

Phil sighed, then reached across the table and covered my hand with his. Of course, it was cold and sweaty. Can there be nothing unrepugnant about this man?

"Plumpkin"—does he even know my real name?—"I can see right through you. You're young, unsure of yourself. You have low self-esteem. People love that fucking word, don't they? Self-esteem? I swear to God, Oprah made that word up in the mid-eighties. Anyway, I know what the problem is. You're terrified. Come on, Plumpkin, you love this celebrity bullshit just as much as anyone else. I can see it in your eyes! You're hungry for the glamour. And some more spring rolls, huh? No? Okay. But I can see how much you want this, and how afraid you are of not being good enough. Everyone I've worked with goes through this, darling. They all want to be in the spotlight, but they're all afraid of illuminating their flaws."

"Why me, though? Why choose *me* to be America's Everywoman?"

"Well, you were the one caught creeping out of Chad's apartment. I don't have too much of a choice, do I?"

"True."

He lit up a Virginia Slim and sighed, streaming smoke through his nose like a tiny Israeli bull.

"Julie"—finally. I was beginning to wonder—"neither of us is exactly Hollywood material. Look at us, huh? Why do you think I'm behind the scenes, instead of working the red carpet? To tell you the truth," he leaned closer to me, "I wanted to dance. Do the hip-hop thing. No, really, had the jazz hands and everything. But, there was a height requirement, of course, and I could never cram myself into the damned unitard."

"Phil, when was the last time you saw a hip-hop dancer in a unitard?"

"Hey, at Lena Barker's Long Island School of Movement, you wore the fucking unitard, okay? I had big dreams, kid, but curly hair and big, floppy bitch tits. I couldn't have been a dancer! So, I moved to L.A., got into promotions. And here I am. Publicist to the stars. Not a bad gig, eh?"

"Big floppy bitch tits? But you're so skinny!"

"I liked the blintzes back then, what can I say? That was long before the low-carb craze."

"Wow."

"So you see, you and me, we're not that different."

"Are you saying I have, big floppy bitch tits?"

"You're missing the point."

"At least they're real."

"Jesus! Your tits are fine, okay? Let it go!"

Hmph.

"My *point*, Plumpkin, is that we're both average Joes with the bug. The Hollywood flu. Think about it; I'm giving you gold, here. This is your chance, honey. Do it for me, do it for the little guys."

"What do I have to do?"

"Just do exactly what you did last night. Have a few drinks, have a laugh. Hang on Chad's arm and be his leading lady. Let everyone get to know you. And when the time is right, we'll branch you out on your own. It'll be a smooth transition."

I couldn't believe what I was hearing.

But I didn't even get a chance to respond, because next thing I knew, there was a hand massaging my shoulder and frogs jumping around in my stomach.

"Hey, you two. Sorry I'm late."

Oooooooh boy, it was Chad. And he's touching my shoulder!

I had to fight to keep that last spring roll from creeping up my throat.

"Hey, hey, there's the man of the hour." Phil cleared his throat and stuck his hand out to grab Chad's briefly. "We were just talking about you, my man."

"The patio, Phil? I'm shocked! Outside dining breeds inside information, you know. Hey, what are you, trying to hold hands with my woman?" Chad teased playfully. He gave my shoulder a squeeze and slid into the empty chair beside me.

I tried not to have an orgasm.

"Hey, um, hey. Hi, Chad. Hi!"

Verbal diarrhea. Verbal diarrhea.

He was stunning in a faded leather coat and shades, even

more attractive now that I knew he had flaws. Somehow, imperfections make a man seem more vulnerable and approachable. I just wanted to wrap him up in a blanket and rock him in my arms for hours. And then shag him rotten, of course. Mmmmm.

"What's the word?" he asked. "Any press from last night? How'd we do?"

"Are you kidding?" Phil lit up another girlie smoke. "They loved her. *And* you, of course, but you knew that. I tell you what, Miss Julie here is going to push your career over the top. Forget A-list; you'll be double A-list, or whatever the fuck you wanna call it. The people want to know more, my friend, and *that* is a great sign."

"Who wants to know more?" Chad furrowed his brow, digging through his jacket and producing a pack of cigarettes. God how I love smokers. It's just so damned cool. Sorry, Mom.

"*Everyone,* babe. The press, the readers, the studios."

"What about Katarina?"

Huh?

Phil's eye bulged. "Katarina? What do you care about what she thinks? Twat."

"She's not a twat!" Chad banged his fist on the table and looked away.

Is that a tear? Uh-oh.

"Chad, she dumped you for a glorified school photographer, for God's sake. A fag. He's a total fag!"

"She did *not* dump me, it was mutual!"

"Chad," Phil hissed, and gestured toward me, "pull yourself together! You're being a fucking pussy. Besides, there's a lady present. Your lady. Remember?"

Oh goddamnit, he still loved her. Did he forget what a conniving little bitch she was last night? *Rubenesque?*

The sad thing was, I thought she meant the sandwich until I looked it up on the Internet that morning.

Chad sighed. "Sorry, Julie. You did great last night, really great. Everyone loved you. It's going to be such a big help."

He reached over and squeezed my knee.

Oh God, I love him.

"That's more like it, kids." Phil rubbed his hands together greedily. "The happy couple. Let's make it happen!"

When I got home, my answering machine was having a seizure, red light pulsing as insistently as a strobe light.

Beeeeeeeep

"Hey, Jule, it's Billie. Just wanted to see how it went last night. I'm still in bed, but I'm going to get the paper in a few. I want details!"

Beeeeeeep

"Miss Jorlamo, this is your cellular wireless company. Please give us a call regarding your past due account."

Shit, forgot about that.

Beeeeeeep

"Julie, thith ith Thtuart from Junebugth." Like I couldn't tell. "The dithtrict manager would like you to call uth today regarding your thchedule. We need to know if you can pick up a few more thiftth."

Beeeeeeep

"*Julie Jorlamo!* This is your mother calling. Or perhaps you've forgotten? You have a mother? The woman who bore you, the woman who's *supposed* to be your *confidante*, not a *total stranger*? Were you planning on telling us about this man? Dating a movie star, and doesn't even tell her mother. I had to find out about it in the papers. If I have to read about a wedding or an illegitimate grandchild in the

Beacon, I swear to God, you're having Thanksgiving out of a can. Oy. Call us. *Now*."

Beeeeeeeep

"*Omigod!* It's Billie again. I just got the paper, and you're on *the front page* and Chad Downing has his *hand* on your *ass*! Oh my *God*, did you do him? Did you do him naaaasty? Girl, you'd better call me!"

Beeeeeeep

"Plumpkin, I know you just left the restaurant, but I wanted to give you a heads-up on your schedule for next week. Call Flan at Fabu Salon tomorrow morning; he's going to fit you in for a consultation. Eat up, sugar bean, and don't you dare drop a single pound. Ciao kid. You're gonna be a star!"

 Twelve

The next two weeks were murder on my poor little feet.
In the midst of attending three premieres, two benefit balls, a charity finger-painting marathon, junkets, press
conferences, grand openings, and a baptism, I was working
endless double shifts at Junebugs. Apparently, the management noticed that customers were waiting over an hour just
to be seated in my section, so they decided I was good for
business.

Kylie and Stuart were less than thrilled; in fact, they
showed me no mercy.

"Wellll," Stuart squeaked Monday morning as I stumbled in ten minutes late. "Lookth like our little thelebrity
thtill thinkth thee's too impooortant to get here on time.
Which page of the paper are you on today, thuperthtar?"

I shot him a look of death and clipped on my name tag
with a vengeance.

Actually, I was on pages three and fourteen of the Social
Notes section in that day's *Beacon*. Chad had dragged me
out to the thirteenth annual "Bar-B-Q for Babies" charity
pig roast, and he'd made me stay until four-thirty in the
morning.

"Just until Katarina leaves, okay?" he'd begged. "I just want her to see me having fun without her. Please?"

I'd been beyond annoyed, but then he slipped his arm around my waist and pulled me close, nibbling softly on my earlobe before planting a sizzling kiss on my lucky lucky lips.

Mmmmmmaaaagggg.

There was no other man on the planet.

My section was already full for lunch, and it was barely eleven o'clock. Nine tables full of adoring patrons, each of whom was anxious for an autograph, or picture, or a story about "my boyfriend." I rushed around like a crazy woman, pouring coffee, taking orders, even turning down a request for my panties from a tiny little Irish octogenarian.

"If I were forty years younger, I'd be chasing you around," he'd lilted with a sigh.

His equally tiny wife elbowed him and rolled her eyes. "Martin," she clipped, "if you were forty years younger, you'd still be forty years too old!"

Kylie led the other servers in a silent rebellion, refusing to help me deliver food or bus any of my tables. Instead, they perched themselves at a bar table and smoked. In my frenzy, I overheard them bitching about their empty tables and my snobbery.

"It's such bullshit." Kylie's voice carried over the buzzing dining room. "She's totally using this place to rub it in our faces."

"Totally!" agreed Gilly.

"And why is she even working here anymore?" Kylie continued. "I thought all this fuss was because she was swept off her feet by a celebrity. Doesn't her man bother to give her any money?"

"Well, Julie probably hathn't thucked hith dick yet," Stuart chimed in. "That'th why he'th holding back."

The pipsqueak was right about that. Not that I hadn't tried, however.

After he kissed me last night, Chad was super affectionate, holding my hand and sucking pork grease off my fingers. The sexual vibe between us was so strong that a photographer asked us if we'd set a wedding date.

When the last party guest had trickled from the barbecue pit, and our host had passed out under the picked-over swine carcass, Chad finally paged the limo driver. I was anxious, antsy, trying to prep myself for boinking a real life megastar. My plan was simple: hop in the car, suck in my gut, and rip off his clothes. Surely he couldn't resist. After all, he couldn't tear his eyes off me (er, my Wonderbra) all night.

Oh, sweet disaster.

It could have been the nine white zinfandels (ordered mysteriously at Chad's insistence), the chitlins, or cracking my head on the door frame as I stumbled into the limo. Maybe it was the Cuban cigar I shared with that reporter, or the benefit's experimental video screening, featuring piles of malnourished baby corpses. Whatever the poison, whoever the culprit, it all added up to one thing.

Puke, baby. Like a sorority girl after a Chinese buffet.

It was instantaneous. It was sniper vomit. Fast, unexpected, from out of nowhere. One minute I was unbuckling his belt, the next, I was blanketing him in an evening of gluttony.

Astonishingly, wretching all over the hottest motherfucker on the planet wasn't the worst of it.

After the heaving subsided, I couldn't look at him. I

couldn't even apologize; I was so unabashedly mortified that all I could do was sink back in my seat and wipe off my mouth. He looked down at the mess in his lap, then back at me. I braced myself.

"You weren't trying to undo my pants, were you, Julie?" he slurred with a smirk. "That's not what this is about," he continued. "And I wouldn't fuck you, anyway. You're a twelve."

He rapped on the tinted privacy glass and the limo lurched to the right, screeching to a halt in front of what I could barely make out, in my inebriation, to be our apartment building.

"See ya," he yawned.

"What?" I joked feebly. "You're not going to get the door for your puke princess?"

"Are you kidding? The night is young, and you smell like a fucking Havana landfill. Dream Gems is having an afterparty; that's where I'm headed."

"But, you kissed me!"

"Well, *yeah*, do you think anyone would believe we were going out if I hadn't puckered up at least once? I'm an *actor*, Julie, I was *acting*."

"But, don't you want—"

"What I *want*, Julie, is for you to stop smelling up the limo! This shindig's going to be crawling with models; I think I can bang at least four. Well, maybe three. Definitely two, definitely. Now, get the fuck out, and try not to slobber on the seats. Oh," he called after me as I crawled, humiliated, from the limo and spilled onto the cold sidewalk. "and take this with you!" It was his dinner jacket, dripping with, well, my own dinner. "Try to get it cleaned tomorrow, would you? I mean, you're the one who messed it up! I'm not touching the damned thing. Ciao."

I was still dragging my left leg out of the limo, but Chad pounded the glass again and it took off, taking my shoe and my dignity with it.

By two o'clock I was wilting. Besides spending most of the morning slipping into the ladies' room to dry-heave, I had waited on close to fifty tables in three hours, and most of them hadn't bothered to tip me.

Finally, the rush lulled, and I sank into a table in the corner of the bar. I was lighting a cigarette when I heard the jangle of the front door.

"Aahhh, another member of Julie's fan club?" I heard Dixie's singsong warble.

"Hi, Dixie." It was a man's voice. "Damn . . . it's packed! What's going on?"

I peered around the booth back. It was Tyler!

I had practically forgotten about him since the kiss, but seeing him walk through the door instantly renewed my attraction; he was looking as cute as ever, cheeks flushed from the heat. I smoothed down my frizz and jumped out of my seat. Finally, the day had a bright spot! Grinning like an idiot, I watched Dixie lead him over to a table . . . not in my section . . . in Kylie's.

In *Kylie's*?

"Julie's tables are all full today, darlin'," I heard Dixie explain as she handed Tyler a menu. "Looks like it's Kylie's lucky day!"

"Well, well, well!" Kylie came out of the kitchen looking like a horny hyena ready to pounce. "Tough luck, glamour girl. He's not your type, anyway. Too commonplace."

I stretched out my leg to try and trip her, but she's not as dumb as she looks. To boot, the bitch spit her gum in my hair as she pushed me out of the way.

Watching her slide into the booth across from him was too much. What did she think she was trying to pull? Tyler came in to see me. Right?

I tried to catch his attention and give him a wave, but Kylie glided right into my line of vision. She pushed her boobs up as she rested her arms on the table, tossing me a "fuck you" glance. I thought Tyler would shoo her off, but instead he leaned forward and said something under his breath that made her giggle hysterically.

Didn't he want to talk to me?

Stuart answered for me. "Thellout!" he whispered while I stood there agape. "Now finith up and go home tho my other employeeth can earn a living."

"I still have tables, Stuart."

"I know that. But you're not getting any more. I'm thick of having to watch people fawn all over you. I don't give a thit whooth girlfriend you are; that doethn't mean I have to like you."

"Do you know how big an asshole you are?"

"Do *you* know how bad you thmell today? What'th wrong, forget to thower after thome big fanthy party latht night? Cry me a fucking river, thuperthtar. Believe me, if the both would let me can you, you'd have been out of here three weekth ago."

It took me a while to get to the employee parking lot when I finished my shift, because a bunch of starhounds were skulking around. I halfheartedly posed for a few pictures by the front window, and out of the corner of my eye, I could have sworn I caught Tyler looking at me. When I went to look, though, a Japanese tourist grabbed me by the cheek and started rambling about my imperfect teeth. By the time I turned my head back to Junebugs, Tyler and Kylie were deep in conversation, and she was scribbling something on a beverage napkin. God, the sight of them was enough to make me puke.

Actually . . .

Huuuuh-bleeeeeeeh

I did. Right in the fucking bushes. Nice shot.

Ooooooh, my tuuuummmy.

Well, at least the autograph hounds scattered.

I retched and heaved for close to five minutes before I was finally able to quell the bile volcano. I perched on the curb, head in my hands, and was about to light a cigarette when I felt a grip on my shoulder.

Oh, please don't be Stuart.

It wasn't. It was worse.

It was Tyler.

Offff course.

"Oh God. Oh God, did you . . . you didn't see that, did you?"

"Um, Julie, you're in front of the plate glass. I think the whole restaurant saw it. Actually, some seven-year-old kid was taping it with his mom's camcorder while she was in the bathroom."

"Oh Jesus."

"You've started a little epidemic, actually. I guess watching someone puke makes other people puke. Your boss had to send someone out to buy more bleach."

He squatted next to me and began to rub my back gently, looking concerned.

"Are you okay? Damn, that was a lot of . . . I mean," he laughed halfheartedly, "you're not one of *those* chicks, are you?"

"Tyler, I'm pretty sure bulimic girls like to purge in private. Besides, did you see me stuffing my face with guacamole and Twinkies?"

Guacamole and Twinkies. Shouldn't have said that. Unnnnnnngh.

I broke free of his grasp and booted in the bushes again.

"Wow! Okay, hang on a second. Let me just . . . there." He eased the googly eye antennae from my head, then pulled sweaty hair back and held it out of my face. "Just an old-fashioned hangover then, huh? You poor thing. Lucky for you, I can handle those."

"At least one of us can."

"Awww." He began to rub my back again, and was quiet while I finished. "Better? Here, have some water. I made Kylie get me a glass so I could bring it out to you."

I wiped my mouth with my sleeve and took the glass gratefully.

"Don't worry," Tyler smiled, "I watched. She didn't spit in it. Oh, maybe that was the wrong thing to say." He frowned as I turned green again at the thought of drinking spit.

Unnnnnnnngh.

"I'm just not going to talk," he said, "and you drink some water and then we'll have a cigarette together, okay? Good girl."

I managed to get a few sips down without retching again.

God, no wonder I can't get a real boyfriend.

"This is why I don't drink anymore." He sighed, using his lips to pull two cigarettes from a pack. He lit them and offered me one, kind of shyly.

"Thanks." I took a soothing drag and held it for a while, hoping the smoke would distract my body into fighting off cancer instead of repelling pickled pork flesh and humiliation. "Wait," I said, remembering our last conversation. "You don't drink? But the other night, you were drinking bourbon."

He sighed. "I only drink when I'm really upset. Sounds backward and unhealthy, I know, but I limit myself, and believe me, I know what the boundaries are. I don't usually drink to have a good time."

"Oh. So, you probably think I'm an alcoholic, huh?"

"You? Nah. I think you're a smart girl with a shitty job who desperately needs some fun in her life."

Interesting.

"I don't know about the smart part, but the rest of it sounds about right."

"I do. Know about the smart part, anyway."

The other times I'd spoken to him, Tyler always seemed so brash and confident. But now—now he was staring at the ground, still squatting beside me, drawing absent-minded circles on the pavement with his finger.

Hmm. Why was he being so shy?

Duh, Julie, he's probably trying not to stare at the barf factory that's poisoning his vision.

"Um . . ." I cleared my throat and began to hoist myself up. "Thanks. Thanks for helping me. It was really sweet of you. But, I should get going."

"Oh, are you sure? Maybe you should sit for a few more minutes."

"No, really, I'm fine, I'm gross, and I'm sorry, and I should . . . whoa!"

Woozy, I lost my balance as I stood, nearly pitching into the very bushes I'd been sick in. Eeeeew.

"Hang on." Tyler stubbed out his cigarette and jumped up, taking me gently by the elbow and wrapping his other arm around my waist. "If you're going to be stubborn and leave, Miss Julie, you should at least let me help you to your car."

"Oh no, that's okay, Tyler."

"No buts. I insist!"

"Um, okay."

Slooowly, we made our way toward my Taurus, Tyler leading the way, with me leaning on his shoulder, trying not to disturb the voodoo vomit gods that were snoozing in my stomach.

"Your chariot, madam."

He opened my door and helped me inside, even putting my seat belt on for me.

"Oh my God," I moaned.

His shirt. His shirt was covered in . . . mess.

"What?" He looked down. "What, this? Oh, this wasn't from you. This is . . . from . . . um, something . . . some-one . . . else."

"You're a terrible fucking liar, Tyler."

"Yeah, that's what my mom always told me, too. Eh, I should throw this T-shirt out, anyway. I mean, look at it. 'Save the Whales'? That's so lame, so totally 1977. I'm such a consignment hippie. Not very appealing to the ladies. Really, Julie, you did me a favor by puking on this shirt. Someone should have puked on this shirt years ago."

"Why are you being so nice to me?" I whispered as he handed me my keys.

"Oh, I don't know," he smiled, "you just look so pitiful right now. It's awfully cute."

He closed the door and gave the roof of my car one of those little giddy-up taps.

I watched as he made his way toward a blue pickup, looking back once or twice, to make sure I wasn't keeled over again, I guess.

Wow.

That was . . . well, that was nice of him. He could proba-bly teach my prick pretend boyfriend a thing or two.

Truth be told, I'm not so convinced anymore that Chad isn't a bit of an ass.

The drive home was a little bit of agony, but I made it, only stopping once to boot on the side of the road.

Naturally, I had a huffy answering machine message waiting for me at home.

Beeeeeeep

"Well, Miss Celebrity, still too busy to call your mother, huh?"

Shit. I hadn't called my mother since this whole thing started a few weeks ago, mostly because I know her too well. She'd insist I bring Chad over to the house for dinner, then regale him with stories and pictures from my geeky misfit childhood. Look, here she is when I bought her first bra. Size triple-A. Didn't want to feel left out, poor thing. Last one in her class to get breasts. Ooh, here's Julie, in her first dance recital. The other girls were in princess tutus, but apparently the teacher saw something special in my Julie; that's why she's wearing the frog costume. The prince, you know. Dear heart. Have some brisket, dear.

Sigh. I picked up the phone.

She always trills when she answers, just in case it's Ed McMahon or the Queen Mum, I guess.

"Helloooooo?"

"Hi, Ma."

"I'm sorry, who is this?"

"*Mom.* It's Julie."

"Who?"

God, I hated this game.

"Your *daughter*."

"Oooooh, hellooooooo! Why, I'd forgotten I even have a daughter! It's been so long since I've heard from her, she's just completely slipped my mind!"

"Ma, don't be mad."

"Why, I'm not mad, I'm just confused, honey. For twenty-four years I thought I'd known my own offspring, but I've just discovered she's living a double life that she has been keeping a secret from her entire family!"

She's gotten really good at the guilt trip thing. That's the Jew in her.

"I've just been really . . . busy."

"Well, I can see that! It's always refreshing to be able to catch up on your daughter's life by reading the papers."

"Mom, it's not like that."

"Then what is it like, exactly? You finally get a boyfriend, and we don't even get to meet him. Is there a reason why you kept him from us? You're ashamed of us, aren't you? My own daughter, *ashamed* of her family! It's because we're Jewish, isn't it?"

"Mom, we're not Jewish."

"Don't let your father hear you say that!"

Sigh.

"I'm not ashamed of anyone. I've just been super busy, and I haven't had time to go anywhere."

"Funny, you seem to have had a lot of time to be in the papers, Miss Movie Star."

"Okay, I'm sorry."

"Sorry doesn't cut it."

"Well what do you want from me?"

"Bring him over for dinner. And bring the granddoggie! I miss my little pooches. Even when you and Chad have babies, I'll still spoil him rotten."

Oy.

"And don't you dare be late for class on Tuesday, or I'll come over there and kick your ass!"

OY.

 Thirteen

Lying to a Jewish mother is impossible.

Fortunately, my mother only wants to *be* Jewish, so it's a little easier. Still, I had a tough time looking her in the eye as a kid, when I skipped my piano lesson to go to the mall or blamed my cigarette stench on the bus driver.

So this whole charade has been *torture*, trying to keep the facts straight, trying to keep my voice from wobbling as I tell Mom the details of how I met Chad, where he took me on our first date, and so on.

She called me again this morning to officially invite us for dinner tomorrow. The woman has a knack for catching me at my most vulnerable. It's either smack in the middle of a REM cycle or just as I'm sitting down to a carton of ice cream and plateful of macaroni and cheese.

She's so excited. *So* excited. Not only that her daughter finally scored a boyfriend who has a steady job, but that the steady job is professional famous person.

"You've *always* had a thing for Chad, haven't you, honey?" She sighed. "No, I didn't snoop in your drawers! A mother just knows these things. Anyway, I caught on when you kids didn't want to rent videos at sleepovers, just watched that tape of toilet paper commercials over and

..

over again. I didn't think you were interested in demo-
graphic marketing strategies, dear."

Besides being zealously, ahem, inquisitive, my mother is
also a fervent hostess. She throws dinners for everything.
Dad gets a raise? Invite the neighbors for seafood! Dan has
a gig? Haul the band in for pasta! Julie has a new
boyfriend? Someone get him over here, quick, so we can
stuff him full of blintzes and slip him a fucking Mickey so
he can never get away!

It's totally just an excuse to check him out, but believe
me, it's much better to get it out of the way so I can still do
it on my terms. Otherwise, if I let her stew in anticipation,
she's likely to show up at my apartment unexpectedly with
a poppyseed coffee cake and a knowing smile.

So when Mom got it into her head that I should bring
Chad over for dinner, what could I say but yes?

"No way!" Chad had protested when I relayed the invitation. "I don't do parents."

The two of us, plus a chain-smoking Phil, were lounging
around the card table in Chad's living room, rehashing our
media strategies for the week. Chad was knocking back
hand-delivered oyster-shooters, while I absentmindedly
swirled breadsticks around a vat of that fuchsia wine-
cheese dip.

It was the same color as the "gift" I had given him the last
time we saw each other. Christ. I still couldn't look him in
the eye.

"Oh. Oh, okay, well, no problem. I'll just tell her that—"

"Hold on a second, Plumpkin," Phil interrupted, silenc-
ing me with an artfully jabbed Virginia Slim in typically
pontifical fashion. He turned to Chad.

"Young Master Downing, life is a sea of opportunities.
When one comes along, you position yourself in the crest

and ride it as far as you can. Either you make it to shore, or get torn apart by bloodthirsty carnal hammerheads."

"Hammerheads? You lost me, Phil," Chad grumbled.

"This whole charade is a tsunami of prospect, Chad. Miss Julie here," he patted my leg, "is going to attract for you an entirely new fan base. Sure, the teenager screamers and panty-tossers will still be around; don't have a heart attack over that one. But right now, your image is very one-dimensional. You're seen as a partier, a flitter. A social butterfly—monarch, of course, babe, but a winged flutterer nonetheless. And while that's very glamorous, doll, it's very shallow."

"It is?"

Phil sighed. "Of course it is. Let me give you an example, okay? Nobody really gave a shit about Prince Charles—you *do* know who that is, right, babe?"

"Uh, he's the one in the can, right?"

"Yeah, fine, the one in the can, whatever. My point is, nobody really sat up and paid attention to Prince What's-his-face until he married Lady Diana Spencer."

"Oh, yeah! She was that teacher, right?"

"Exactly, my dear boy. She was a teacher—an *ordinary* citizen, and then, *poof!*—she was a princess, and suddenly people couldn't fucking get enough of them. Why would a royal heir, a man so laden with money and power that he can't even walk normally, pay any attention to some commonplace nobody? Why, she must be someone special! Someone so unique and so striking that the fucking Prince of England had to have her for himself. He was able to see beyond her normalcy. And *that*, Chad-doll, *that* made the whole fucking world sit up and pay attention. To *him*. To the *prince*."

"Um," I interrupted, "I thought that everyone sat up and

paid attention to *Diana*. And she wasn't *really* a nobody, was she? I mean, Prince Charles was just—"

Phil shot me a poisoned glare.

Oh, duh. Shut up, Plumpkin.

"Sure," Phil continued, after I slumped back in my chair, "you and Katarina ruled the scene together for a little while. Went to premieres, sucked face at a few afterparties, did some sunbathing in the Hamptons, that whole thing. But did you spend a lot of time with her family? Did you even *meet* her family, Chad?"

"Well, um, no . . ."

"Let me tell you something, babe. I've been in this business a long time, and I've learned some valuable lessons. One of them, of course, is that Jacob the Jeweler has these big German guys that will *hunt you down* if you miss a payment, but slightly more important is this: housewives in the Bible Belt like their celebrities wholesome and family-oriented. And they're a huge market! Think about it: there's nothing to do when the butter is churned, the pig's been barbecued, and church isn't for another two days. Nothing to do except watch TV, Chad. These women love their televisions; they rely on them for gut-wrenchingly pertinent, global information, like who shot J.R.? Who's dipping their fingers into whose Hollywood honeypot? Who values their family, and who's out at the strip clubs while their pregnant fiancée embroiders her veil for the shotgun Vegas wedding? Inquiring redneck housewives want to know, Chad, and by God, you're going to give it to them!"

So I guess that's how I found myself buckled into the all-leather interior of an orange Hummer, racing along the freeway toward the vanilla doldrums of the suburbs.

"Welcome!" my mother's harpy soprano trilled from the screen door as Chad cut the engine off. "Eli, the kids are here! Welcome, hi! Hi! Hello! You must be Chad! Oh it's so nice to meet you! Come in!"

Of course, Mom let the door slam in my face in her rush to welcome Chad into the foyer (and the family). Typical.

I cleared my throat and made my way into the house.

"Ma, we can't stay for too long, so I hope you didn't go all out."

"Take your shoes off, Julie. Go all out? Whatever do you mean?"

Oh, I don't know, like the time I brought my college boyfriend home to an entire aquarium's worth of lobsters crawling frantically around the kitchen. Mom was bidding each an individual good-bye, soothing them with lullabies before bidding them farewell and plunging them to boiling, shrieking death.

"In you go, Seymour."

That's right, Seymour. She names them. She *names* them.

"In you go, Erwin. Come on, that's right. Oh, you're going to taste so good with a little sherry! Yes you are. Mmmm, okay, alley oop, in you go."

And then there was the time I brought one of my suitemates home with me from college over winter break. Lelani was from Hawaii, and she was stopping over in L.A. for a few days before continuing the flight to Maui.

Mom greeted us at the screen door with homemade leis, crafted from freshly plucked hibiscus and English roses.

It was actually kind of a sweet homecoming gesture, until we got to the kitchen and discovered the roast pig, apple and all, smirking at us from the center of the dinner table.

She carved the spit herself, you know.

"Well come on, Julie, don't just stand there in the foyer! Come in and introduce us to your friend here!"

Making my way into the airy kitchen, I could smell dinner simmering. It was a foreign bouquet; spices that crept up my nose and tangoed across the back of my throat. Was that . . . cinnamon?

"Mom, Dad, this is my . . . um, this is Chad."

"Chad Downing," he said with a confident grin, grasping my father's hand in a smoothly choreographed shake. "What a pleasure it is to meet you! Julie's gushed about you for weeks, but I can tell right away she hardly does you justice. Mrs. Jorlamo," he grinned, turning to my blushing mother and encircling her hand with both of his, "whatever you're cooking smells absolutely incredible. Can you give us a hint? I'm dying to know what that enticing aroma is!"

Wow. He was good.

I could tell Mom thought so, too, because, giggling like a bookworm at a Beatles concert, she led Chad (by the hand!) to the stove, pointing out various bubbling dishes while I looked on, flabbergasted.

Dad immediately gave me the thumbs-up. He *never* does that.

"Indian curry?" Chad remarked, "Well that's fantastic! You see, I brought the most delightful Riesling." *He did?* "And it will complement a curry *splendidly*."

"Mom . . ." I started, joining them at the stove.

There were pots filled with exotic-looking food; chicken and vegetables swimming in vibrant, orange sauce, crispy, triangular dumpling-looking things, a pink, pungent soup garnished with cilantro that was making my eyes and mouth water.

"Mom, what's all this? You've never made, um, food like this before!"

Domestically brilliant as she may be, the most my mother has ever deviated from Western cuisine was the time she served bok choy to accompany a meat loaf with plum sauce. (My brother brought home a Chinese girl to study one night. Mom explained, to our chagrin, that the fusion of American and Chinese flavors paralleled my brother's biracial romance. I don't think Mei-Ling ever came over for dinner again.)

"Well, it's Indian cuisine, Jule! I thought we'd try something new. I had a feeling that our guest has a more seasoned palate than some of your other friends. I imagine you eat a lot of exotic foods, Chad?"

"None that have ever smelled this delicious." Chad smiled. "Now, let me run out to my car and grab that bottle of Riesling. You can relax with a glass while Julie and I serve dinner."

He dashed out of the kitchen, leaving me agape. Was this the same man who booted me from a limo? Who plucked my eyebrows and sneered at my plus-sized curvature?

Maybe there's hope for me after all?

"Julie!" my mother hissed, glancing out the large bay window to make sure Chad was still outside. He was, rooting busily through the backseat of his Hummer. "Julie, he's unbelievable! Oh my goodness, what a gem! Wherever did you find him?"

"Ma, I told you, we met at the restaurant."

"I can't believe that a famous movie star is *in my kitchen*! Oh my stars, the ladies in the Rotary club are not going to believe this!"

"You did good, beaner," my Dad chimed in, "he seems like a very nice young man."

"And he's even better looking in person!" Mom was still stage whispering, fanning herself with a pot holder. "You know, you're so lucky to have found him! I mean, a straight one! My friend Barb says that these days, all of those Hollywood hotties are gay!"

"*Mom!*"

The screen door banged, and Chad came strolling back into the kitchen.

I gave my mother the "One word about your friend Barb and I cut your throat with the edge of my hand" look, and turned to my charming, doting, fake boyfriend.

"Found it!" he announced, making sure my parents were looking at him before planting a chaste peck on my forehead. "Want a glass, honey? I know you prefer wine coolers, but this is really high-end wine! German vintage. It's smooth and lovely and a little bit sweet, just like you!"

"Ooooh," my mother gasped under her breath, "Eli, isn't that adorable?"

"Huh." Dad was *beaming* at us, stroking his beard thoughtfully and sizing us up.

Damnit. They never liked any of my *real* boyfriends. Well, at least if Chad decided to really love me, he'd already have won over the parents.

"Now," Chad continued, "why don't you grab the opener, honey, and I'll pour. Just had a manicure yesterday; I don't want my cuticles to get all agitated!"

Ah, and there's the dad I recognize. Bemused. Skeptical. Not willing to leave his little girl alone in the company of what is clearly an unbelievable schmuck.

"Did you say you had a *manicure* yesterday, son?"

"Why, yes, Mr. Jorlamo, I did."

"Huh."

Grimacing, I caught my mother's eye.

Gay! she mouthed. *Gaaaaaaaay!*

I shook my head furiously.

No, not gay, just coddled and pampered like an American Kennel Club Alsatian.

"No, really, Mr. Jorlamo, they can be quite masculine. In my line of work, unfortunately, we're held to this impossible standard of beauty. Flawless, not a hair out of place, not a hangnail in sight. It used to be just the ladies, you know, those Hollywood epitomes of glamour. Men were supposed to be rugged, a little rough around the edges. But now," he sighed, "we've been gussied up a bit. Not that I'm complaining, of course. I think we could take a few cues from contemporary women. After all, behind every great man is a woman who's shaking her head in disbelief, am I right?"

Wow. Wow, that was actually the right thing to say! Dad's chuckling again, and Mom looks positively relieved. Chad threw his arm around me casually.

"Now, honey, why don't you pour your parents a nice glass of wine, and I'll keep an eye on the stove. Mom, Dad, take a load off."

My mother added a few final dashes of spice to her various creations, and moved to take her apron off. Suddenly . . .

Snap!! Flash!!

"What in the world was that?" she cried. "Eli . . . Eli, I think there's someone out there!"

Sure enough, under the pallid cover of dusk we could see a man lurking in the bushes outside the kitchen.

"Eli!" my mother hissed. "Eli! Call the police!"

"Calm down, Bonnie," my father said. "He's not here to hurt us, he's here to . . . what is he doing?"

It was, of course, a photographer. And from the increasingly frequent bursts of light coming from the front lawn, I could tell that he wasn't alone.

"Well, I never!" My mother reached up to her strand of

pearls, fingering them nervously. "Those vultures can't just plant themselves on my lawn! Goodness, have they no *decency*, no *shame*? It's *dinner* time, for heaven's sake. Don't they realize how *rude* that is! Oh, it's worse than those telemarketers!"

"They must have followed us here," Chad said, moving to the window to size up the situation.

Snap!!! Flash!!!

I could hear the buzz of inquiries through the windowpane.

"Mr. Downing! Is this the house of the Jorlamo family?"

"Chad? Chad! Are you here to ask for Julie's hand in marriage?"

"Are you in there, Julie? How do you feel about introducing Chad to your parents for the first time?"

"What's for dinner, Mrs. Jorlamo?"

Chad turned to me. He didn't look surprised; I'm sure Phil, or even Chad himself, for that matter, sent out a heads-up press release to the papers so that we'd be followed. Jesus. I just hoped those slugs would leave my parents alone after tonight.

"I think," Chad turned to my mother, "under the circumstances, our only option is to comply."

I snorted. "What do you mean 'our only option is to comply'? We're not dealing with terrorist negotiations here, it's a bunch of snooping media weasels."

"Well, honey," Chad put his arm around me again, this time squeezing in a "wink-wink" kind of way, "I think what they want is a picture of you, and me, and your family. And if we give it to them, nicely, then they'll go away."

"A picture?" Mom looked at my father. "What kind of picture? Do I have to take my apron off? Wait, let me just go change my dickie."

"Did you plan this?" I asked under my breath.

"Just help me out here, okay, Julie?"

You'd think Sears and Roebuck themselves had hand-selected my family to pose for the International Domestic All-Stars Great American Family Portrait.

"Eli, my hair, my hair!" Mom was running around the kitchen squealing like a ferret let loose from its cage. "I can't *believe* I skipped my appointment today so I could perfect the tandoori! Have you seen my purse? Oh, I'm going to look as pale as a poltergeist if I don't put some rouge on! Oy, where's the Aquanet?"

"Bonnie! Would you calm down for *two* seconds? Jesus! Now who exactly are these people, Chad, and where are they planning on publishing these pictures, *if* we agree to pose for them?"

Chad had whipped out a bejeweled compact and was gazing at his profile while expertly piecing his hair into sculpted spikes.

"Well, sir," he peered at his teeth and snapped the compact closed, "I don't know that they'll make the *front page,* necessarily, but definitely the Social Notes section."

"Which paper?"

"The *Beacon.*"

"Oh."

Now Dad looked interested. He respected the *Beacon.* He read the *Beacon.* And so did his colleagues.

"Well," Dad straightened his tie, "I guess a picture or two can't hurt anybody. And then they'll leave us alone, you say? Bonnie, did you find the Aquanet?"

Five minutes later, picture perfect, we were reigning the front porch with Windsor-worthy dignity.

"Just look over here, everyone! That's right, smile!"

"Chad, could you put your arm around Mom for us?"

"Mr. Jorlamo, sir, do you have a pipe you could be smoking?"

"So are things getting serious between you two?"

"This is so exciting!" Mom squealed under her breath. "And you two get to do this all the time?"

"Believe me, it wears a little thin after a while," Chad muttered in return, "but they're being awfully nice to you, Mrs. Jorlamo. I've never seen a photographer so respectful of boundaries. I mean, look, those goons are practically hurdling your zinnias to avoid trampling them!"

We posed for a few more minutes, letting Chad field most of the questions, and then, in a shocking move, the photographers thanked us politely, retreated to their respective cars parked on the street, and vanished.

"Well!" Mom patted her hair and smiled at Chad warmly. "If that doesn't send the Rotary club into a tizzy, I'll eat my hat. Come on everybody, supper will get cold. I've got garlic pistachio *nan* waiting in the oven!"

"How did you get them to leave so quickly?" I whispered to Chad as he held the door open for my parents.

"Easy," he whispered back. "I had Phil tell them that Sol Solstein would be proposing to his teenage girlfriend around seven-thirty tonight at a hush-hush location. Fake address, of course. Right now, they're probably hauling ass to some random crack shack across town."

I'm starting to think that Chad is maybe a little schizophrenic.

Points to consider: he's condescending, he's accommodating. He's affectionate, he's disdainful. He's unaffected and detached, he's absolutely fucking lovely.

Just pick one already, Sybil. Just pick one and go with it.

Well, Mom was pretty smitten, I'd say. By the time we sat down to dinner in the dining room, she was chatting with

Chad like they were old friends, exhibiting none of the
awkwardness her daughter suffers, but instead bantering
and giggling like a snappy little pepper pot.

"Well," she smiled, lifting her wineglass in a toast when
we had finally settled down at the table, "let me say this: it
is so delightful to have company that is, well, just so refreshing."

Here we go.

"Chad," she continued. "I'm just thrilled that my daughter has finally, finally found herself a gentleman. Welcome
to the family, honey. *L'chayim!*"

"*L'chayim,*" Dad and I repeated. Sometimes we indulge
her.

"*L'chayim!*" Chad chimed in. "This curry looks delicious.
Geschmak!"

Excuse me?

Mom blinked. "What did you just say?"

Chad grinned sheepishly, "Oh, I'm sorry. *Geschmak.* It
means 'delicious.'"

Oh?

It appears the Grand High Shiksa Baleboosteh had met
her match.

"Well, I . . . of course! Of course I know what it means.
Eli, did you hear him? Eli, would you put the paper down,
please? Eli! Anyway," she cleared her throat, "are you . . .
are you Jewish, dear?"

You have got to be kidding me.

"I mean," she continued, an ecstatic gleam in her eye,
"um, 'Downing' isn't really a—"

"Sounds kind of waspy, huh?" Chad chuckled. "That
was the whole idea, I guess. No, 'Downing' is a stage name.
My real name is Chad Liebowitz."

Mom dropped her fork.

So did I.

This was just too much. Not only am I sitting at my parents' dining room table with the man of my dreams, but now, as it turns out, he's the man of my mother's dreams, too.

Except, *oh yeah*, I had to practically drag him here against his will.

And, you know, he's not *really* my boyfriend.

Details.

"Well . . ." I could tell my mother was trying to contain her excitement, but I caught her and Dad exchanging a triumphant look. "What a nice surprise. Let's dig in, everyone. Hopefully our little impromptu photo shoot didn't ruin my chicken tikka masala. Chad? Can I offer you a samosa?"

"Please!"

Mom heaped his plate with piles of fried dumpling-looking things, and Chad got to it, heartily.

"Mmmmm! Mmmmm, oh boy, Mrs. Jorlamo," he raved through a mouthful of food, "this is just incredible. Right, *bubeleh*?"

Did he just wink at me?

I can't believe this. Not only is he sexy and successful and charming the *hell* out of my parents, but he's Jewish, too. How did I manage to find this guy? Or, more appropriately, how can I manage to get this guy?

Maybe it would help if he were actually attracted to me.

Actually, one of the most frustrating things about the past few weeks has been my own ambivalent attraction to Chad. It's pretty overwhelming. Before I actually knew him as a person, you know, when he was just the pretty man on TV, I couldn't imagine a guy who was more perfect. On-screen, Chad seemed like every woman's dream. It's not that he isn't in person, either, but . . . okay, so I can tell he's arrogant, sure, and completely self-centered. But most of the time he's *wonderful;* sweet and considerate and gracious . . . I've just been going back and forth about the whole thing. At least I've managed to calm down around him a little.

I really need to just stop picking him apart. So he's a little cranky sometimes. Big deal! I mean, nobody can be suave and charming *all* the time.

"*Bbbbrrreeeeeeeeeccccchhhhh.* Hoo boy, that was a good one!"

Nice. Curry doesn't smell so good on the return trip.

We ended up staying at my parents' place way longer than originally anticipated. Mom didn't pull out the baby albums, thank God, but she *did* whip up some cherry blintzes in honor of my "Hebrew honey." Yes, yes. She actually called him that.

By the time we piled into the Hummer, it was almost midnight.

"Damn. *Bbbbbbrrreeeeeccchh.* Oh man!" He beat at his chest with a fist. "Your mother sure can cook, Julie. We should go over there more often."

I rolled down the window.

"Do you want to? I mean, I know she'd love to have you."

"Oh yeah! Those were the best damned samosas I've ever had. Shit, if she's going to feed me like that, I'll tough it out and head over there once or twice a week!"

Tough it out, huh? Was he kidding? That was the most pleasant dinner I'd had over there in years.

"Well, I'm so glad you had a good time. You know, I . . . um . . ."

Oh God, he makes me nervous.

"Not going to throw up again, are you? Do you need me to pull over?

"No, I . . ."

"Really, just tell me if you do, because I just had this re-upholstered and I don't need to spend the rest of the night tracking down someone who can clean custom Italian leather. That suit was bad enough; I thought Phil was going to kill me. It was on loan, you know."

I'm never going to live that down.

"I'm *fine*. And I'm sorry. I was just going to say how nice it was to see you and my mother getting along. I thought she was going to fall over when she found out you're Jewish. I should have picked up on it by now. She really fine-tuned my Jew-dar when I was growing up. It must be really awful to have to keep your true identity a secret, though! I can't believe someone convinced you to change your name. Do you still go to temple?"

Was he laughing? Why was he laughing uncontrollably?

"Don't tell me you actually fell for that?" Chad sputtered. "I knew I had your mom and pops going pretty good, but I hoped you were at least a little smarter than that!"

Excuse me?

"*L'chayim!*" he giggled. "*Kol tuv! Mazel tov!* Holy shit!" He lifted both hands from the wheel to wipe tears from his eyes, and shook his head. "That was good. That was really good; I should get an Academy for that one. And you! You couldn't even tell!"

Son of a bitch.

"Mind clueing me in a little, here?" I began slowly, afraid of what might come out of my mouth. "So, clearly, you're *not* Jewish. Wow. Okay. But who the fuck cares? You didn't have to *actually* make a good impression on my parents. You got your picture with the happy family, what do you care if they actually like you?"

He shrugged, still chortling to himself.

"And how the hell do you know all of those phrases if you're not Jewish?"

"Well, clearly you're not a diehard Chad Liebowitz, excuse me, *Downing* fan, because if you were, you would have seen all of my movies, including the ones that went straight to video."

"What?"

"*Tender Is the Semite.* I played an undercover FBI agent living on a kibbutz, trying to wrangle inside information. Not a bad flick, actually. Zora Nichols costarred. Man, what a rack on that chick."

"So you thought you'd just make a mockery of my mother."

"Oh don't be ridiculous. She's a perfectly nice woman, I'm not an asshole."

"Then why?"

"Think about how much it helps, Julie, if your parents actually like me. Just picture this, for a second. I go to your house, I let them see how bored and unimpressed I actually am, I don't pay any attention to you, and I fall facedown asleep in my chicken tikka. What's the first thing your parents are going to do? Hm? Call the *Beacon* and spill the dirt. Tell them all about our little charade and how I'm just using an innocent woman to trick the entire world into loving me even more."

"What? But my parents wouldn't do that. They're not vindictive people and they don't *care* if my boyfriend is famous. They just want me to be with someone who treats me well."

"Fake boyfriend," he corrected me.

Right, right.

"Do you honestly think my parents would have rung up

the fucking media if you hadn't pulled my chair out for me?"

"Listen, toots, I'm not taking any chances. The last thing I need is a bitter mommy blowing the roof in on this thing."

I see.

You know, I think I was a pretty good sport about the whole limo incident. Actually, I'd been a pretty good sport about this whole thing. Yeah, I get to be in the spotlight and wear pretty clothes and whatever, but I'm doing a whole hell of a lot more for Chad Downing than he's doing for me.

And now, it was extending *beyond* me.

I myself think it's a pain in the ass to have to go to my parents' house for dinner. My mom is totally weird and annoying, Dad just sits there and grunts from behind the paper, I eat too much, I get harped on for eating too much, I feel bad about eating too much, and then I go home with a week's worth of leftovers.

But I would never, *never* exploit them.

Okay, sure, I've led them to believe that this guy is my boyfriend. But what choice did I have? They read about me every week in the papers; they would have been hurt and angry if they never got a chance to meet him. And, true, this whole relationship is fake, but it's not like he's *imaginary*.

The rest of the car ride was silent. By the time we got to my neighborhood, I was just plain pissed off. Okay, so he exploits and uses and lies about *me,* but at least I allowed him to do that. I gave him my fucking permission. But to use an innocent dinner invitation from my mother as his own personal suburban junket . . .

I didn't even say good-night to him when I slammed the door shut and stomped into our building. He wouldn't have heard me anyway, he was too busy having a marathon belch session while trying to rebutton his pants over a belly full of angry Indian gas.

As expected, my answering machine was blinking when I got in.

Beeeeeeeep.

"Helloooooo, *bubeleh!* Oh, your father and I just had the greatest time tonight. He's really something special, Jule. Anyway, I'll see you in class this week, but I just wanted to say good-night, and say 'Hi, Chad!' because I know he's probably there with you. I'm not that old-fashioned, dear. So good night, kids! Hope you had fun; I know we sure did."

Was that the curry, or guilt, that was making my stomach turn?

THE DAILY BEACON

ALL IN THE FAMILY?

It seems Chad Downing has carved another niche for himself. If it wasn't clear before that the heartthrob is getting downright domestic with his damsel, just check out the adorable family portrait above. That's Chad all right, making nice with Mom and Dad Jorlamo. Seems the elder (and equally lovely!) Lady Jorlamo whipped up a home-cooked feast for her daughter's new beau, garnished with a little family bonding. What do you think, Chad? Can you say, "future in-laws"?

Fourteen

Riley may actually be a greater love connection than
Chuck Woolery.

Once in a while I get the urge to spoil the dog like a Nu-
bian princess, so I'll load him into the car and take him to
Super Pooch, the FAO Schwarz of pet stores. The aisles are
filled with goodies for every conceivable canine palate;
rows and rows of rubber pork chops, kitty-flavored chew
toys, rawhide pig ears, and rubber spiked contraptions that
resemble medieval torture devices. Dogs are allowed in the
store, so to walk Riley down an aisle of peanut butter moocow hooves is a true test of athletic prowess. You can also
get gourmet vittles that come in vacuum-sealed pouches
and actually contain identifiable meat (instead of that questionable shit from the grocery store that probably hides the
pony I was supposed to get for Christmas).

Okay, so I'm usually prompted to spoil him when I open
my cupboards and find the "dog" shelf empty, like I did
this morning. I buy his food in bulk so it lasts for-e-ver, so I
never think about restocking until it's too late and I have
nothing to feed him but oyster crackers and American
cheese.

Which vanished in half a second. Poor Riley looked up at

me like, "Well, that was a nice little hors d'oeuvre, Ma, but bring on the horsey!"

My little heart broke. I grabbed his leash. Good thing he's not a kid or DSS would have sent me to the pokey by now. Poor thing. No man will ever love me the way he does.

Riley might be mostly clueless, but let me tell you—the dog *knows* when we're headed to the pet store. He almost dislocated my shoulder pulling me through the building. When we got to the car, I thought he was going to lose it. He was so excited he couldn't make the jump into the backseat, like the sheer glee of it all was distracting him from being able to execute a simple leap.

I finally just grabbed his butt and hoisted him in like a sack of potatoes.

Super Pooch was crowded. I've noticed that people really do tend to look like their pets, so everywhere I turned there were freaky little couples cavorting around. In aisle four, a schnauzer was trotting happily alongside a gentleman with a frizzy, gray beard. By the Snickerpoodles (obnoxious gourmet bakery treats; Riley adores them), a tiny little pudgy woman with an upturned nose was lingering with her pug. And of course, there's always at least one old lady coiffed to match her smarmy little French poodle.

Riley was having a field day, sticking his nose up every butt that crossed our path. I could barely keep up with him as he made the rounds, mingling with every spaniel and shi-tzu he could get his mitts on. Sex would be so much easier if we took our cues from the pooches. Hey baby, you smellin' fine. Mind if I hop on? Great. And a-one and a-two, and I'm done. See ya around.

On second thought, I think that's a pretty common approach. Never mind.

We browsed around for a little while; I filled the basket with chewy toys and made awkward small talk with the owners in our path. The whole pet experience is so fucking parental, it makes me want to have my ovaries vacuum sealed. You find yourself talking about poo and skin rashes with total strangers. Shudder.

I finally wheedled my way out of a conversation about tapeworms and tugged Riley away from a blasé ménage-a-trois with a Pekinese and a Great Dane. They looked sorry to see him go. Glad someone's getting some action.

I dragged him down an aisle toward the front of the store, and stopped dead in my tracks.

Oooh, bijiggity.

Our path to the cash register was blocked by a pacing, rabid wildebeest.

I mean, this was the biggest dog I've ever seen, even more impressive than Riley on a fat day, and believe me, that's saying something.

I think it was a pit bull, black as Italian coffee, with wiry fur and a leather studded collar. Its left eye was twitching like it had just swallowed something sour, maybe a lemon or rotten human flesh.

Riley whimpered. The beast approached.

"Daisy!" a male voice shouted from another aisle. "Daisy, where are you, girl?"

The creature's ears perked up.

Daisy?

"There you are, babe. You can't just take off like that! I'm so sorry, I hope she wasn't bothering—"

We locked eyes.

It was Tyler.

"Well," he smiled, "hello there."

Eased into faded jeans and a black shirt that nonchalantly showcased his biceps, the sight of him launched the butterflies in my stomach into a frantic lambada.

"Hi . . . hey. Hey!"

Pull it together, Julie.

"What are you doing here?"

"My old lady dragged me here." He tousled Daisy's head and clipped a leash to her collar. "And believe me, she gets what she wants."

"I can see that." Right now she wanted Riley, apparently, because she had mounted his head and was humping away.

Riley looked nonplussed. Even for a dog.

"Daisy, Daisy! I'm sorry, she gets a little, uh—."

"Excited?"

He grinned. "I guess that's one way to put it. Daisy, come here. Now."

She disembarked, shaking her head and sending doggie foam all over the place.

"So, what's your dog's name? He's cute. Looks a little shaken up, but cute."

"Yeah, Daisy's a whole lot of woman. Riley's used to being the one in charge."

"Of course he is, if he takes after you. You look different without your uniform,"

Did he just check me out? I could have sworn he swept his eyes over me, but whether it was appreciatively or not was totally up in the air.

"Yeah, horizontal stripes and googly eyes do a lot for me."

Tyler laughed.

"No, you look . . . you look really pretty."

Urp?

"Uh, thanks."

And, I don't know what to say, aaaaand awkward silence.

Tyler cleared his throat. "Much better than yesterday, that's for damned sure. Are you feeling better this afternoon?"

"Oh. Haha, um, yeah. Yeah, definitely a lot better."

"Good. I hate to see a lady in distress."

"Ha! After yesterday, I wouldn't exactly call myself a lady, would you?"

"I can't think of a better description, actually."

Ahem.

Awkward silence *again*. We stood for a minute, each of us nodding like bobbleheads on the dashboard of a Pinto.

"So—" I began.

"So, I—" he did, too. "Oh, sorry! You first!"

"No, you!"

"Oh, um, okay. So, when I came in to see you at work yesterday, I noticed that, um, I couldn't get anywhere near one of your tables! What gives, you shelling out free lap dances to customers, or what?"

"Not free, just cheap."

"Ah, so that's why they all had cameras."

"Hey, I'm a popular girl."

"I guess so."

He ran his fingers through his already unruly hair, making it stand on end. So hot.

"So, how popular are you?"

"What do you mean?"

"I mean . . . do you go out a lot? With guys?"

Is he kidding?

"Are you kidding? I mean, uh, no, no not really."

"Really?" He raised his eyebrows. "Because I was thinking, you know, if you're interested, that—hey, hey, hey! Ow! Jesus Christ, get the fuck off of me!"

I looked down and saw that a French poodle had latched

itself onto Tyler's ankle, hissing and flailing like a defunct Macy's Day balloon.

"What the—mauled by a fucking poodle. Are you kidding me? When lapdogs attack. Daisy, why aren't you eating her?"

At the sound of her name, Daisy perked up and finally noticed that her master was being viciously assaulted by a curly-haired rat beast. A growl curdled deep within her throat.

"Peanut? Peanut? Oh there you are, sweet pea!" A tiny little blue-haired lady, complete with hairnet, shuffled around the corner, waving her finger in mock reprimand. "There's my little Peanut!"

"Um, do you think you could get Peanut to release the death grip on my calf?" Poor Tyler now had the mongrel by the back of the head and was trying desperately to keep it from sinking its needle teeth any further into his flesh.

"Watch out! You'll hurt him! Oh somebody, somebody help! This man has my little Peanut by the hair! Oh, Peanut! Listen sonny, you'd better let go of him right now! My grandson is a yellow belt in tae kwon do, he'll make you sorry for hurting my little baby! Peanut? Peanut, it's okay, Mommy's here!"

"Ma'am . . ." I could tell Tyler was getting pissed, but was trying to be patient. "Your little Peanut has bitten a chunk out of my leg the size of a large rodent. Now unless you want *my* dog to return the favor, you'd better call him off. *Now.*"

The old lady started to squawk, but was interrupted when a store employee came running down the aisle.

"Mrs. Wilkins? Mrs. Wilkins. How many times have I told you not to bring Peanut in here without a leash? This is really getting to be a problem!"

The old lady rolled her eyes.

"Listen, young missy, I keep telling you, Peanut is too strong for me! Why, he'd be dragging me all over the store if I had to cling onto one of those confounded leash thinga-majigs."

"Mrs. Wilkins, be that as it may, store policy strongly indicates that dogs must be on a leash if they're to be allowed in the store. We have this problem every week, ma'am, with someone else getting chewed on by your poodle. Now get your basket together, and get Peanut, and we'll ring you out at the register. If this happens again, you won't be allowed back. Understand?"

Mrs. Wilkins muttered something dirty under her breath and bent to scoop up Peanut, still clinging to Tyler's ankle with every ounce of poodle might he could muster.

"*Nnnrrrghhaaaaahhhh!*" He screwed up his face in pain as old lady Wilkins ripped Peanuts fangs through his skin. I looked down and noticed blood trickling down his shoe.

"Jesus, Daisy, what do I keep you around for? That poodle was trying to eat me alive, and all you could do was make eyes at Riley. Julie, your dog has hypnotized her into a state of total apathy."

"I guess I taught him well, then. Are you okay?"

"Yeah, I guess. Lousy bitch-ass poodle."

"Sir," the Super Pooch employee squatted down to examine his wound, "this could require stitches. Super Pooch will gladly pay your medical costs if you'd like to go and get this taken care of. And I do apologize, tremendously. I've told that woman to keep that goddamned dog chained up. I'm going to have a conversation with the district manager as soon as I get you taken care of."

Tyler winced as she reached out to dab at his leg with a tissue.

"Really, I'm okay. I just need a cigarette and some bourbon, and I'll be set. I'm more embarrassed that my dog is a lovesick wuss, actually, than I am anything else."

It's true; Daisy was so enraptured that she had totally ignored the poodle attack, instead gazing adoringly at Riley, who was innocently licking his balls.

"Maybe I should take you to get that looked at?" I asked, leaning in for a closer look. The bleeding had slowed, but it was still a nasty cut.

"You should listen to your friend." The employee smiled up at him, and then swiveled to talk to me. "You're right. He needs to . . ." Her voice trailed off. "Hey. Hey, you look familiar."

Who, me?

"Ummmmm," I stammered, "familiar? Well, yeah, I mean, I come in here all the time!"

"No, no, that's not it," she mused, stroking her chin. "How do I know you?"

Oh God, lady, pleeeeease don't say what I think you're about to. Please, please, please. I was just about to get asked out on my first legitimate date since flannel was chic. Please, please, please don't mess this up for me. The last thing I need is for Tyler to know about—

"Chad Downing!" she exclaimed. "Oh my God, Chad Downing! You're Julie Jorlamo!"

Oh for fuck's sake, lady.

Tyler was clearly confused. "What? Julie, how does she know—"

"Oh my God, I can't believe it!" The employee jumped to her feet, looking around wildly, like she couldn't believe her luck. "In our store—in *my* store! I'm the shift manager, you know. My name's Cheryl, Ms. Jorlamo. Wow, wow! I can't believe you're here!"

"Ms. Jorlamo?" Tyler looked at me and raised his eyebrows.

Cheryl, unfortunately, showed no signs of abandoning her rant. "Jessie!" she screamed to another employee who was passing through the aisle, restocking. "Jessie! Look! Look who it is!"

Jessie looked at me, unaffected.

"Jessie! You know who this is! We were just talking about her this morning! Julie Jorlamo? From the papers? Chad Downing's girlfriend?"

"Ohmigod!" Jessie shrieked, "You're right! *Wow, wow!*"

Oh, for fuck's sake, lady.

I looked sheepishly up at Tyler, who was watching the ensuing chaos, mouth dangling in disbelief.

"Chad Downing." He was nodding his head slowly, like suddenly it was all crystal fucking clear. "Chad Downing's girlfriend. That cheeseball actor? Chad Downing, that fucking celebrity bottom feeder? You're his girlfriend?"

"Well, duh!" Cheryl looked at Tyler like he'd been living in a Twinkie for the past century. "Of course she is! It's been all over the papers, I mean, *hello*. They're totally adorable together!"

Oh no, no, nononononono.

Tyler looked torn, like he was debating whether to break down and cry or hack me to death with a pooper scooper.

"Well, where the hell have I been?" he spat. "And you, I mean, my God! You *definitely* don't get out a lot, do you?"

"Tyler—"

"No, no, please. I mean, what the fuck is my problem? I'm the one who bought all that 'poor little waitress' nonsense, like a fucking fool. Following you around like a puppy, thinking you actually gave a shit. And asking you out? Jesus, I, wow, I mean, I'm an asshole." He shook his head and tugged on Daisy's leash. "A total, total asshole."

"Tyler, wait, I can—"

"You can what?" He stared at me with icy, expressionless eyes. "You can laugh it up at the party tonight when you tell your superstar boyfriend that a piddling little working man had the audacity to ask you out? God, I bet you . . . did you think I was some, some *fan,* some crazy fan, like, stalking you or something? Because, I'm not. You know, I didn't even . . . No, please, don't look sorry, I'm the sorry one. Jesus, I'm an idiot."

An infantry of mimes could have drowned me out.

I watched, dumbstruck, as Tyler dragged a whimpering Daisy away from me, Super Pooch employees now crowding around me like a pack of hyenas circling a carcass. I wanted to run after him, to throw myself at his feet and explain the whole ridiculous charade. I wanted . . . I don't know.

And then it hit me. I just wanted him.

Instead, I'd committed myself to playing dress-up with a pretend boyfriend who thinks I'm fat and ridiculous.

What the fuck was my problem?

He didn't look back as he marched through the automatic doors, pausing briefly to light a cigarette before hopping into his midnight-blue pickup and peeling out of the parking lot.

I could have sunk to the floor and bawled my eyes out, but instead I signed autographs for an hour. Like a snotty little bitch.

And oh crap. I would be late. Late for motherfucking kickboxing.

"Vun, two, vun two! Furchtbar! Oh, you are *terrible,* young Miss Jorlamo! Vat, you not practice ze keecks I show you?

Ach, do it like Mama, like Frau Bonnie. Bonnie, ve show her, no?"

Ooooh God, this was toooorture!

Like it's not bad enough that I work as a food flunky in a quirky, corporate hellhole. That I wear googly eyes, and big, bad, boob-embellishing horizontal stripes. That I make enough money to buy white bread and peanuts. That I spent a remarkable portion of yesterday spewing pork and vinegar into the bushes of my terrible, terrible place of employment. That I also puked in the lap of a beautiful movie star. That I'm trapped in a pretend relationship with said movie star, who will never, ever love, or even screw me. That I sort of hate him, but can't make myself walk away. Things were bad enough yesterday.

But now, now it's really bad.

Now, I've committed myself to eight weeks of kickboxing classes with my crazy, crazy mother and a crazy, crazy German.

Now, I think I want to be with the only person in the world that wants nothing to do with me.

Well, maybe not the only person, but Stuart and Kylie don't count, really. Technically, I think you have to have a soul, or perhaps a spine, to be considered a person.

Oh, and Chad wants nothing to do with me, but only sexually. And socially. And . . . okay, so Chad wants nothing to do with me, either.

Sigh.

I suck.

Lucky for me, Timmy brought out the punching bag next.

"Okay, Miss Jorlamo, now ve work on ze punches. Ze vay ve do eet here, ees ve pretend zat ze bag ees someone ve hate. Confidentially," he made sure no one was listening, and leaned in, "ze hardest part for me vith zis exercize ees deciding whose face to picture!"

Okay! Now I'm starting to like this guy. Because, frankly, I was having a hard time choosing between a few fatheaded foes of my own.

I beat Chad's face in for a while, then Stuart's, then Kylie's. I switched between them with a fervor.

"Good, good, *ja!*" Timmy clapped me on the back as I launched into yet another tireless round of beating the lisp out of Stuart. "Your punches, zey are looking much better! Ooh, you must be mad at someone veeeerry much, *ja?* Ooh, zey are gonna get eet."

"You really *do* look mad, dear!" Mom whispered to me as I moved in for the kill. "I hope it's not Chad! Your father and I just can't get over how charming he is! When are you coming for dinner again? I just picked up the most delightful cookbook about nigiri sushi. Oh goodness, he didn't dump you, did he? I knew that Katarina woman was bad news. Well, don't look at me like that, didn't you read the *Snoop Scoop*?"

"The huh?"

"The *Snoop Scoop*! You know, that magazine, comes out once a week, has all the juicy stuff about everyone?"

"No, I . . . no."

Apparently, I'm hopelessly out of touch with cutthroat celebrity grapevine tabloids. Heaven forbid.

"Jeez Louise, Julie, your name is even on the cover! Well, it's only a rumor, dear, you know how the paparazzi like to get everyone in a tizzy. I think I have a copy in my minivan. I'll show you after class."

"After class? What Katarina—Katarina Conrad?"

"Oh, dear, I shouldn't have said anything."

"Mom?"

"Oh, you want to see it now?"

"Do I want to . . . of *course* I want to fucking see it now!"

"*Julie Jorlamo!* May Jesus help your black and tainted soul! Talking to your mother with a mouth like that! Where in God's name did you learn to talk like a sailor? Probably your father, the fucking moron. Oopsie! Hahahahaha. Well, come on, don't look at me like that, let's go out to my car! Bye-bye, Timmy, see you next week!"

"*Mom,*" I growled, "stop trying to make pretty eyes at the *obviously* homosexual *kickboxing* instructor, and let's *go!*"

"Sheesh, someone sure got up on the wrong side of bed this morning! How can you be so grouchy when you have my little *gwanddoggie* to cheer you up?"

THE SNOOP SCOOP

REUNITED?

Say it ain't so, Chad Downing! Just when we were starting to love her! Wonder what Miss Julie Jorlamo thinks of her man's late night cavorting with none other than the Dreaded Ex, catty Katarina Conrad! The two were spotted snuggling in secret the other night, at the exclusive Dream Gems afterparty following the "Barbecue for Babies" charity hoedown. The party was *so* exclusive, apparently, that not even Miss Jorlamo herself was in attendance! Something smells bad, and we at the *Scoop* don't think it's the barbie. Naturally, Downing insists the two are friends, merely hamming it up to promote the duo's latest joint project, *Fancy Pants*. Sure, but didn't anyone tell him that the flimsy film has already fled the box office?

Jesus. Does anyone else want to break my heart into a million pieces? Anyone?
Anyone?

 **Fifteen**

"Only in Hollywood can a man get his ass waxed and soothed with cucumber essence, and not be considered a total fag. What, I can't say 'fag'?"

I think Phil's ideas of what is socially appropriate have been marred by years of dealing with the exalted untouchables.

He called me this morning while I was still trying to fumigate my morning mouth. I sat up with a bottle of cheap vodka until four in the morning, sniveling like an idiot and cursing my own romantic ineptitude. I smelled like misery and rancid Russian potatoes.

"A surprise, Plumpkin! A treat! No, you can't eat it! Now, get your dimpled keister out of bed and put on a track suit. I'm sending a car in two."

I've learned to anticipate his surprises with a touch of wariness. Last week he got me hyped up about an "unexpected treat." I got all fluttery and excited, and motherfucker was I disappointed when it turned out to be a photo shoot to endorse tube socks. So, I take Phil's allusions with a grain or two of salt.

A shaker, really.

So, when I got into the limo (thankfully, not the same one

that I had booted in—yep, still a little sensitive about that one), I wasn't expecting too much. Didn't even bother with makeup, actually.

Which turned out to be okay, I realized, when my ride pulled up in front of Chut-Spa.

Oh joy, oh joy!

Chut-Spa is the ultimate, chi-chi, decadent, snobby, exclusive, girlie spa, specifically designed for millionaires who believe that seaweed and rocks were put on earth to make pretty people look prettier.

I've only read about and pined over it about a bajillion times. Rumor has it, the spa charges $600 just to wax one eyebrow. (One!) Their phone number is impossible to find; unlisted, of course. Supposedly, the waiting list is eighteen months long.

And I get an appoiiiiiiinment!

Mwa-ha-ha.

I get the feeling that this is Phil's way of apologizing for the complete and utter exploitation of my parents' hospitality. Or it should be, anyway.

Hmph.

An enormous coffee-skinned man in a white turban held the door open for me as I entered. His name tag read PUN-JAB WELCOMES YOU TO CHUT-SPA. He nodded as I whispered hello, then gently closed the door behind me as I entered the spa and was swallowed into the immaculate foyer.

Yowsa.

Now, the closest I've been to an exclusive spa is the Korean nail place in Pacific mall, but I could tell just from the lobby that this was the real deal. The real, astronomically expensive deal.

The walls stretched thirty feet above me to a pristine glass ceiling, tinted palm-reader blue and speckled with sil-

very, celestial flecks. It was futuristically stark, boasting
only a few white-cushioned blond oak chairs and a hostess
stand, like you'd see in a restaurant. The floors were white
marble; any shoes besides sneakers would have clacked
like Civil War gunshots, footsteps amplified one thousand
times by the vast acoustics of the room.

Wowwww.

I looked around some more. No employees in sight.

Maybe I'll just check out these magazines over here.

Doo da doo, still no employees.

Um, where am I supposed to go? Punjab? Puuuunjab?

After some more awkward confusion, I was preparing to
about-face and chase down my limo when a barefoot employee (er, probably a "beauty consultant" or "relaxation
specialist") emerged from a nearly invisible door and
padded toward me.

"Aah, Miss Jorlamo! I hope we haven't kept you waiting
for too long. Now let me see . . ." She mused over a large
book on the hostess stand, flipping through a few pages
and running her finger down a list of items. "Ah, yes of
course, you're having the *Deluxe à Deux*. Follow me,
please."

"*À Deux*? I'm sorry, is there someone else here?"

"The gentleman, ma'am."

Certainly it wasn't Chad; the woman would have recognized him. Unless she was trying to be discreet . . .

"The . . . gentleman?"

"Yes, Miss Jorlamo. The man . . . with the . . . eye."

Great. Now he's my freaky little chaperone.

"Oh. Right, my publicist."

She looked relieved. "Yes, yes of course. Your publicist.
Well, welcome to Chut-Spa. Please, there's a dressing room
right over there." She pointed to a white curtain hanging to

the right. "And here, of course, is your robe. Spun by hand-fed Guatemalan silk worms; we don't use synthetics here. All natural."

"Hand-fed? What did they eat?" I joked. "I only wear silk spun by worms fed an organic diet!"

Well, I *thought* I was joking.

I chuckled and looked at her to reciprocate, but she looked uncomfortable. Then I realized that this probably wasn't an outrageous claim around these parts.

"Kidding. I'm just . . . kidding."

"Oh," she sighed, again looking mighty relieved. "Oh. Because I could find out for you. I'm new here, you know, but I'm pretty sure the worms only eat macrobiotic."

"No, really, I'm . . . I'll just go put this on, okay?"

I darted into the dressing room, shed my track suit and sneakers, and slipped into the robe. When I came out she was still standing there, probably wondering if I was going to throw a hissy fit over the lighting or the angle of reflection in the three-way mirror.

"Ready!" I smiled.

She took my clothes from me and led me through the lone door, down another impossibly white marble hallway. The spa smelled like Moroccan pond water; aromas of salt, algae, and exotic spices filled my nostrils as I followed her to another inconspicuous doorway.

"Your companion is in here." She opened the door, beckoned me through, and departed, leaving me ogling a reclining figure that resembled a gigantic lump of nougat dripping with beluga whale snot.

"Ah, Plumpkin, is that you? You made it! How's your mother? I hear she's the best cook in town."

"Hi, Phil. Yeah, I'm—no, no, don't roll over! Phil, I can—awww, you're *naked*, dude! Aw, put a towel on! Jeeze!"

He had been lying facedown on a massage table, but as I entered he shimmied to flip himself, revealing a seaweed swathed torso, and one happy little fella.

"Oh come on," he yawned, "no secrets here."

"Yeah? Speak for yourself. Here, would you mind?" I grabbed a towel from a nearby table and tossed it at him, careful not to get too close in case I accidentally brushed against his, um, chilly willy. Yuuuck.

I noticed too late that his good eye was covered with a tea bag. The towel hit him in the chest. "Careful, dumpling. Don't smear my wrap. It's still fresh. There, it's covered. Happy? Now come and have a seat."

When he'd covered his naughty bits, I sat gingerly on the massage table next to his.

"You're gonna love this," Phil said. "Inga is the best, I tell you, the best in the biz. Hands of a goddess. What I wouldn't give for a house call!"

"Phil, I . . . well, this is great, but . . . I didn't expect you to, um . . ."

"What? Enjoy a spa treatment or two? This is mainte-nance, Plumpkin, it's like getting your oil changed. How do you think I manage this glowing peaches and cream com-plexion? It ain't that wheatgrass bullshit of Chad's, I'll tell you that much. It's the delicate, loving touch of that hot lit-tle German mama. Inga? Inga, my dear, is it time for the warm stones? You know I love it when you heat my rocks up! That's a little joke, Inga, my darling, now where are you?"

A door in the back of the room opened, and in shuffled who I presumed to be Inga, a teeny redhead sporting blue eye shadow and an enormous rack.

"*Ja, ja, ja,* Herr Phil. Ah, Fraulein Julie. I start on you. Lie down, please. Robe off."

"Robe off? Um . . ." I gestured to Phil and made a grossed-out face. Inga nodded in agreement.

"Okay, Herr Phil, tea bag or no, you look at ze lady, I vill knock your teeth out, got it, hot zhtuff?"

"Oh, anything for you, Inga." Phil giggled like a manly schoolgirl. "I'll never look at another woman, never ever again."

Oh, wretch.

I forgot all about Phil (and everyone else on the planet, for that matter) when Inga began my treatment. I was facedown on the table, so I couldn't really see what was going on, but I was in heaven. First she ran a sandpapery stone over my back ("Pumice, to take off ze dead zkin"), then followed by slathering a wonderful warm sludge all over me.

"Ees brown zhugar mango wrap," Inga informed me. "Ees first step. Then, ve rinse and massage. Twenty minutes like zis. You relax, please, I finish Herr Phil's rocks."

Phil giggled again, and I tried to ignore his rasp as I melted through the massage table, floating on a pillowy cloud of sunshiny happiness.

I had ten minutes of blissful, gooey silence.

"So, Plumpkin, what do you think? Chut-Spa is the bees' knees, huh?"

"Phil, you talk like a dork sometimes."

"Hey." I couldn't see him, but I could tell Phil was feigning shock and disdain. He likes it when I screw with him. "I resent that, Plumpkin! I make you famous, I give you the world on a string and a fabulous day at the spa, and you mock me? What gall, what nerve! Are you sure you're not Jewish?"

"I'm half."

"The *good* half."

I chuckled. "So, how'd you get us these appointments, Phil? I've heard that you have to be royalty to get in here!"

"Honey, *that* doesn't even work sometimes. Nope, I just pulled some strings. I'm sort of a regular. I refer a lot of up-and-comers here, in exchange for some press. Works like a charm. So, they owe me once in a while. And I told them I had a special client who needed to relax a little bit."

That's for damned sure.

"Well . . . I appreciate it. I've never been to a spa before. You know, I don't think I've ever had a massage, either."

"What? Oh honey, no wonder you look so haggard all the time!"

"Hey!"

"I'm teasing you, Plumpkin! You're fabulous. Gorgeous. Jesus, grow some self-esteem! I'm going to have to give you a crash course in self-confidence."

You know, he *was* awfully confident, for a twitchy little toady.

Ew, ew, ew! What was he doing?

"Phil, what are you *doing*?"

He had raised his left hand and was poking at the glass eye with a pinky, swiveling it in place and making it squeak.

Sqqqqrrrrrreeeeeeuuurrrrk

Oh God, oh God, it was like nails on a chalkboard.

"I was thinking," he said, "about updating my look."

What, from Cro-Magnon to Homo sapien?

"You mean like a haircut?"

"No," *sqqqqqrrrrreeeeeuuuurrrrrkkkkk*, "I was thinking about doing something really," *sqqqqqqrrrrreeeeuuurrrkkkk*, "unique."

I could feel my own eye start to twitch in Tourette's-like fashion.

"Unique?"

"Yeah," *sqqqqqqqrrrrrreeeeeuuuuurrrrrkkkkkkk*, "like, I could—"

"*Would you cut that shit out?*"

"What?"

"*Your eye. Stop. Touching. Your. Eye. Nooooowwww!*"

Oh God, thank you.

"Sorry. Nasty habit. Anyway, I was thinking about getting a different eye."

"What?"

"You know, make it more of an accessory, like a Clockwork Orange, jumps-out-at-you kind of thing. It could be the talk of the town! You know, different colors, patterns, change it up for different outfits, that kind of thing."

"Um . . ."

"Or," he continued, "what could be *really* fab is if I had a whole bunch of them made up with pictures of my clients. You know, like those New Kids marbles. Remember those things? Brilliant. Well, maybe didn't work out so well for them, but I could take it to a whole new level. Can't you just eat it up? Little pictures, of my clients, in my *eye*! It's the ultimate marketing tool! And nobody else can do it! I think Chad would absolutely *nut* over something like that."

Inga returned, thank God, to scrape off the warm goo and rub my temples with saffron.

"Do you bring Chad in here, too?" I yawned. Mmm, spices making me sleeeeepy.

Phil snorted. "That airhead? I tried, once. Got all pissed off because they don't have magnets. Made like a tree, muttering something about his chakra."

"Airhead? I thought you liked Chad?"

"Plumpkin, just because I adore having someone as a client does *not* mean that I have to enjoy their company.

And anyway, I'm extremely pissed at him for pulling that Katarina Conrad bullshit the other night. He was supposed to go straight home with you, not flit all over the fucking town and jam his tongue down his ex's throat! Do you know how much scrambling around I had to do to make sure nobody printed a picture of them diddling around in Solstein's hot tub? Oy, it's a good thing he remembered the 'friends' routine. Not to mention pulling all that method acting crap with your parents. I swear, Plumpkin, I didn't tell him to do any of that. Do you see what happens when he tries to think for himself? God, he should just stick to the routine. Fucking circus monkey."

"Circus monkey, huh?"

"Jesus, I'm like the fucking puppet master with that man. He usually does whatever I tell him to, you know. I mean, that's how it usually is between a publicist and a client, but, Chad? Chad's a special kind of dimwit."

Wow, this was about to get good.

"I can get him to say whatever I want!" Phil sat up and began to wave his hands excitedly. "To whoever I want! I don't think he even pays attention to what he's saying! Just takes it in and spits it back out. All I have to do is feed it to him, and he's off and flapping his mouth like a pet parrot that you teach holiday greetings to. 'Rah! Happy Easter!' 'Rah! Season's greetings!' 'Rah! Solstein's a genius!' It's like programming my goddamned answering machine."

"Are you telling me that every time Chad gives an interview, he's just repeating what you tell him to?"

"Well what did you think, Plumpkin, that he's naturally eloquent and quick on his feet?"

"So what, do you, like, feed it to him through an ear piece or something?"

"I wish! That would make everyone's life easier. You

know for an actor, he sure is lousy at memorizing lines. Do you know how many hours of rehearsing we have to do before he goes on late night? Good God, it's like prepping a witness for prosecutorial testimony! At least he's learned to smile and just make a pretty face at the audience when he can't remember the appropriate thing to say. He comes off as looking discreet, which doesn't hurt. Fucking amoeba."

He finally plucked the tea bag from his eye, recoiling at the flood of light, then fixing his creepy unigaze on me.

"You know," he continued, "it's kind of a turn-on sometimes."

"Um, *ew*, please don't continue that sadistically homo-erotic train of thought!"

"No, I'm serious! It's empowering, being totally in control. I tell him what to say, what to wear, who to date, what to eat, when to pick his nose, when to light a smoke. If it weren't for me, he'd be running around like a blind puppy, ramming into walls and weeing on the carpet."

"You really don't like him, do you?"

"Oh, he's such a putz. Same as all the other pretty boys, lots of teeth, lots of girls, no common sense. If I hadn't taken him on he'd still be co-starring with a cartoon, hawking ass wipes."

Yikes.

"He can't be *that* dumb."

"Oh my God, honey, he's got the know-how of a rutabaga. Do you know how often I've wanted to fuck with him, just for a giggle? It'd be so easy. Just feed him some absolute fucking nonsense, and let him run with it? He would, too, that fucking monkey. He'd tell the President to kiss his exfoliated white ass, if that's what I told him."

Phil was sitting up ramrod straight now, all evidence of relaxation tossed out the window. He had a spiteful, mischievous look in his eye that I hadn't seen before. It was sort of scary.

But then again, it was sort of awesome. After all, I was beginning to loathe Chad like a stepsibling.

"Um, Phil? You okay, buddy? You're starting to sweat. Is that going to counteract the seaweed?"

And like that, I'd lost him. I could tell by the way he was nodding to himself that he couldn't even hear me anymore, only his own flamboyantly manic ravings.

"You know why I like you, Plumpkin? Because you're just like me, kid, one and the fucking same. We're in it for the glamour, all the fucking bullshit glitter that we never could have had on our own. Nope, had to latch onto these clowns in order to have our fucking day in the sun. But I'll tell you what, cream puff, it's all worth it."

"It is?"

"Of course it is!" he barked. "Because you get to know what it feels like to have everyone love you, to have super-fluous megastars crouched at your mangled tootsies and practically beg you to make them bigger, make them better! They depend on me, on me! I'm in total control, sweet potato. *I'm* the important one, *I'm* the maker."

Great, the freaky fuck had run amuck and I was stuck.

God, I'm brilliant in a panic.

I tried to be subtle as I shifted my gaze around the room, frantically looking for an exit sign. Goddamned spa and their goddamned sense of chi and balance. Why do the doors have to blend in with the scenery?

No luck. Damn.

"Um, Phil?" I began cautiously. "You sound a little, um, stressed out. Maybe you should lie back and try to relax, huh?"

Please, *please* relax, little man?

Oh good, Inga was back. Maybe she could calm him down, give him a happy ending, or something.

He paused mid-twitch when he noticed the redhead, and cocked his head, flicking a stray cucumber seed from his thigh.

"You're right, Plumpkin. That man gets me in a tizzy every fucking time. Aaaah, my Inga. That's good, my dear, that shoulder feels a little tense. Yes, goddamnit, Chad always seems to get me worked up. Not the same thing he does to you, of course, but all worked up nonetheless."

I blushed. (Thankfully, I don't think it was noticeable underneath the avocado paste that Inga had begun to smear on my cheeks.)

"Worked up? What do you mean? I, uh, I don't get worked up!"

"Angel cake, when he's around, you turn into a sixth grader with a crush on her math teacher."

"Ummm."

"Oh, please, who the fuck doesn't? The man has more teeth than a Chinese phone book!"

Huh?

"And he certainly knows how to flash 'em. That, of course, would be the charm classes I put him through, *naturally*. Fucking monkey."

"You know, Phil, to be honest, I did have a little crush—"

"A *little* crush! Ha!"

"—on Chad," I continued, "but, you know, after that stunt he pulled at my house, I think it's starting to fade."

"Well, thank God for that, Plumpkin! You seem like a nice girl. Don't need to get all mixed up in *that* fucking train wreck. You know," he mused, "it *would* be nice to have the last laugh on him, just once."

"What do you mean, the last laugh?"

"Oh, you know, make him say something dumb. Just for my own personal satisfaction."

"Isn't that kind of unethical?"

He snorted.

"Unethical? Honey, please. Everybody does it! Britney Spears? Oh child, her people are definitely out to get her. Nobody's that fucking oblivious, not even Mouseketeers. Honestly, I'm probably one of the only ones who hasn't snuck in a little self-deprecating jab here and there. To be a promotional muse, well, it's a powerful thing, cupcake. Easy to let it go to your head, especially when a client gets all high and mighty. I always swore up and down I'd stay one of the good guys, but, you know—Ooh, Inga, rub right there, sweet pea. Yessss, that's the spot—you know, just once I'd like to feel like I've come out on top. Reeeeally stick it to 'em. Does that make me crazy?"

"Actually, Phil, what makes *you* crazy is the way you froth at the corners of your mouth when you say the word 'self-deprecate.' "

"Ahahahahaha! Ooh, you're a feisty one, Plumpkin, I like that. That's gonna be good TV, my dear. Good TV. I'll make sure Chad lets you get a word or two in. Fuck it, the whole thing will be about you. It's about time, anyway!"

"TV? Whole thing? What whole thing? What are you talking about, Phil?"

"Your big debut, sugarplum! Why do you think I brought you here, silly? You need to be all relaxed and glowing for your big night! Studio lights are terribly harsh, Plumpkin. Make your pores look like fucking polka dots."

My whats look like *what*?

"What do you mean 'big debut'? I've been on camera with Chad lots of times!"

"Oh-ho! A few red carpet interviews and she thinks she's

an old pro! Isn't that adorable! No no, I'm talking about late night, snickerdoodle, the cream of the crop. And I got you a half-hour block, which is golden stuff."

"Late night? Half an hour?"

"Cookie Ferris-Clayton, Plumpkin. The real deal. Ooh, I'm tingling! I swear to God, if we pull this off, I'm buying you a pony. No no, don't look so nervous! If you back out on me now, Plumpkin, I'll set the fucking dogs on you! Kidding, kidding! But seriously, this is my career we're talking about, please don't fuck me in the ass. Oh my God, TV! You're in it now, Plumpkin! Up to your chinny-chin-chin!"

Oh, bajeezus.

 Sixteen

Ready or not, here comes my close-up.
    Figures that just when I'd finally become comfortable with this spotlight bullshit, Phil decided to up the stakes.

I hope he's making a lot of money off me. Someone should be, for all of the nonsense I've put myself through.

And after tonight, someone deserves a raise.

For tonight's the night; the pinnacle of potential publicity disaster; my big TV debut, you see. *Potent Notables*, a snazzy, jazzy, late night talk show, has apparently been champing at the bit to get Chad and me on their show.

Me?

Still haven't figured that one out, although between throwing up and going over flash cards with Chad, I haven't had much time to think it over.

I think he's even more nervous than I am.

"Now remember, this part's critical!" He snapped at me over lattes on the morning of the studio taping. "You have to make sure to say that we met while you were finishing up a night shift *four* weeks ago, okay? If you fuck up that number, I'm going to look like an asshole."

I stared at him blankly for what seemed the fiftieth time since we'd started my cram session.

"Julie, if we met *five* weeks ago, then it was while I was still dating Katarina, and suddenly I become a cheating bastard. If we met *three* weeks ago, then that photographer took your picture right after we met, and I'll look like a male slut for fucking you too quickly."

"Ha." I muttered, "male slut. Always a tragic reputation."

"Excuse me?"

"Nothing." I sat up straight.

My ego was still sore from the last time we went out in public, that fateful pukey limo ride when he told me I wasn't fuckable. It's hard to maintain the same level of attraction when you know for sure that a man wants absolutely nothing to do with your cooter. And I'm mad because of the mockery he made of my parents. (Wait until Mom finds out. A mother scorned is a dangerous, dreadful thing.) Add on that he's fooling around with his ex, when I'm supposed to be his girlfriend . . . well, not really, but everyone thinks I am, damnit. The least the penis-head could do is *not* make me look like a damned fool *or* a clueless, throwaway, has-been celebrity girlfriend wannabe.

Not that I care, or anything.

"Earth to Julie. Hello? Are we doing this, or what?"

"What? Oh, sorry."

I was bored to tears. I don't know why Chad was making me do this, anyway. It wasn't like he ever let me get a word in edgewise when anyone asked me a question.

"Now my favorite color is . . . blue—come on, say it with me—and my mother's name is . . . Brenda."

"Chad, who is going to ask me what your mother's name is? You don't even speak to your mother."

"Which *nobody* needs to know, got it? Jesus, I'd lose an entire fan bracket if word got out that I haven't spoken to her since I was seventeen."

"Seventeen?"

He took a casual sip of his latte.

"Yep. The bitch tried to siphon half my money away into some ridiculous college fund."

"A college fund for who? You?"

"Yeah."

I snorted. "Wow. What nerve. You poor thing."

"I know. Horrible business sense. Glad I cut the cord when I did."

"Uh-*huh*."

"Anyway, let's focus, okay? Phil's coming over in an hour to give you an outfit."

"Oh goodie. I hope it's cool."

"Oh my God. Did you just say 'Oh goodie'? Try not to be such a two-shoes on the show tonight, okay? I know you're supposed to be basic and everything, but for Christ's sake, we're not appearing on *Howdy Doody*."

I can't believe that two weeks ago I wanted to jump this guy's bones. Now I wanted to crush them to smithereens in a cement mixer. Make paste out of the rotten creep.

"What about me, Chad?"

"What about you?"

"Don't you need to know anything about me? I mean, all right, I get it. You like long walks on the beach and spending all day at the go-cart track. You hate polyester, and think flannel should be outlawed in forty-nine states. Your favorite ice cream is chocolate chip, your pecker's name is Yoda."

"Hey! That's not public information."

"Do you actually tell women 'May the force be with you' right before you stick it in?"

"Are you trying to be funny?"

"Am I being funny?"

"Well, it sounds like someone's a little bitter that they couldn't get laid in the back of a limo."

I swear to God, when this was all over, I would lace his low carb beer with liquid Ex-Lax. Stupid fuck.

"Chad, what's my middle name?"

"Huh?"

"What's my middle name, Chad? No, better yet, how do you *spell* my last name?"

"I'm missing something."

"Exactly, you're missing everything. You know my first and last names, you know my dog, and you know my dress size. That's it. Aren't you worried that someone will pick up on that eventually? Like tonight, for example?"

"Julie, you're forgetting yourself. Everyone expects *you* to be enamored with *me*. Everyone expects *me* to be witty and charming. Jesus, I could tell the audience that you were raised by purple coon hounds in a Transylvanian bomb shelter, and no one would question it. No one would give a shit."

I hate his stupid, famous guts.

The host of *Potent Notables* is Cookie Ferris-Clayton, a transsexual piranha masquerading as a sweet-talking Georgia peach. She's fruity, all right.

When we got to the studio, we were greeted by a bevy of production assistants, all brunette indy-looking chicks sporting Buddy Holly glasses. If you ever wondered why there are no nerdy looking people in Hollywood, you've clearly never been behind the scenes. Sets are chock full of them. All stumbling all over themselves to please the bigwigs, each eternally doomed to the tail end of the closing credits.

I watched them forlornly as they fluttered around Chad, bestowing him with cigarettes and espresso, Belgian liquor chocolates and minty body lotions. Poor little plain girls. I sort of miss being one of them.

"Chad-doll! Plumpkin! There you two are! Glad to see you!"

"Hey, Phil," Chad barely looked up from the doting production flunkies, "did you get the preshow bullshit finished?"

"Hey, is the Pope a gentile? Of course I did. Don't worry, Cookie's not going to ask you about Katarina, or your mother, or your nose hair."

"Nose hair?" I giggled.

Chad shot me a filthy look. Meow.

Phil winked at me and cleared his throat.

"And don't worry, Chad, your coffee will be brewed with microinfused springwater, and be sprinkled with Indonesian cinnamon. No, really! Fresh off the plane, I watched them cart it in. Plumpkin, did you take those vitamins I bought you at the spa? Got to be pep-pep-peppy for tonight!"

On our way out of Chut-Spa, Phil had paused in the gift shop to buy me a *ginormous* bottle of some kind of ginko-bijiggity supplement. Truth be told, I'm pretty sure they were just caffeine pills, because I couldn't stop jiggling my right foot if you fucking cut it off.

We didn't even meet Cookie until twenty minutes before the interview. I'd only seen her show a couple of times. It's more like a tabloid than anything else; one of those nitty-gritty gossip shows that rips apart the very celebrities it exalts, biting the hand that feeds it. Cookie likes to make her guests feel comfortable, then yank the rug out from under them by asking them mortifying questions about their personal lives.

Maybe she'd go easy on me.

I had my hair and makeup done for the first time since this whole ordeal started. Finally, a chance to look glamorous. Chad couldn't say anything about it because there were a thousand people milling around, so he just sulked in the corner while three stylists ruffled his hair with pomade.

I was having my nails buffed when Cookie finally appeared to introduce herself.

I should use the word "herself" loosely.

S/he was a vision of androgyny, short and solid, built like a brick of cheddar cheese. Teetering in her heels, she swaggered like a frat boy. Rumor had it she was still undergoing treatment to make the full blossom into womanhood. Amazing. They can make a pill to give you breasts, but still not a goddamned thing for the flu.

Cookie was festooned like a Chanukah bush; adorned with stars of David and glittering like a prism under the hot studio lights. Her orange hair was an avant-garde sculpture, defying any conventional form, but still recognizable as some sort of style.

The hormone therapy had done nothing to affect her voice, which conjured a donkey grazing in a tobacco field.

"Darlings, you're here! You're here! I'm Cookie! Kiss, kiss, my little snow peas!"

Oh boy.

"Chad," she continued, "always a pleasure, love. But you?" She turned to me. "You I have not met before." She approached me with outstretched arms. I thought she was going to embrace me, but instead pinched my cheeks with her purple talons as though I were a long-lost niece.

"Look at you. Look at you!" she exclaimed. "Adorable. Oh my God, what are you, twelve? Fabulous. You did good, Chad, you did real good."

"I like to think so." He strolled over to join us and cupped my chin in his hand, so my face was now being pulled in three different directions.

"I ruruhhh rurrmneu yru."

"What's that, darling?"

"Reh rrroh. Rrreeeh rrrroh!"

Jesus, what am I, Scooby Doo?

"I can't understand you, darling." Cookie finally released her death grip and patted me on the head. "But that's okay. You're still toooo adorable. Now. Questions. Let's review."

She snatched a pen and clipboard from a nearby production assistant and scribbled a few notes.

"Hmmm . . . right . . . okay . . . right. Basically, I'm just going to ask you the same old: how'd you meet, how's everything going, that sort of thing. You know the drill, Chad, I'm sure. And of course, we'll want the sappy stuff. Make some shit up, I don't care. The audience likes a good anecdote. Tell some stories, get us to laugh, cry, crap our pants, that kind of thing. What time is it? Two minutes? Gotta dash, buttercups. See you after my monologue!"

And she was off, leaving us in a wake of cheap perfume and nerves.

One of the nerdy androids appeared at my side. "You're on in ten minutes, right after the first commercial break. I'll cue you."

"Swell," I muttered nervously.

When the time finally came to go on, I had gnawed away my new manicure and was pacing like an antsy house cat.

"Let's go!" the android exclaimed. "Downing and Jorlamo, in five, four, three . . ."

"Let's get this over with," Chad sighed under his breath.

". . . two, one . . . cue Chad and Julie!"

Chad grabbed me by the hand and led me through the stage door to the set.

It was just like I'd seen on TV; fuchsia armchairs, abstract skyline backdrop, hundreds of scorching lights, and a screaming, rabid audience. Only this time they were screaming at me.

Gulp.

Somehow I made it to Cookie, kissed her on the cheek and sank into my chair without wiping out or tearing my pants. I looked over at Chad. He was totally calm, maybe even bored, grinning his plastic robot grin at the swooning audience. Some actors launch into an "aw shucks" routine when they get in front of an audience, but not Chad. He's a whore for attention, the Jezebel of late night.

"Well! Well, welcome!" Cookie crowed. "Welcome, welcome, Mr. Downing! Yeah!" She encouraged the audience, who were still whooping it up over their unbelievable luck. Ah yes, I remember the days when I would have been thrilled to be in the same room as him, too.

"Yes! And who do we have here, Mr. Downing? Hmm? Why, it's your lovely lady! Isn't she, ladies and gentlemen? Huh? Yes! Miss Julie Jorlamo! Yes!"

Ooh, they're clapping for me now. Ooh, that's kind of cool!

"Great to see you Cookie," Chad oozed. "You look fantastic!"

The audience cheered again.

"Oh, well thank you, thank you! Aren't you the cat's meow? And believe me, I do mean meow. *Meeeeeow.* Good lord, you're delicious, isn't he, folks? Yes! Yes he is! Ooh. Oh, Mr. Downing. So, anyway, how are you? What's been going on? Busy beaver lately, huh?"

"I sure am! We've been doing some reshoots on my upcoming feature, *John Dough*—" The audience broke into applause *again.* "Thank you! Thank you so much! Yeah, so that's going pretty well, and, I've got a new project in the works with Dream Gems Pictures, so things are looking pretty good!"

"Well, you know what else is looking good, Mr. Chad Downing? Your lady friend! Isn't she? Isn't she?"

Oh God, it's my turn to talk. Uhhhh . . .

"Why, thank . . . ahem . . . thank you, Cookie," I squawked. "That's so nice of you!"

"Julie, we're all dying to get to know you. I mean, we hear about you everywhere, but nobody knows a thing! You're like the Taliban, honey, honest to God. Now, let's hear it. What's your story?"

My story. My story?

There were gigantic cameras all over the place, and they were all pointed directly at me, like bazookas holding off their fire.

Chad nudged me with his foot.

"Umm, well . . ." I didn't know which camera to look at, so I swiveled my head like a lawn sprinkler. "I grew up here in Los Angeles, and went away to college, and now . . . I'm back. Here. In Los Angeles."

"Uh-huh. College you say? How interesting. See the man over there, honey? He'll cue you where to look. And you're working . . . as a waitress? Right, right? She works as a waitress?"

"Well, Julie's not exactly the academic type," Chad interjected. "She's more your *everyday* kind of girl, you know?"

"Didn't like to crack those books, huh, Julie?" Cookie winked at me. "Well, I can certainly understand that! So do you have any plans for the future, now that everyone knows your name?"

I opened my mouth to respond, but Chad jumped in again.

"Julie's pretty happy with the way things are!" he said pointedly. "She's a laidback, *normal* person. Perfect for me," he smiled, sitting back in his chair, "because she keeps me grounded. Brings me back down to earth after doing the Hollywood thing all day."

"I see, I see. Isn't that great, folks? Yeah, yeah! Wow! So, I think the whole world wants to hear it from you, kids: how *did* you meet?"

Chad caught my eye and shook his head ever so slightly. I guess that meant I was supposed to shut up. Fine. Prick.

"Well, Cookie," he beamed, grabbing my hand and bringing it to his lips theatrically, "it was a very special day. For me, anyway. Just another *normal* afternoon for Miss Julie here."

Okay, they get it. I'm run of the mill, for Christ's sake. Stop rubbing it in.

"So, I was absolutely dying for a tuna fish sandwich— you know, that flaky stuff, comes in a can?"

Oh, come on.

"Anyway, I get so tired of haute cuisine, so I slipped into this chain restaurant to grab a bite and hang out a little. Well, I'm sitting there looking at the menu, when over walks the cutest little waitress I had ever seen. I just had to have her!"

"*Aaaaawwwwwwwwww!*" the audience sighed collectively.

"I know," he continued, "it's a great story! I was incognito, of course, so she didn't recognize me, and I asked her out as soon as she brought me my sandwich. When she realized who I was, well—"

He turned to me now, for dramatic effect, of course, and gazed into my eyes.

"—it just didn't matter to her. She liked me for, well, just being *me*." He turned back to the audience and dropped my hand, "And that's why I'm so crazy about her, Cookie. Because around Julie, I don't have to be Chad Downing, celebrity. I can just be Chad Downing, everyday Joe. A lot like the character in my upcoming film, actually."

I knew that was coming.

"Well, Chad, we hear that a lot from celebs who date nobodies!" Cookie chuckled. "I'm sorry, 'nonactors.' And they usually turn out to be gold diggers, don't they, Miss Jorlamo? I'm kidding! I'm kidding! You don't want to be an actress, do you Julie?"

"Um, no. No, of course not."

"Well, you're not going to be a waitress for the rest of your life, are you?" Cookie turned to the audience for agreement. "I mean, that wouldn't be too exciting for a girl who's had a taste of the spotlight, hmmm? It's sweet, isn't it honey? Like a goddamned drug."

Just what is the haggard old queen trying to imply?

"I guess, but—"

"I'm sure you can snag a guest spot on the WB, sweet pea. Better do it soon, though! Fifteen minutes, and all that."

"But I don't—"

"I'd just like to clarify," Chad jumped in quickly, "for the record, that Katarina Conrad and I are *just friends*, and that anything the papers say is—"

"Well, folks, we've got to take a break, but when we come back, we've got Zara Winters and her dastardly Brazilian circus monkeys! Boy, those things can whip through the air! Chad, Julie, it's been a pleasure. We'll be right back."

Cookie adjusted her clip-on microphone and turned to us.

"Okay, well thanks, kids. Chad, make sure to stop by with a clip when you get that movie finished. And Julie, well, the WB, right? We'll squeeze you in for a quick one-on-one. Have some girl talk. Sound good? Okay, it's on to the monkeys, darlings. Ciao! Come back and see me!"

That's it? We were done?

"Come on," Chad whispered as he grabbed my elbow to steer me off stage.

"I can't believe that woman," he exclaimed when we made it back to the green room, "or man. Whatever. I just can't believe he did that to you!"

What's this? Sympathy?

"For God's sake!" he continued. "I need the public to actually like you, or this whole charade will never fucking work! Of course, maybe they'll feel bad for me, but I'd rather have their blessing than their pity! I'm going to have to release a statement. Let me find Phil. I thought we had a half hour, anyway? That she-man gypped us. The fucking nerve."

THE DAILY BEACON

CHAD'S LEADING LADY:
GOLDMINE OR GOLDDIGGER?

Late night head honcho Cookie Ferris-Clayton played hostess last night to the delectable Chad Downing and his new love. Or is she? Cookie was crisp on last night's showdown, making Miss Jorlamo seem a little questionable! Maybe that explains Chad's recent shenanigans with exotic ex Katarina Conrad? Chad's people say it's nonsense, that Kat is splat, and his new lady is a class act. Seems their love is here to stay; though in Tinseltown, who knows for how long?

 Seventeen

The chic has hit the fan.

I thought this famous nonsense was going to be easy. Just hang on Chad's arm, look pretty, and try not to pick my nose. Simple, right? Well now this bullshit's out of control, and it's starting to fester, and I hate it I hate it *I hate it*.

I needed to take my mind off of my disastrous TV debut, so Billie and I went to the mall today. I thought we'd do a little browsing and enjoy a food court feast of nachos, corn dogs, teriyaki beef rolls, and a few of those frothy orange smoothie things.

"What do you think of these?"

"I don't . . . do those have stirrups?"

When we got to the mall, Billie had immediately dragged me into Total Eclipse of the Haute, an eighties novelty store and her own personal nirvana. I've told her a thousand times to just get a job there and be done with it, but she's afraid that the downfalls of working in retail will taint the merchandise, maybe even the decade. God forbid.

The shelves were filled with nostalgia: shoulderless sweatshirts, sweatbands, leg warmers, Members Only jackets, those shirts that change color when you blow on them. Most people shopped here for Halloween, or if the runways revived Chuck Taylors for half a second. Billie, of course, purchased ninety-six percent of her wardrobe here.

The pants in question were stretchy purple Lycra, littered with iridescent sparkles. And they did indeed boast teal ankle stirrups. Yikes.

"Well, you'd have no trouble keeping them tucked into your moon boots, if that's the look you're going for."

"Oh yeah! Dude, I totally forgot about moon boots! You're a genius; that'd be fabulous!"

Aaaand, she's off, scavenging the racks for silver space shoes.

I shook my head, left to sift through a bin of mismatched tube socks.

Usually I feel pretty nondescript at the mall. There are a million people everywhere, and who pays attention to a plain-looking brunette carrying a department store brown bag and a handful of soft pretzel twists? If Billie joins me, it can get a little fishbowlish; preteen goths giggle and point at the eighties gear, soccer moms steer their strollers away so that curious toddlers don't scream something rude. Men don't pay her much attention, but she's a bright shining beacon for lesbians, who I gather appreciate the showcase of every color in the pride flag. But gawking and homoerotic wooing aside, our shopping trips are generally uneventful.

How I long for the days of anonymity.

My browsing stopped short when I felt the eyes. You know, you get the creepy feeling like someone is watching you, like maybe you've got a nice ass, or you've got something disgusting or inappropriate on your face? I looked up from the bin and made eye contact with a teenage salesgirl who was staring at me the way a supermodel would size up a turkey dinner. Contemplative. Hesitant. Wildly famished.

What the fuck, dude?

I swiped at my face. Was it latte foam? Mascara streaks?

She smiled uncomfortably when she realized that I'd caught her looking, and went back to folding her pile of pleated chinos.

"Jule? Jule. Hello, earth to fabulous?"

"Wha . . . sorry."

To my left, Billie was hopping up and down, waving the coveted moon boots frantically.

"Check it out! They have some! Only . . . they're sixty dollars, and I only have a ten. Could I borrow some cash? I'll pay you back on Friday!"

"Yeah, I'll just put it on my card. You can get lunch."

"Cool! Thank you, pookie! Oh, and I found these fabulous pants that you *have* to try on. No, don't look so horrified, they're pretty tame. Well, yeah, they're orange, but you have to visualize before you reject them. You could *totally* tone them down with a black blouse. Here, go put them on and show me."

I glanced up at where the salesgirl had been staring me down. She was still folding clothes intently. Hm. Weird.

There's a tactful art to shopping with Billie. If she sees something that she thinks will look fabulous on someone else, she's like a dog shaking a toy; she just can't fucking let it go. How many times she's made me try on outlandish clothing, I couldn't tell you. I learned years ago that it's better to indulge her, try on the pants, and pretend they don't fit. Otherwise, I end up unwrapping geometric windbreaker pants on Christmas morning.

I hate trying on pants in general because of my hips. I'm not that uncomfortable with my body, just the hush-hush conspiracy devised by the fashion industry to make all women stop eating. I'm pretty sure it was a tactic contrived in cahoots with the government, to help curb famine in third world countries. Why, woman want to fit into pants! The United States has all this extra food that nobody's eating! Here you go, Botswana! *Mangia bene!*

Oooh, but I don't have to fake it with these. Besides being the same shade of the puke someone might produce after a pumpkin-pie-eating contest, I could barely get them over my ass. Stupid baby fat. That's right, baby fat. It's hard to shed, damnit. I've been working on it for years.

"How'd it go?" Billie asked brightly, practically crossing her fingers.

"Nope, didn't fit. Too bad; they're so, uh, cute."

"That sucks. Want to head to another store?"

I heard her ask the question, but I couldn't concentrate on her face. Instead, I was distracted by two women standing behind her, watching me and whispering to each other. Goddamnit; what is everyone staring at?

"Huh? Yeeeah, let's go somewhere else. Come on." I grabbed Billie by the elbow and began to steer her toward the front of the store.

"Hold on, Jule. My boots! I, er, you haven't paid for them yet."

"Oh yeah. Sorry."

I shifted direction and made my way toward the cashier, who was idly winding a long string of chewing gum around her finger. When I plunked the boots down on the counter, she snapped to attention.

"Wowww, I, like, totally love these boots!" she exclaimed jealously. "I've been trying to save my money for a pair, but, like, my paycheck totally flies out the window, like, every week!"

Tell me about it, sister.

She rang up the boots and I handed her my already

groaning credit card. Oh well, maybe if I picked up a few extra shifts, I—

"Oh my God!" the salesgirl yelped. "I, like, totally knew it!"

"Excuse me? Knew what?"

"I knew it was you. You look just the same on TV!"

Ooooh, man, you've got to be kidding me.

"Look, uh," I stammered, glancing around to make sure nobody had heard her exclamation, "I really just need to get the boots so I can get out of here. Can you do that for me?"

"Oh my God. Oh my God, I, like, totally can't believe this!"

"Well," Billie cut in, "*I* can't believe that you're going to make her pay for these boots! I mean, you guys will get fantastic publicity when people learn that Julie is wearing moon boots that she bought *here*. And that's worth *waaay* more than sixty dollars!"

"*Billie!*" I nudged her, but she'd found a fun new game for herself.

"Like, oh my God!" The salesgirl hurriedly stuffed the boots into a bright plastic bag and shoved them at me. "Totally, *totally!* Here you go, Miss Jorlamo! Thank you sooo much, I mean, for, like, shopping here! That's, like, sooo awesome!"

"Um, no problem. Um . . . thanks."

As we made our way, amid incredulous whispers and stares, out of the store, I hissed to Billie, "I can't believe you just did that!"

"What? That was fabulous!" she exclaimed. "Let's see if we can get more free shit!"

Oh man, did we ever. Ten pairs of silk panties, four leather bras, six pairs of thigh-highs, countless lipsticks, and one glass frog paperweight later, Billie was breathless with greed.

"Look at all this shit!" she crowed as we clacked our way down the mall corridor. "It's the motherfucking mother-lode! Ooh, look at those pants! Ooh, can we try to get those pants?"

She dragged me over to a store window in which a man-nequin proudly donned a pair of red and yellow plaid wool pants, held up by blue bottlecap suspenders.

"Of course," I laughed, "come on, let's go in, and then we can . . ." I trailed off. There, in the reflection of the store win-dow, I saw a shadowy figure lurking behind us. Another joined him. Then another. And another.

"Um, Billie?" I hissed, nudging her rib cage with my elbow. "Don't turn around. *Don't!* Listen. Look at the glass. Are those people . . . looking at us?"

She squinted and leaned closer to the reflection.

"I can't tell . . . why would they be looking at us?"

"I don't know. But it's creeping me out."

"Let's just go. Come on."

We turned around.

"Look honey, it *is* her!"

"Oh my God, it's Julie what'serface!"

"No, is it? It *is*!"

"Julie? Julie? Is Chad with you?"

"Omigod, *Chad Downing*!"

The next thing I knew, people were screaming and run-ning toward me like I was handing out first-class tickets to heaven. Girls were in a frenzy, jumping up and down like monkeys and clutching at their faces in mock agony. Out of nowhere came the paparazzi, snapping away and pummel-ing me with questions.

"Julie? Julie? Where's Chad today?"

"You two are still together, right?"

"Ms. Jorlamo, what are you shopping for today?"

"Was Cookie right about you? Are you only with Chad so you can be a star?"

"Who's your friend, Julie?"

"Are you and Chad going to stay together?"

"Did you dump him because you're having a torrid affair with this drag queen?"

Ah, she must be from *The Weasel*.

"Drag queen?" I thought Billie would punch the woman's lights out. "Watch it, bitch, or you're gonna need an OB/GYN to retrieve that tape recorder!"

On and on and on these people squawked at us, shoving microphones and pens and paper and posters and panties (?) and children in my face. If they didn't want an interview, they wanted an autograph or a picture. I was terrified. Billie, however, was in her element.

"One at a time, one at a time!" she screeched over the impatient mob. "She's only got one fucking voice box, you know? Can't answer all your questions at once. You want an autograph? Who's it for? Your husband? No dice, that's sad and perverted. How about you? Your six-year-old daughter? Okay, honey, step on up and we'll get your dolly signed. Sir, is that a twenty dollar bill you want her to autograph? The only paper you have? You ostentatious bastard! Go to the back of the line! I said one at a time, people!"

I thought it would never end, but thankfully, mall security arrived and broke up the mob. When at last they'd shooed away the last autograph hound, I sank to the floor and beat my head against the display window.

Billie plunked down next to me.

"What the fuck was *that*?" she breathed, reaching automatically for her cigarettes, then, remembering where we were, shook her head.

I plunged my hand into her orange shoulder bag and grabbed the abandoned pack of Marlboros. Fuck it, let them kick me out. If ever I needed a smoke, this was the time.

"I—I mean, I—I—I don't know," I stammered, striking my lighter furiously but having no luck. My hands were shaking. Billie reached over and lit my cigarette for me.

"Thanks. Thanks, I . . . wow. Wow."

"Has that ever happened to you before?"

"No! I mean, people come into the restaurant, but I've never been mobbed like that. Even when I'm with Chad we don't get mobbed like that."

"Hmm. Well, frankly, I'm not surprised."

"What? Why not?"

"These people see you in magazines every single day, Julie, living the life that most people can only dream about. You're the most interesting person in the press."

"But I'm *not*—"

"But you *are*. Think about it, Julie. You're a waitress. You make no money. You're not perfect looking. You don't have fake boobs and hair extensions. But every day your picture is all over the place. You get to go to cool parties and date a movie star. Okay, so that's not real, but nobody knows that. People get obsessed, dude, they watch TV and movies and secretly wish they could be as glamorous as the people they see in front of them. You're like the new blue collar hero, kiddo. Bruce Springstein for chicks."

"Why does everyone keep telling me that?"

"What, that you're the female Boss?"

"That I'm 'normal,' so people like me. It's ridiculous!"

"But why? It's hilarious! Your life is a giant practical joke."

"Are you trying to make me feel better, or worse?"

"I'm serious! How many people do you know that live a

total lie and get rewarded for it? You're lying to the entire country, and you're a fucking national treasure!"

"I guess."

"Who could blame them?" she mused, ruffling my hair with orange taloned fingers. "You're fabulous. And you're showing the world that you can *be* fabulous without having an eating disorder. It's about time someone did."

"This whole thing is just so fucking stupid, Billie."

"You thought it was pretty great a few weeks ago. Jaded already, Jule? That didn't take long, you Hollywood snob!"

I sighed. "I'm serious. I feel like I don't even know who I am anymore. I'm so busy making shit up and living my life for someone I don't even like."

"Who, Chad?"

"Yeah."

"What's not to like? He's rich, he's hot, gets into good parties. Sounds good to me."

"Well, for starters, he's inconsiderate. . . ."

"Inconsiderate how, like when you puked on him? Honey, I would have booted you to the curb, too!"

"Ahem!" I sniffed. "You promised not to talk about that, bitch. *Anyway*, he's also self-centered, narcissistic, and to-tally rude."

"True," Billie mused, "I sort of got that impression from your talk show last night."

"Oh God, you watched that disaster?"

"Of course I did. I taped it for your mother."

"Great, so I'll have to relive it year after year at every family holiday get-together. It's bad enough that the bitch ruined my night; now she's ruined turkey and chocolate Santas for the rest of my life."

"It wasn't all Cookie Ferris-Clayton, Julie. Chad wouldn't let you open your mouth! Jesus, could he promote himself any more? He sounded like he was getting paid by the word."

"He probably was. Prick. He made me feel like such a dumb asshole. And then getting accused of being a fame leech? You'd think he would have stuck up for me!"

"But I read in the paper today—"

"He did that for himself, so that his fans wouldn't pity him."

"Hmmm," Billie sniffed. "Well, could be worse. At least he's not your real boyfriend."

"That's another thing. He's hauling me around like an accessory, and I'm not even getting anything out of it."

"What are you fucking *talking* about, dude? You're getting to be glamorous! You're on every newspaper and magazine cover in publication! You're getting freebie dresses, and Cristal poured down your throat!"

"It's gotten really old, Billie. I thought . . . I don't know. Jesus, Chad Downing has been the sun and moon and stars since I was in high school! I thought this whole charade would be the best thing that had ever happened to me. But it's turning out to be . . . I don't know. Shitty. Just really fucking disappointing."

"Well, why don't you just stop?"

"Stop?"

"You know, stop! Quit, resign, turn in your badge and get the fuck out. You didn't sign your life away, for fuck's sake. Jesus, you didn't actually sign anything, did you, Jule?"

"No, of course not." I lit up another cigarette and ignored the glare I got from a security guard. Bring it on, beefcake, I dare you to tell me to put this thing out.

"I didn't even tell you about Tyler." I sighed.

"Who?"

"It's this guy, comes into work all the time."

"Creepy."

"No, he's really sweet. And so hot."

"Hmph," she sniffed. "That's what they said about Ted Bundy, too."

Groan. Billie always assumes that if a guy exhibits any sort of habitual behavior, he must be a serial killer. I guess I won't tell her that Tyler orders the same thing every time he comes in to see me.

"I fucked it all up, anyway, so don't worry, Lieutenant."

"What'd you do, fuck him in the meat cooler? Drop a pen under the table and accidentally get your mouth stuck on his dick? He never called, right? Are you surprised?"

"Ha ha, bitch. No, I've definitely steered clear of one night stands since you got scabies from that art professor."

"Hey fuck you, that was body lice. It's very common."

"They're supposed to tell you that so you don't feel like a dirty whore."

"Yeah yeah. Go on. Tell me about lover boy."

"Well . . . everything was great, we were flirting, and he sort of almost asked me out."

"Come again?"

I sighed and stared at my lap.

"I ran into him at the pet store, and I think he was going to ask me out, but then some dumb bitch recognized me and made a big deal out of Chad. Tyler got so pissed, he just took off."

"Why did he get pissed?"

"Because he didn't know."

"How could he not know? Does he live in a petri dish? You spend more time on television than my grandmother's cat."

"I don't know. It was kind of nice, actually. He was totally clueless about it. God, I hate this."

"Hate what?"

"This! This famous bullshit. I hate fans, I hate photographers, I hate hate *hate* Chad Downing. Can you believe I had like seven hundred posters of him all over my bedroom? Now I feel like throwing up every time I have to look at him."

"Well, then if you're so miserable, what are you doing still going along with this bullshit?"

Good question.

"I don't know. It's a few things, I guess. I loved this, at first. I've never felt important before in my whole life. I've never been popular."

"That's because you hung out with me, jackass."

"True."

We giggled.

"I'd feel kind of guilty about bailing, too, I guess. Because of Phil."

"Phil? The Cyclops barracuda? The creepy little eel who's constantly referring to you in bakery lingo?"

"Yep."

"What the fuck?"

"I don't know. I feel bad for him. He poured his heart out to me one day. He said he sees a lot of himself in me."

"Yeah, I bet there's one thing of his he'd like to see in you. And I bet it's not a lot, either."

"Billie, eeeeewwww."

"What? You don't owe him a thing, Julie. He's just using you to promote his own career. He's worse than Chad in that department, I'd say. Chad's too dumb to orchestrate this whole thing."

"That's true. I don't know. There's something about Phil. He's so sad and deformed. He's kind of grown on me."

"Like a fungus," Billie sighed. She stood and brushed off

her violet Palazzo pants. "Come on, let's get something to eat. Do you think you can make it to the food court without causing another ruckus?"

"God, I hope so."

"Good, because I'm going to die if I don't have spicy cheddar nachos in like five seconds. Maybe you can exploit your fame and get us some free grub. Come on, Boss."

THE DAILY BEACON

SIGHTINGS

Looks like even hunk-worthy chicks like Julie Jorlamo need some girl talk every once in a while. The luminous Ms. J was spotted window shopping with a sassy gal pal (shown here, on the right) at the Pacific Mall early yesterday afternoon. The dynamic, dudeless duo checked out panties at Bou-drawers, dabbled in makeup (at a department store! Gasp!), and munched their way through the food court. Miss Julie even paused for a gracious autograph session, before onlookers (and the *Beacon!*) were shooed away by mall security.

So nice to see that fame hasn't gone to her head! We can't wait to see more of this sassy sweetie-pie . . .

Eighteen

I swear, if it weren't for this newly discovered "free stuff" phenomenon, I'd probably be eating my own eyebrows by now. I wonder if all the gratis goods are what keep celebrities pacified? Or at least, keep them from disappearing, Bobby Fischer style.

I had an epiphany at the mall yesterday. I hate my life. I hated it before this whole charade, but at least I was living it for myself. Now, I'm in a twenty-four-hour fishbowl, and everything I do is put on display to be revered, or judged, or ridiculed.

But I can't give it up.

Think about it: if I blew my own cover now, I'd be the laughingstock of the entire country. Not to mention I'd lose my job, I probably wouldn't be able to get another one right away (and I'm *not* posing for a nudie magazine), and my parents would be unbelievably disappointed in me.

No, can't give it up quite yet. Have to lie in wait for the right time to make itself available.

In the meantime, however, I'm milking this for all it's worth.

It's about time Chad Downing did something for me, anyway. I mean, besides publicly rendering me one-dimensional, he has plain out *ruined* any chance I had of re-suscitating my flailing love life. That thing's been struggling to keep afloat for years! So, if he's not going to sleep with me or at least be nice to me, I will, in turn, exploit his name so I can have myself a good time.

What better time to start than a Friday night?

And I didn't have to ask. I was actually given Friday night off (probably because it's a good night to make money, and Stuart hates me with a passion), so I decided to take Billie (who else?) out to wrangle some more perks.

Chez Naw-T, here we come again.

Only this time, we don't need no stinkin' Dragon Dick Denny.

I was hoping to get in touch with Phil, see if he could score me some duds and a fancy car, but Chad *refused* to give me his cell phone number.

"You don't need to call Phil," he'd grumbled, "he's *my* publicist, not *yours*. He works for *me*. Besides, you have no business being in a limo if you're not with me, on a way to a premiere or something. You're supposed to be normal, remember?"

"How could I forget," I'd snarled sweetly, "when you keep reminding the whole world every ten seconds?"

Well, we'd just take Billie's car, since I drove last time. The last time, to be more precise, that I'd gone out and actually needed to drive myself. You know, despite the hassle, I could get used to all of this famous stuff. The pampering, anyway.

Billie pulled up in "Cinogen," her aptly named piece of shit, at around nine-thirty. I could tell it was her because she honked. As one might expect, a honk from Billie is easily discernable. Rather than the standard angry, monotone blast, her horn, when leaned upon, blares "Turning Japanese." Apparently, she was dating some A/V guy who had a thing for incorporating eighties music into rush hour traffic patterns.

So, I heard the ditty, patted Riley on the head, and raced out the door, clad once again in my blue pleather ensemble. I wanted to breeze into the club in some chi-chi designer frock, but, alas, Chad put a damper on the outfit for the evening. Oh well. This tube top was pretty successful the last time.

I gotta tell you, each ride I take with Billie, however brief it may be, is like inching five steps closer to death.

First of all, it's a cancer risk. The smoke is perpetual. Even when she's not puffing, which is never, the residual smoke accumulated over the years is enough to choke a moose. No matter how good I smell when I leave the house, inevitably, I will reek like an airport lounge after a mere thirty seconds in Billie's car.

Secondly, the girl drives like a fucking maniac. Forget bat out of hell; it's the same speed and aggression as an entire cave's worth of bats. Every bat that ever flew out of anywhere even remotely warm; that's how Billie drives.

I don't know if it's because she tries to smoke, adjust the radio, put on mascara, paint her toenails, talk on her cell phone, give everyone the finger, and drive with her knees all at the same time. It could also be because she has anger management issues, and finds weaving and cursing to be therapeutic. What I especially enjoy is the manner in which she maniacally screams at surrounding commuters, and occasionally tries to intimidate eager passersby into the oncoming traffic lanes.

"Holy bajeezus!" She'll scream at the family of four who

travel leisurely along in the lane in front of us. "Your kids will be done with puberty by the time you get to your fucking exit! There's a *slow lane*, you know!"

"Billie, why don't you just pass them?"

"It's the *principle* of the goddamned thing! They're in the *middle lane*!"

Nobody is safe from her ranting and cursing, no classification of driver is sacred.

"Oh my *God*, the speed limit is *sixty-five! Sixty-five!!!* Could you speed it up a little?"

"Billie, that's a handicapped driver! Don't be an asshole?"

"*I'm* an asshole? If you're too handicapped to *drive* the *speed limit*, then don't *drive* at *all*! That guy's the asshole!"

Personally, my favorite is when she starts referring to her targets by their respective license plates.

"Nothing to see here, Oklahoma! If you're looking for whistling wind, you're in the *wrong* place mothafucker! No, no, don't slow down . . . Oh, oh *come on*! I know there's no electricity where you come from, but pick a better place to look at the pretty lights! Pennsylvania? You've got a *friend* in mothafucking Pennsylvania, why don't you go *back* there? Oh, bajeezus!"

Goddamn, that girl's a treat.

The ride to Chez Naw-T was no less exciting than usual, the journey finding its crescendo when Billie decided to drag race a bunch of teenagers on Sunset Boulevard.

When we finally got to the club, my nails were a little shorter.

The place was hopping, as usual. I wonder if people think that P. Diddy will actually be here? The line stretched around the block was definitely not the Martha Stewart crowd. No turtleneck sweaters on these broads.

"Damn, Billie, look at that line! It's twice as long as the last time."

"Not to worry; we have secret weapon celebrity status! Well, you do, anyway. This'll be a blast!"

I tugged at my miniskirt nervously.

"Do you think Brian will be here again?"

"Dude, who cares? We'll probably be in the VIP room; he'll never see us!"

"Billie, you're wearing a vest made out of reflective bicycle tape. How could he miss us?"

No lie. For some reason (and it's always fun to guess), she had chosen an industrial themed outfit for the evening, sporting pants made from duct tape and a searing, canary yellow vest that captured and mutated every available light refraction.

"It's all part of my strategy. Everyone will be too busy averting their eyes from the glare to even notice you! Then, when we get around the rich and fabulous people, I'll take it off."

"What are you wearing underneath that?"

She pulled the vest apart. Ah, a black T-shirt with a shiny silver handprint on each boob. Claaaaassy.

"Do you want to say hi to your man on our way in?"

"Man? Oh, Denny. Nah, I'm over it."

"Aw, I'm sure he'll be heartbroken."

"Ha! Hardly. The dude's a walking petri dish. Different chick every night. All club kids, too. Dirty bitches. I can't see him up there anyway. I don't think he works Fridays."

"Billie?"

"Yeah?"

We had stopped short a few feet from the velvet ropes.

"How am I, um, supposed to do this?"

"Do what?"

"Am I supposed to, like, um . . ."

She rolled her eyes. "Oh you are so ridiculous. You clearly haven't learned to exploit your fame, have you? And no wonder, with that publicist doing everything for you. Here, I've been dying to try this."

With a flick of her cigarette, Billie charged toward the entrance, on a different mission this time.

"'Scuse me, 'scuse me! Coming through, celebrity coming through! Wipe that face off your face, sister, and move your candy ass outta my way. Damn!" she huffed when she finally reached the bouncers, "you'd think people would be a little more *respectful* when there's somebody *famous* involved!"

The bouncer, not Denny, and clearly not amused, looked her up and down, arms crossed over his solid barrel chest. "And who exactly would that be, lady? I sure as fuck don't recognize *you*, toots."

Oooh, bad move, wise guy. I watched from my shy stake-out on the curb, horrified, as Billie leaned in for the kill. She grabbed Frankenbouncer's hand, gave his palm a sly little lick, then stubbed her cigarette out on the wet spot.

That's her signature torture move.

"As I was saying," she purred menacingly, "famous person, coming through. Now are you going to let us in, or not?"

"Hey, what the fuck's going on up there?" an angry voice piped up from the crowd.

"Yeah, you can't just cut the line!"

This, of course, provoked a collective irritation.

"Hubbub!" the crowd grumbled angrily. "Hubbub! Hubbub, hubbub!"

"Hey, hey hey hey *hey*!" Billie yelled over the din. "Just settle down, all right? Jesus. Julie, could you get your ass over here so I don't get trampled by a bunch of floozies in pink pleather? Come on." She waved me over.

Okay. Here goes.

I joined her at the head of the line.

"*Huuuuuuhhhh!!!*" the crowd gasped. "Hubbub! Hub-bub!"

"Miss Jorlamo!" The bouncer actually smiled, revealing muddied teeth and enormous equine gums.

"Mmm-hmm." Billie, satisfied, lit a smoke and smiled.

"Well, why didn't you say so?"

"Julie!" It was the same girl who had squawked a minute earlier, "Julie! We love you!"

"Julie, you're the best!"

"Julie? Can you say hi to Chad for me?"

"Hubbub! Julie Jorlamo! Hubbub, hubbub!"

"Hang on a second, please." The bouncer touched a hand to his ear and spoke into an invisible headset. "Johnny? Yeah, I'm gonna need an escort." Billie nudged me with her elbow. "No . . . no . . . yeah. Yeah, VIP. Yeah. Okay. Well, ladies," he flashed me another horsey grin, "welcome to Chez Naw-T. I hope we can make you comfortable this evening. Ronaldo is on his way, to escort you through our private VIP entrance. Ah, and here he is! Enjoy your evening, and please, if you need anything at all, alert one of our staff. It's a pleasure to have you here."

"Well, of course it is!" Billie grinned. "No cover, right?"

Oh, ho ho! We all shared a little chuckle over that one.

Phew. I mean, it usually costs thirty bucks to get in.

And I have thirteen.

In my bank account.

But, no matter, because here's Ronaldo, and we're in!

Having been to plenty of VIP functions, but never a specific VIP entrance, I was curious. It seemed a little silly; I mean, we'd already entered the foyer of the club, and it was clearly no secret that we had arrived; I could still hear the excited line-dwellers chanting my name in unison.

I have to admit, it's nice to hear people calling my name without it prefacing "You're grounded!" or "We need ketchup!" or "You have the right to remain silent!" (Aaah, high school memories.)

The lobby was standard venue: dark, blacklit, littered with bored-looking Asian chicks waiting to check their bags, tapping their feet lackadaisically to the generic thump of a club mix. There didn't seem to be anything "VIP" about our entrance at all, until Ronaldo took me by the elbow and steered me toward a door I hadn't noticed before, tucked nonchalantly between the ladies' room and the cashier.

He ushered us through in a hurry, keeping an eye on the lobby behind us to make sure nobody tried to follow, I guess.

Wowwwwww.

We had entered a realm of infinite shimmer.

The room was octagonal, majestic, tinged with soft, rosy lighting that cast a tranquil glow upon my outstretched arms. Oblong chandeliers dangled above our heads, twinkling with endless prisms. The walls were entirely mirrored (either an indulgence or mockery of celebrity narcissism), and stretched endlessly above our heads, rendezvousing passionately with a cathedral ceiling that was detailed with millions of tiny crystals.

"Swarovski," Ronaldo said simply, speaking for the first time.

It sure did sparkle. I felt like a raccoon in a recycling center, eyes widened in unabashed delight.

The pièce de résistance was the elevator in the center of

the room, an ornate, platinum cage that hovered effortlessly several feet above the ground.

"Ladies." Ronaldo spoke again, gesturing toward the elevator as it descended from its aerial linger.

Too awed to crack a joke, we glided over the Spanish tile, careful not to make a sound for fear of tainting the VIP brilliance with our cloddish presence.

Our journey was brief.

There were no buttons aboard; we simply stepped inside and the cage swallowed us, shooting smoothly upward as we reclined upon black velvet chaise lounges.

The room that awaited us was even more magical.

I know—I sound like a wide-eyed dweeb—but really, sometimes I just can't believe the shit that people come up with.

This room was swathed in blood-colored velvet, equally sparkly as the first floor entrance, but much sexier. The ceilings were low, bedecked with Moroccan tapestries and laden with delicate wire lanterns. Famous faces were scattered about the room, relaxing in enormous booths littered with pillows and leaning against the bar (actually a mahogany slab atop a gigantic aquarium filled with exotic fishies). Everyone, I mean *everyone*, was drinking Cristal like it flowed from the tap.

"Holy bajeezus," Billie whispered next to me. "Motherlode."

"What are we supposed to do?" I whispered back. "Just sit anywhere?"

"Don't ask me! You're the famous one."

Right. Shit.

"Miss Jorlamo!"

Oh thank God, a maître d'.

"Um, hello. Table for . . . um . . . two?"

"But of course. Where would you like to sit?"

I took a quick look around. Besides the bar stools, every seat in the lounge was taken.

"Oh, well . . . um, I don't see any tables, so—"

"No no, Miss Jorlamo, where would you like to sit? For you, well, *you* may sit anywhere you like. Perhaps by the aquarium?" He swept his arm to the left. "Or maybe, a view of the club? You have not been here before, correct? Come, come with me and see."

We followed as he strode toward the only naked wall in the room, made of smoky glass.

"Lots to see tonight." He smiled.

Upon closer inspection, we discovered that the wall revealed a view of the dance floor, several levels below us.

"They cannot see you, of course," the maître d' continued, "but if you'd like to hear the music better, the glass slides up like this," he demonstrated, "only a foot or two, but it brings the club atmosphere into the lounge. We have opera glasses, of course, if you're feeling voyeuristic."

He handed me a pair, and I spent a minute watching the sea of heads bob up and down in time to a P. Diddy remix.

"So, here, I think, would be good for you?" he asked.

There were only two tables with access to the view, and they were both occupied. I started to protest, but Billie elbowed me.

"Ah, good. A moment, ladies."

He casually strolled over to the smaller of the tables, a zebra-patterned mosaic accented by mohair recliners, and leaned into the center of the conversation. The patrons, a china doll brunette and a slick looking banker-type who could have been her father, looked *extremely* put out. When Daddy started to protest, however, the maître d' nodded toward the bar and clapped him on the shoulder. They rose immediately and skulked over to a pair of bar stools, throwing us a couple of wounded glances.

"Now," continued the maître d' when he returned, "my name is Simon, and I'll be taking care of you this evening. I like to look after our special guests myself. Let me clear this table for you, and you may have a seat. There. Please, Miss Jorlamo." He pulled a chair out for me, and I sank into it, giggling. He did the same for Billie.

"You'll be wanting Cristal, I imagine? On the house, of course. Unless you'd prefer another cocktail?"

"No, no," I said quickly, "Cristal will do just fine."

"Make it two!" Billie piped up.

"Very good. I shall return in a moment, ladies. Enjoy the view."

We settled into our chairs and peered down at the frenzied crowd below.

"Dude, do you think I can smoke in here?"

"Um . . ." I glanced around the room. Two tables over, a soap opera heartthrob was staring at the ceiling as a trio of doting blondes took turns holding a joint to his lips. Behind him, an alarmingly skinny actress was chain smoking bidis and nursing an enormous cappuccino. Not far from her, the teen pop punk band of the month was clustered around a large hookah, sucking down great billows of pink smoke.

"I think you're safe."

"Excellent. You know," she mused, lighting up and bringing a pair of opera glasses up to her face, "I could get used to this. Why didn't you get famous years ago?"

"I don't know what I was thinking."

"This is so cool, Jule. I mean, look at this! Look at the crowd in this joint. She's on TV. She's a model. He's on TV. *He's* on TV. She was an intern. I mean, God, can you believe people actually live like this?"

"I know."

"And you didn't even have to do anything!"

"I know."

"Jesus, did you see how the staff here is, like, falling all over you? Like you're the Queen of France, or something."

"Yeah, that *would* be unusual."

Simon returned, wielding *two* bottles of Cristal.

"Ladies." He popped one of them open and poured each of us a flute of the golden fizz. "And, compliments of the kitchen, of course, a selection of tapas created by Martha herself. These are autumnal acorn canapes, here we have Spanish gherkins pickled in a champagne brine, and on this plate, miniature Philly cheesesteaks made from brie and black angus, drizzled with truffle oil. Bon appetit, ladies, and please," he set an antique telephone on the table, "call if you need anything. All you need to do is pick up the receiver, and it will set off my pager."

With a bow, he retreated, leaving us with steaming plates of sumptuous food and two thousand dollars worth of bubbly.

Wooohooooo!

"This iiiissss the life," Billie sighed, popping a tiny cheesesteak into her mouth, "You should aim for never having to pay for anything, ever again."

"That'd be nice," I agreed, swigging from my flute and mulling over the appetizers. That Martha. How *does* she carve melba toast into the shape of oak trees? "Might as well get *something* out of this bullshit."

"What do you mean, 'get something'? You've got everything, Julie!"

I didn't want to whine about my misery, since it seemed so selfish and, well, *wrong* to be unhappy with the way life had been treating me lately. But this whole fame thing had gotten to be way too much. It was actually becoming stressful, putting on the girlfriend act for the world to see.

"I guess."

"You guess?" Billie leaned forward, hard to do in the squishy chair, and peered at me. "You get to go to fabulous parties, wear fabulous clothes, hang on the arm of a fabulous man, and get fabulous things *for free*. Everyone knows who you are, everyone adores you. Christ, everyone wants to *be* you." She swigged the rest of her Cristal. Out of nowhere, a tiny little goblin man appeared, refilled her glass, and disappeared as quickly as he emerged. "What's there to guess about? What's missing?"

Sigh.

"Nothing. Nothing at all."

Ha. Lies.

Truth be told, lately I've been feeling like *I'm* missing. I mean, maybe everyone else knows who I am, but, quite frankly, I still don't.

And who wants to be known for who they *know*, anyway? I'd rather be known for what I am, whatever that is.

Of course, if I ever said that out loud to Billie, she'd smack me into next Tuesday. I can just hear her now:

"You're being a pretentious existentialist wannabe, dude! You know exactly who you are! You're a fabulous superstar, and right now, your famous ass is parked on the hair of rabbits that were hand-fed organic soy pellets cultivated on Mars! Suck it up, and cut out the 'poor me' bullshit!"

Of course, she'd be right.

Or would she?

"Hey!" She jolted me from my wallow. "Is that . . . who *is* that?"

"What? See somebody super famous?"

"No . . . I can't tell . . . hand me those opera thingies,

wouldja? I'm not sure. . . ." She guzzled the rest of her glass *again,* and hiccupped.

"Billie? How many glasses is that?"

"Um . . . four. *Hiccccccup!*"

Oh boy. Billie's no good when it comes to champagne. After a few New Year's Eves of trying to keep up with the revelry, I thought she had learned her lesson. The last time she drank more than one glass of bubbly, it was 1998, and she got a little Auld Lang Asinine, chasing some poor guy around with a sprig of leftover mistletoe and begging him to "frost her cupcake." It wasn't pretty.

"It *is!*" she yelled triumphantly after a minute of squinting down at the dancers.

"Billie! Shhhhhhh!"

"Oh fuck you. Don't you even want to know who I see down there?"

"I want you to try to . . . oh never mind. Who, who do you see down there?"

"Brian."

Gulp.

"Brian . . . my ex, Brian?"

"Yeppers. And guess who's pulling his leash around tonight?"

"Gosh, I can't possibly imagine."

"Jesus, even from up here she looks plastic. Do you think there's some factory in the middle of Idaho that mass produces these bimbos? I swear, Jule, they all look the same. Maybe Hef's buying in bulk."

"Does she have the dog with her?"

"I don't know, I can't . . . oh yeeeeah, yeah, the rat dog is there. This time it's in a tiny little backpack. Is it wearing sunglasses?"

"Let me see."

Sure enough, there they were, grinding away on the dance floor while the dog perched aloofly in the bag strapped to Naomi's back. Funny, Brian would never dance with me while we were dating. Only in my dorm room, if there was nobody looking. And it was a Thursday. But not a full moon, and only if I was wearing socks.

Good lord, I'm an ass.

"What I don't get," Billie was beginning to slur now, "is how he went from *you* to *her*."

Good question.

And a familiar sounding one.

"You know, Jule . . ."

Oh God, she had that look in her eye. The "I'm about to do something totally embarrassing, but you'll still love me in the morning because if you don't I'll do something worse to you" look.

"Whaaat?"

"I'm a pretty good shot."

"What do you mean, good shot?" I asked warily.

There was nothing I could do to stop her.

Before I knew what was happening, she had popped the cork on our second bottle of Cristal and had slithered it out the tiny window that opened over the dance floor.

"Oops! Ohh noooo!" She giggled. The bottle tipped, and an expensive stream trickled from the neck onto the dancers below.

I can still hear the screams.

And the crowd wasn't too happy, either.

"Take your hands off of me!" Billie shrieked as two brutish security guards clamped her by the wrist. "Don't you know who she is? You can't treat me like this! Julie? Julie! Do something!"

"I'm so sorry," I murmured to Simon as I scurried behind

the trio. Billie was hissing like a wildcat, twisting and spitting and just generally being an asshole. She's a feisty one, though. All those months dating a Krav Maga instructor paid off, I guess. The security beasts were having a hard time dragging her out. *Not* via the VIP elevator, might I add, but a barren concrete staircase.

Naturally, we had our picture snapped when her ass landed on the pavement outside.

Son of a bitch.

THE DAILY BEACON

BEAUTIES BEHAVING BADLY!

Oh dear, Miss Jorlamo, what company you keep! It just isn't Julie Jorlamo's week. Chad Downing's lovely lady has been putting up with her fair share of shenanigans, starting with her man's rumored hanky-panky with former offscreen flame Katarina Conrad. Besides her raucous romance, however, Miss Julie can't seem to stay away from troublemakers. She was spotted last night at the exclusive Chez Naw-T, in the company of one très troublemaking trollop, who apparently had a hard time keeping her liquor down; er, in her glass, anyway. Let's just say that a couple of patrons found themselves all wet. Miss J seemed to be an innocent bystander, but someone should teach the poor thing how to pick and choose her pals.

She apologized, of course, as soon as her hangover cleared up the next day.

Eh, who am I kidding? I would have done the same

thing, if I had as much confidence in my aim. I can't stay mad at her.

Besides, I have enough mortal enemies. I need allies like my grandma needs a girdle.

"And *then* I heard that she's getting a nose job so their faces can match! Can you believe that?"

"Well, who wouldn't want to get rid of that schnoz?"

"I know! It's like, the size of my car!"

Ah, another rewarding shift at Junebugs. Kylie was leading a bitch session, clustered around the bar during a busy (for me, anyway) lunch hour. Of course, I was the topic of conversation yet again. I was surprised, actually, that it had taken this long. My last feature headline was last week, after the champagne incident, and I'd been trying to lay low since then. I'd expected the grapevine to wither if there was no fresh gossip to keep it nurtured. Silly Julie.

"Did you know he met her here? *Here?*" Kylie stamped out her cigarette angrily and sneered in my direction. "Where the fuck was I that day? He should have sat in my section; he'd be a lot happier, that's for damned sure. Have you seen how miserable he looks on TV lately?"

"Probably because he's embarrassed that his *girlfriend* won't quit her tacky waitress job." Toni rolled her eyes.

"Well, she should," Gina piped up, "I'm so sick of sitting around and not making any money. Did you know that last week there were actually people waiting *two* and *three hours* for her tables? The rest of us were foaming at the mouth to wait on people, but nobody gave a shit. They should just rename this place 'Chad Downing's Girlfriend Works Here' and be done with it. I swear to God I'd quit if I didn't have the health insurance."

And five children with four daddies. Ho.

I marched up to the table of catty wenches, hands on my hips, poker face in place.

"Excuse me. There's like forty plates of food backed up in the kitchen, and Armando is screaming at me. Since I only have two hands, and since *you* girls aren't doing anything, maybe you could help me out so that lunch doesn't get out of control."

Most of them stared at their hands, a few even started to get up. Kylie, however, put a stop to that. She looked me square in the eye.

"Can't. We're busy."

"Busy. Busy? What in the fuck are you doing, Kylie, that makes you so busy?"

"It'th a thtaff meeting."

Stuart came up from nowhere and wedged himself between me and the table of adversaries.

"What?"

"A thtaff meeting."

"Sorry, come again?"

"A *staff* meeting," Kylie spat at me. "God, you're so insensitive! Do you think you could consider anyone else but yourself for, like, *two seconds*?"

"Why would there be a *staff* meeting in the middle of lunch? You're not making any damned sense!"

"Excuse me, Julie? Miss Jorlamo?"

I could hear my customers getting antsy in the dining room behind me. Oh, screw 'em.

"Miss Jorlamo? I need honey mustard!"

"Julie, can we have some more fries?"

"Hey Miss J, got time for a picture?"

"Your public awaits," Kylie snorted, pulling out the chair next to her for Stuart to park his porky ass on. "Good luck with that, Hollywood."

Why do I put myself through this?

Like a fool, I hauled ass to make everyone happy, delivering burgers and finger foods at record speed. You'd think being a celebrity (sort of) would make customers a little more patient, but noooooo. Everyone needed ranch dressing and napkins and silverware and autographs and diet sodas and hugs and pictures at the same time, and *everyone* got pissy when their needs weren't satisfied immediately.

I managed to catch a few more snippets of the bitch session while I fluttered around the restaurant, but I didn't really pay attention.

Until I heard "Tyler."

My heart sped up. My pace slowed down.

I perched at the end of the bar, pretending to review a check on the ancient computer. Kylie's mouth was flapping furiously, like a chicken trying to fly the coop.

"Can you honestly believe he's so hung up on her?" she was saying, "After *all* the times I've waited on him because she's too busy, after *all* the tables I gave up just so I could pay extra attention to him! Jesus, he spent the whole time he was here yesterday practically *crying* into his chowder!"

"Ith he crazy?" Stuart jumped in.

"I don't know! It's not like he's spent any time with her, or anything. He just comes in to the restaurant and talks to her, for God's sake. Or he did before this whole Chad Downing thing started. I guess he's upset because Julie led him on the whole time. Poor thing, had to find out she had a boyfriend by reading it in the paper!"

"Oh my God, she's such a bitch!" Gina exclaimed.

"I *know*! I mean, what does she think this place is, anyway, a fucking singles' bar? Like it wasn't enough that she got to meet Chad here."

"I *still* don't get what Chad sees in her," Toni sighed. "I mean, he's sooooo fucking hot! And she's so . . . average."

"Well," Kylie spat, "that's probably why she keeps flirting with everyone in the first place, just trying to make herself feel like hot shit. Probably has no fucking self-esteem. I wouldn't, if my hips were that big."

Ooh, you're gonna regret that one bitch. On the day I quit this wretched job, I'm going to dig out your larynx with a soup spoon.

"Can you imagine?" she continued. "She's been toying with Tyler for months, and the whole time she's got this big, famous boyfriend! I still can't believe she managed to keep it a secret. Fucking snob. Probably thought we'd be jealous. Jealous! Of her! Ha! She's probably even been laughing at Tyler with her stupid celebrity friends this whole time."

"Oh my God! Tyler's so sweet. What a whore!"

"I *know*! I'm trying to convince him that he needs a girl who's closer to his level, you know, someone who's had to struggle to make it on their own. Someone sensitive, someone who can understand him. Like me!"

I perked up, ready to rumble. No way, there's *no way* I'm letting Kylie get her mitts on Tyler. He might hate me right now, but goddamnit, he'd hate me more if I let him get sucked into the dismal, wretched vortex that is Kylie.

"Tho athk him out, Kylie! What are you waiting for?"

"Do what?"

"Athk him out."

"Athhhh . . . oh, *ask* him out! Well, yeah, I want to, but I don't know if he's gonna go for it. He seems pretty broken up about Miss Hollywood."

He does?

"Why would anyone be broken up over her? The's tho . . . plain. And thtupid!"

"Beats me. Fucking bitch. I bet she slept with him. Some guys get really attached when you sleep with them. Well, nobody I've slept with, but that's what I heard."

"Figureth. Julie lookth like a whore."

How could you look like a whore in this uniform? If anything, I looked autistic.

I kept fumbling around the computer, ignoring the shouts of my impatient, starstruck customers. This conversation was getting good.

"I really wanted to fire her, but the dithtrict manager wouldn't let me. Thaid thee'th good for buthinethth."

"*Whose* business? I'm not making any money."

"For the rethtaurant, Kylie."

"Oh. Well, she still sucks. I mean, look at her! She's been standing at that computer for ten minutes, trying to figure her shit out. So stupid. I swear, if I had this many tables, I'd be fine. I could take twice as many. *Three* times as many! She thinks she's so fucking great."

I let their cattiness fade into the background as I contemplated what had just been revealed. Tyler was broken up over . . . me? Me?

I had absolutely no idea what to do.

When he stormed out of the pet store, I wanted to kick my own ass. I couldn't believe . . . goddamnit, men are *never* attracted to me! And now I finally interest one (who's not a perv or totally wasted) and I'd fucked it up.

For a man that I hate, and another that I pity.

Jesus, I'm self-destructive.

I think what bothers me the most is that, in her own, roundabout, fucked-up way, Kylie was sort of right about me. I definitely have confidence issues. Granted, she thinks I'm really in a relationship with someone way more attractive than me, but . . . well, I guess I kind of am. It's more like a marriage, really. An old, stale, sexless, stay-together-for-the-kids union. Only my kid is in his forties and can use his left eye for rainy day indoor recess games.

I waited around after Stuart finally cut me from the floor, hoping that Tyler would show up to confide in Kylie again. I chain-smoked and stuffed myself halfheartedly with stale chips and guacamole, just . . . hoping.

Of course, he never showed. I'd probably never see him again.

Well, who needs love, anyway? I've got . . . image.

# Nineteen

Laissez les bons temps rouler, so they say. . . .
Further proof that I can do nothing to mar my reputation as America's cream puff, this week I have continued to make a fool of myself, yet have had nothing but great press. I'm starting to feel like an Osbourne.

Cajun Persuasion; the latest in a string of nonprofit organizations to erupt serendipitously on the charity scene. Last week the heavens dealt a devastating blow to the South, pounding Louisiana and parts of Mississippi with three consecutive hurricanes. Entire communities were flooded and demolished, leaving thousands of people stranded on the rooftops of their submerged mobile homes. Of course, nobody in Hollywood gave a rat's ass, until word got out that New Orleans was so badly damaged that the city would have to abandon its annual Mardi Gras debauchery. This, of course, sparked an outrage. No Fat Tuesday? No Bourbon Street? No king cake, no tacky beads? No rum runners, no parades, and, God forbid, no titties? This, *this* is the stuff of national disasters. No titties? Pshaw. Let's get a bunch of celebrities, slap together a nonprofit, and have a fund-raiser.

And so, someone did.

Phil called me the morning of the party to fill me in.

"Hello, my little gold mine. Feeling glamorous today?"

I ran my tongue over two days worth of cigarette grime that was festering on the back of my teeth.

"Sure."

"Great, Plumpkin, because there's this thing tonight—a big thing, actually—and I need you to be there."

"What kind of thing?"

"Oh, raising some chunk change for Mardi Gras, darling. National disaster, you know. Can't let American tradition suffer because of lousy weather. Unpatriotic."

Uuuuuurgh. The last thing in the world I wanted to do was get dragged to another one of these overhyped bullshit fund-raising schmoozing snorefests.

Phil's gotten good at sensing my disdain.

"It'll be fun, my little danish! There'll be people, and food, and bright lights, and glitter, and chandeliers—"

"I'm not a raccoon, Phil. I can't be enticed by shiny objects."

He sighed.

"Please, cream pie, do it for old Phil here. You and me, kid, we're one and the same, remember? Only you get to crawl out from the woodwork every so often. You know I love to live it through you—you get to cross over and hang with the lovelies, not like Faux Phil, the glass-eyed wonder schlub."

"Jesus, Phil. Did they teach you to guilt-trip at college, or do you get standard issue cue cards when you join the guild?"

"Does that mean you'll do it?"

Sigh. "Yes."

"That's my girl! I'm sending a car to take you to Rodeo. Big night for you, calls for a big outfit. I'm thinking something fresh but attainable, like Betsey Johnson. Pink, maybe, with ribbons. Festivelike."

"What's Chad wearing?"

Phil paused.

"Actually, Chad won't be able to make it. You're flying solo, honey, which is why I need you to be extra fabulous."

"Phil! I can't go there by myself!"

"And why not, Ms. Julie? You haven't figured it out yet? You're hot, babe, totally smokin'. Tell me you're not, after that little scene at the mall last week."

"Phil, who am I going to talk to if I go by myself? Most of the time I only get acknowledged because I'm practically surgically attached to Chad. I'm going to look like a total loser if I go alone. What the fuck, anyway? Why isn't he going? I haven't seen him all week."

"And you're complaining about that?"

"Well, no, but . . ."

"He's been tied up with casting sessions. Still trying to find a leading lady for *John Dough*. He's starting to sweat a little, actually. Anyway, let's get back to tonight. First of all, you're a winner for even getting in the fucking door, Plumpkin. Secondly, this is just the chance we need for you! Talk it up to the A-list, charm them, outwit them, show them why Chad's so goddamned smitten with you. And if that doesn't work, find a Hilton sister! They're good times, they'll hang with anyone who's wearing a label."

"Grand. Can't wait."

Phil sighed. "Who's that crazy friend of yours from the *Beacon*? The fiberoptic-looking one?"

"You mean Billie?"

"There's a chick with a personal style if I ever saw one. She looks like a goddamned disco ball. She'd be good. Just warn her that the nightclub is nonsmoking unless you're fucking a mogul. *And* that if she makes you look like an ass-hole again, I'll make sure she has one of those tubes in her throat before it's absolutely necessary, if you catch my drift."

"Billie can come? Really?"

"Really. It'll be good press for you. Get to let loose with the girls, live it up a little more than usual. When Chad's away, the chicks will play. Oooh, good tag. Yeah, bring Billie, but try not to make out with any pop tarts. Unless it's a chick."

I thought Billie would need a catheter when I told her.

"What? No. No! Oh my God! Yeah, fuck yeah I'll go! And I won't drink champagne this time, I promise. I'm still really sorry about that, you know. Holy shit, holy shit! I was wondering if you were ever going to ask me along to one of these things, you schmuck. Is Chad gonna be pissed? You know, since I'm a tagalong lunatic and all. Am I going to be stuck drinking by myself in the corner while you two make the rounds? 'Cause that's cool, as long as I get to make out with someone. Someone famous. Oh my God."

"Um, actually, Chad's not going."

"Oh . . . Is that why you want me to come?"

"What do you mean?"

"You're stuck going by yourself, so you need someone to talk to, right?"

"Billie—"

"Because I've been pretty patient about this whole god-damned thing, you know. You get to go to fancy bullshit parties every night, and you're all over the papers, and I'm stuck hanging out with Margo, and it's not even *for real*, and I can't even tell anyone—"

"Billie!"

"What?"

"Stop. You know as well as I do that I can't just invite my friends along whenever I go to parties or premieres or whatever. That's not why I'm there. It's not my call, you know?"

She sighed.

"I know. I know, it's your job to go along and smile and pretend to be a trophy girlfriend who's madly in love with her famous beefcake."

"And I don't even like him!"

"And you don't even like him."

It's true; Chad was getting more and more obnoxious with each appearance. He actually got pissed at me last week for offering my opinion in a heated political discussion between Warren Beatty and Emmanuel Lewis.

"Julie," he hissed under his breath as he steered me away from the conversation.

"What? Ow, you're hurting me!"

"Sorry." He released his death grip. I rubbed my elbow and cursed under my breath. "It's just that . . . well, you sound like you know what you're talking about!"

". . . And? So what? I've always felt strongly about affirmative action, and if that man—"

"Julie, you're not here to make conversation. You're here to make me look good, remember? That's why we started this whole thing."

"What, my participation in an intelligent conversation makes you look bad? I'm *bored*, Chad. I'm sick of just standing there and smiling like a fucking goon while you charm the hell out of everyone. I thought you wanted people to be impressed with me?"

"I do! They are. It's just . . ."

His eyes were shifting around nervously now. I followed his gaze and saw Katarina across the room, flipping her hair and puffing on a cigarette that was the same pastel shade of coral as her gown.

"*What*, Chad?"

His eyes snapped back to meet mine.

"If you keep flapping your goddamned mouth about politics and other boring shit, people are going to think you're smarter than me. And how does that make Chad look, huh? Like a fucking idiot."

"Well, Chad, if you ask me, you look like *more* of an idiot by pulling me away like a naughty child. People are going to think you're a control freak."

"No, people are going to wonder why such a smart woman is working as a waitress."

"Well, I've been wondering that myself. . . ."

He rolled his eyes.

"I *mean*, they're going to get suspicious. Wonder if you're really who you say you are. Julie, if my cover's blown, I'll be the laughingstock of this town. You think I want to be known as a liar?"

"No, I think you're doing just fine as a conceited prick."

Chad paged the limo soon after that.

Frankly, I was sort of excited about going to an event without him breathing down my neck. And Billie and I hadn't been out together in weeks, since our headline-making scene at Chez Naw-T.

"So you'll come with?" I cajoled. "Pleeeeeeease?"

"Of course I'll go with, schmuck. But what am I supposed to wear?"

"I don't know. . . ." I teased. "I guess we'll have to ask Betsey what she thinks will go with your hair. What color is it this week, Rodman?"

"Purple. What do you mean, ask Betsey? Betsey who?"

I chuckled. "I'll be at your place in half an hour. Put on comfy shoes. Oh, and smoke as much as you can, because the party's at a nightclub."

I could hear her wheezing as she raced through her apartment.

"Shit, where are my cigs? I thought I left them . . . aaaaaah, here they are. Half an hour? Good, I've got time to smoke seven. That should hold me for a while."

Ick.

Betsey Johnson was a *dream*, an absolute doll. She didn't give a shit that Chad wasn't with us, either, just welcomed us into her boutique and bounced around like a cartoon tiger. A fuchsia cartoon tiger. Love her hair.

After a few hours of giggling and wiggling into dresses, I ended up in a turquoise strapless number with little pink bows around the hemline. Betsey was so taken with Billie that she kept dancing around her in little circles, snatching at her purple hair and giggling like a birthday girl.

"Look at this personality!" Betsey kept shrieking. "Fresh as a buttercup, this one is. Oh my God, is your belt made out of old Barnes & Noble gift cards? Love it! *Love it!*"

Billie walked with two mohair shoulder shrugs, Astroturf stilettos, a pair of electric blue leather gloves, and a minidress woven from cinnamon dental floss, all gratis.

"Later doll babies!" Betsey said as she hugged us each good-bye. "Come back and see me! Billie, don't forget to seal that dress with hair spray before you go out tonight, okay? Otherwise you'll be sticking to the bar stools. Ciao, darlings!"

"Wow," Billie sighed as the limo pulled away from the boutique. "Is that how you get treated all the time?"

"Pretty much."

She whistled, and began sifting through the minibar.

"Not bad, Jorlamo. You tell Chad to call me if he needs any more pretend girlfriends."

"Don't tempt me. I'm about fed up with this bullshit."

"What do you mean?" Billie looked up from a fistful of gin.

"Don't you think it's annoying that we can't even go to the mall without being ambushed by photographers and people who want my autograph? My fucking *autograph*, Billie."

"I don't know," she shrugged, "I think it's kind of fun."

"I did, too, at first. Now I just think it's a pain in the ass. I'd hate to be famous for real."

"At least you get to go out with Chaaaaad," she teased.

"Oh, please."

"What? Two months ago you were so desperate to sleep with him you could barely see straight. And now you're spending all this time with him and you don't even mention his name anymore!"

"Don't tell me you're serious, Billie. I think it's pretty obvious that I can't stand him. He's arrogant. And obnoxious. And he cares too much about how things look."

"Of course he does, Jule, he's an actor. He makes his money off of looks."

"No, but I mean, my looks, too. It's this weird, fucked-up trophy girlfriend thing."

"Except you're the booby prize."

"Fuck you. Why are you sticking up for him? Whose side are you on, here?"

"Well . . . look at it from my point of view, Jule. Which one of you is more likely to lend me a million dollars when I can't make my rent?"

She laughed and poured another generous drink.

"You are such a dumbass, Julie. You know I'm just kidding, don't you? I think Chad Downing is a completely self-centered moron. I'm not sticking up for him, just rattling your chain."

"Hmph."

"I do like all the royal treatment, though. You think I could wrangle some Dior for my birthday?"

"Hmph!"

"Oh, come on, it's no fun to tease you if you're going to get all pissy. Here you go, sunshine." She handed me the drink she'd just poured and quickly mixed herself another, raising the glass to the roof of the limo.

"Ahem. A toast, Miss Julie Jorlamo. Here's to you being utterly fantastic, even though you're not really a famous person and your whole life is a charade. Drink up."

She's so twisted.

But she makes a damned fine cocktail.

"*Aaaaah.* Thanks, Billie. You know, I haven't had a real drink in weeks. Chad always makes me drink white zinfandel when we go out."

"Oooh, another reason to hate his guts."

"No, but seriously, I don't even get a chance to order! He just snaps his fingers and I'm stuck with girlie wine for the rest of the night."

"Weird. Maybe he thinks you like it."

"That can't be it. He doesn't care what I like."

"Hmm. Can I smoke in here?"

"I don't know. Yeah, just go ahead."

She lit up. "Speaking of what you like, how's that guy from work?"

"Oooooh, Tyler?" I slumped back against the leather seat and promptly spilled half my drink down my shirt. "He's sooooo hot."

"Yeah? He like you?"

"Oh, I totally blew it. Didn't I tell you? It's such a disaster."

"What? What happened?"

"He found out about Chad and he got pissed because I've been leading him on."

"Leading him on?"

"Yeah, I told him I didn't have a boyfriend, and then he saw me with Chad on the front page. He got really mad at me. Called me a liar. You know, you never realize how much you like a guy until he's pointing out your character flaws in the middle of a pet store."

"So . . . tell him what's really going on! I'm sure he'd understand."

"What, tell him that I'm only pretending to be Chad Downing's girlfriend? He'd think I was a total nutcase. Besides, he won't come anywhere near me."

"He doesn't come in anymore?"

"Well, no, he does, but he sits in Kylie's section."

"Wait, he still comes into the restaurant?"

"Yeah."

Billie grinned and lit up another cigarette. "Well then he likes you. He likes you so much he can't stay away. You've got to do something about this!"

"What can I possibly do?"

"Well you like him, don't you?"

"If by 'like him' you mean, 'want to ride him like a circus pony and spend the rest of my life rolling his socks,' then, yes."

"Then it'll work itself out."

"Billie, the last time I liked a guy and it 'worked itself out,' I ended entrapping myself in a fictional relationship with a stuck-up celebrity who makes bad movies and thinks he can score a record deal for farting in time to 'Afternoon Delight.' "

"Really? Ew!"

"I live the glamorous life, huh? Oh, here's my building. Come on, we've got to be back on the road in an hour."

In record time we were dolled up, boozed up, and ready to cause a scene. (Totally Phil's fault; he sent over a huge bottle of Bombay with a note that said, "Have fun, Plumpkin. Remember, you're not driving!" I think he was itching for some drama to stir things up in tomorrow's *Beacon*.)

The party was at some underground nightclub not too far from my building. Lately it's been the thing to rally in obscure hot spots that are totally antithetical to the people who attend them. So, celebs flock in droves to decrepit factory buildings and rickety abandoned buffet restaurants, the perfect deterrent to the unwanted little people. I guess that's how I found myself staring up at the shell of what was once a fish-gutting warehouse, evidenced by the decaying sign that still swung from hinges above the entrance.

"Um, Jule?" Billie said weakly. "Are you sure this is it?"

"Nope."

"It's just that, you know, this isn't really what I imagined a Hollywood party would be like. I mean, there's no red carpet."

"Nope."

"There's no photographers."

"Nope."

"There's . . . nobody else here."

"Nope."

"Are you sure Phil's not fucking with you?"

"Nope."

I turned around to ask the limo driver if he was sure about the address, but the motherfucker was peeling away from the curb like a bat out of hell. Probably didn't want to be the only witness when Billie and I were skinned alive and sodomized by the gang members who shacked up across the street.

But wait . . . what's that noise . . . ?

Billie started to speak, but I held my hand up and shook my head, straining to hear. . . .

Sure enough, it was the remote thump-thump-thump of techno music.

"We must be close." I turned to her. "Come on, let's go in."

She looked at me like I'd just asked her to eat a pickled turd.

"Are you fucking kidding me? You want me to go in *where*? In *there*?"

"Can't you smell that? It smells like—"

"Death?"

"It smells like food, Billie, like sausage or something. This must be it."

"Smells like fucking guts to me," she huffed. "Fucking fish guts. And little girl guts. Fucking A."

I grabbed her by the hand and led her to the door.

Which swung open.

"Mees Jorlamo!"

A pasty man in a sparkly purple Jester's outfit sprung from out of nowhere and tossed a handful of glitter at my face.

"*Iiieeeeeeeeeeeeee!!!!*" In a flash, Billie was wielding an economy-size can of pepper spray and was crouched in front of me like a Technicolor panther, ready to pounce.

"*Non, non, non!*" the Jester cried, throwing his hands up to protect his eyes. "I am eere to welcome you to ze partee! You are eere for ze Mardi Gras, no?"

Billie lowered her arms.

"Come een! We ave been waiting for you!"

He bowed deeply, and held open the heavy door.

It was like entering French Oz. Complete with the munchkins.

"This is more like it," Billie whispered in awe.

Little people in iridescent pantaloons were scampering around all over the place, wielding trays of crawfish and crystal goblets of jambalaya. Some were wearing papier-mâché masks festooned with ribbons and gigantic phallic chins and noses, turning cartwheels and tossing beads at ir- ritated A-listers. The place was a vision of purple and green, bursting with confetti and twinkling lights, be- decked, I imagine, to recreate Bourbon Street festivities. Everyone was dressed to the nines, even the teen starlets who kept lifting up their designer tank tops to flash their goods. One redheaded sitcom darling, already stacked to the gills with gaudy plastic baubles, kept chasing this one midget around, taunting him with her chest.

"Lookie here, little guy!" she slurred. "Gimme those teddy bear beads and I'll let you pinch my boobie!"

"Claaassy," I muttered to Billie, who handed me a snifter brimming with green liquid.

"Ten bucks you'll be doing the same after a few of these!" she giggled.

"What is it?"

"I think it's absinthe."

"It's . . . what?"

"Dude, just drink it. It's totally illegal in this country."

Rock on. I sipped. My mouth was consumed by pungent licorice, which stung like hell on the way down.

"Nasty." I shuddered.

So of course, I took another one.

And that was the beginning of the end.

The rest of the night was pretty blurry, but I'm pretty sure I did the following: flashed my tits to a reporter from the *Beacon*, danced on the bar with Billie and showed off my Strawberry Shortcake panties, ate an entire king cake, spent half an hour sucking the heads off of crawfish with some fucked-up rock singer, tried to stuff a midget up my dress, blew spit bubbles at the teen queens, smoked two packs of menthols, and threw up in Katarina Conrad's hair. (Ha.)

I guess Phil got what he asked for.

I awoke the next morning to six banshees trying to squeeze themselves out of my eardrums, crawfish doing step aerobics in my stomach, and my phone ringing off the fucking hook.

Beeeeeeeep, wailed my answering machine

"Plumpkin, what have you done? Check out the *Beacon*, front page, and then pages four, six, eighteen, nineteen, and twenty-four. You little rascal."

Beeeeeeeep

"*Caaaaaauuuunggggh*. Hey Jule, it's—*caaaaaaauuuuunnnggghhhh*—me. Just wanted to make sure you got home okay. When I left, you—*caaaaauuuunnnggghhhh*—were still scavenging the leftover drinks on the bar. *Caaaaaaaaaaaauuuunnnnggggghhhh*. I think I'm in a hotel with Axl Rose. Call me later."

Beeeeeeeep

"Julie Jorlamo, your father and I are *beside* ourselves. Oy, what were you thinking? I just hope Chad hasn't seen the papers yet, poor young man. I'm at kickboxing until two. Wash your face; you looked like hell in the paper."

Beeeeeeeep

"Plumpkin, me again. Listen, I just had a call from *Vogue*, and another from E!—they can't get enough of you! Apparently, you were the life of the party last night. Well done, well done, my dear. You're gonna be huge. Bigger than Chad—but don't tell him I said that. Call me."

Beeeeeeeeeep

"Hello Julie, this is Chad. Looks like you did just *fine* without me. I heard all about it from Katarina this morning. She's been at the salon since seven-thirty, trying to get the smell out. I really don't appreciate—well, why don't you just get out of bed and take a shower. Meet me for lunch at one."

Sigh. I rolled out of bed, almost puking on Riley as I groped on the floor for my slippers. He raised an eyebrow at me.

" 'Morning, boy," I croaked. It's a bad sign when your breath is so bad that even the dog backs away in horror.

Coffee. Coffee coffee coffee coffee coffee.

I made a pit stop in the bathroom to disinfect my mouth with Listerine, and then stumbled to the kitchen.

Hm, wonder if the paper's here yet?

I threw back the front door, and was greeted by a gigantic picture of myself, staring drunkenly up from the welcome mat.

JOYFUL JORLAMO, The headline screamed. WHERE HAS SHE BEEN ALL OUR LIVES?

Huh?

I frantically scanned the article, flipping through the entire paper in disbelief.

THE DAILY BEACON

JUMPIN' JULIE JIVES THE NIGHT AWAY

Who knew that Julie Jorlamo was so much fun? Chad Downing has finally stopped reining in his better half, much to the delight of the famous attendees

at last night's *Cajun Persuasion* fund-raising extrav-
aganza. Ms. Jorlamo, joined by longtime gal-pal Billie Twix (keep your eye out for this one, folks),
outsparkled every jewel on every actress in sight,
dazzling the crowd with her wit, spunk, and refreshing devil-may-care attitude. It was great to see
Chad's mystery woman finally let loose and be herself. The only mystery remaining? What this dynamic dame sees in dreary Downing.

Shit. Unbelievable.

Phil was right. I made an absolute asshole out of myself
last night, and look where it got me. Terrific front page
press, extolling me and totally ripping Chad apart.

Lunch, like my photo spread, would not be pretty.

 Twenty

I ran late for lunch, thanks to a stubborn crawfish shell that wouldn't come out of my teeth. I had a little trouble finding the place; Asian Invasion, the latest "it" spot wedged among its peers on Sunset. Like last night's venue, this café was so exclusive, it wasn't even forthright about being a restaurant, but rather, fronted itself as a Chinese laundry. The first floor was nothing but rows of tired looking washers bedecked with handmade "out of order" placards. Wannabe patrons were screened from hidden cameras, and if you passed the notoriety test, a rickety door at the back of the laundry would swing open, revealing a marble staircase. Climbing the steps, I felt like Miss Scarlett, creeping through the secret passage on my way to bludgeon Colonel Mustard.

The fragile looking hostess greeted me with a bow.

"Ah, Mees Jorlamo. You are remove shoes, then you are follow me, okay?"

You are follow . . . oh. Duh.

"Thank you," I muttered, kicking off my sandals and feeling gigantic as I waddled behind the snapdragon.

We padded through a spacious dining room, bedecked with flickering lanterns and ivory hummingbirds. The crimson silk carpet lapped at my feet as I wove past the dining tables, shielded by delicate rice paper screens. Geisha girls darted, pantherlike, about the restaurant, pausing to flirt silently with gaping gentlemen.

"Mr. Chad here already. Out in sunshine. Sunshine is okay?"

Sunshine is . . . "Chad's here?"

Chad operates within his own narcissistic time zone. He usually proposes a meeting time, but really just uses it as a guideline. But nobody complains. I learned very quickly that nobody minds waiting for Chad Downing to show up.

So it surprised me that he was here already. True, I was fifteen minutes late, but I expected to be left waiting for at least twenty more.

She led me to exquisite paper *shoji* doors and slid them open, revealing a balcony with a glaring view of the boulevard and a cluster of petrified wood dining tables surrounded by bamboo thrones. Contrary to the intimate theme of the restaurant, these tables offered a ghastly view of traffic and passersby, and, even less appealing, offered *them* a view of *us*.

Chad sat stirring a gimlet, staring into space.

I cleared my throat.

"Oh. Hey." He half smiled, tipping his chin up toward me.

I obliged, pecking him on the lips, which were fuller than usual.

Chad glanced at the lingering hostess, "Oh come on," he hissed, "try to look like you mean it, for God's sake."

I sighed, held my breath, and pressed my lips to his. He tasted like onions and saline.

I broke off the half-assed kiss and whispered, "The cameras aren't on us *all* the time, you know. And did you get some work done, or what? Is that why I had to go alone last night?"

"Actually," he began, but was interrupted by a perky teenage waitress who practically trilled a hello.

"Ms. Jorlamo! Welcome to Asian Invasion. Like, I'm Kippy." Kippy? "And it's my pleasure today to make sure that you, like, have everything you could possibly need! I've already been watching over your wonderful boyfriend—no, it's my pleasure, Mr. Downing! Now, what may I get you to drink? Like, on the house, of course."

Chad looked annoyed. "Just bring her a white zin."

Kippy floated away before I had a chance to correct him.

"Have a good time last night?" he started, with a sneer, but I cut him off.

"I am perfectly capable of ordering for myself," I hissed, "and why the fuck do you always make me drink white zinfandel? I hate that girlie shit!"

"Because you're a waitress and a commoner, Julie, and commoners don't know a damned thing about wine, so they drink what looks pretty and sounds exotic. I swear, women hear 'zinfandel' and they think it's a utopic French elixir."

"Be that as it may," I snarled, "*I* would prefer a Bombay and tonic."

"Too classy, Julie. Don't forget who you are."

"You mean, don't forget who I'm supposed to be?"

Chad yawned. "Same thing."

His cell phone screeched from the confines of a Gucci backpack.

"Hello? Yeah. Yeah, she is. Nope. No. Uh-huh. Okay. Phil says hi." He set the phone next to his napkin and rested his forehead in his hand, rubbing his temples and wincing.

"Oh, great. Is he going to be at the premiere on Tuesday? I need to ask him about this manicurist I heard about."

"Julie, you do *not* need a fucking manicure. You're a *waitress*, for Christ's sake. What do you think that's going to *look* like?"

I was tempted to reach across the table and squeeze the Botox out of his new lips, but Kippy chose that moment to set a tumbler of pink wine in my way.

"So, are we, like, ready to order? We have a totally excellent salmon special today. It's got, um, those little green things on top . . . what are they, like, coppers?"

"Capers," I said through clenched teeth.

"Capers." Chad looked amused. "Do they serve those at Junebugs, honey? You girls pick up so much knowledge at your jobs, I'm a little jealous! The only thing I ever learn on set is how many sugars it takes to make the craft services coffee tolerable!"

"Oh, honey," I spat, "you know how we waitresses are. We don't have lines to memorize, or outfits to plan, or really anything important to remember, so we just fill our little brains with bits and pieces!"

"Yes." Good, he looked pissed.

"Yes, *honey*," he continued, "your cache of useless trivia never ceases to amaze me." He turned to Kippy. "I'll have the salmon, and just bring the lady a grilled cheese."

I slammed my menu shut, "You have got to be *fucking* kidding me," I snarled.

Kippy giggled nervously.

I narrowed my eyes. "Do you really believe that 'the common people' only eat processed cheese and Wonder bread?"

"Julie—"

"No, do you actually, honestly think that a lowly, dirtbag waitress would go to a restaurant and order a motherfucking *grilled cheese sandwich*? You have no *fucking* idea about what it's like to be the other 99.9 percent of the population, do you?"

"Julie—"

"Do you, like, want me to come back?" Kippy asked.

"No. Chad, shut your six thousand dollar mouth for ten seconds. I can't believe you think you're *so* highly elevated over everyone else on the planet that you're the only person in the entire world who knows how to order off of a god-damned menu. Like you're the only motherfucker on the planet who has any class, any clue at all. Grilled cheese. Grilled cheese sandwich my ass. I'll take the almond-encrusted snapper, Kippy. And start me off with Peking foie gras, ginger oysters, and a motherfucking Bombay and tonic. Take this pink sugar water out of my sight. You got that?"

". . . Yes ma'am."

Kippy bolted from our table, and raced back in thirty seconds with my drink, still giggling. Chad leaned back in his bamboo throne and peered at me.

"How did you know? Did Phil tip you off? That fucking prick. I'm still pissed about his little Mardi Gras scheme."

"Did Phil—-what?" I sputtered, still livid, "What do you mean, tip me off?"

"Because that was great, Jule, I mean, wow! That plays in perfectly."

What was the arrogant prick talking about?

"Chad, what are you talking about?"

"Great prelude. I mean, I was going to start a fit about how you've been cheating on me, leaving me home alone while you cavort around, but we can run with this, too! Nice approach. Doesn't give me as much sympathy, of course, but nice angle. From the wrong side of the tracks, touchy about the crossover. It's an old trick, but it works."

"Cheating on you—-what? What do you mean, nice approach?"

"Julie, doll, do me a favor and take a look around. No, I don't mean at the pretty lanterns or the geisha models, I mean take a look at where we are. Nothing? Hello? We're on the *veranda*, Julie."

"So?"

"So, what have I said six million times about going out in public?"

I thought about it. "Outside dining breeds inside information."

"Exactly. Only sit outside at a restaurant if you want the whole world to know who you're fucking and what you're digesting. Now, why do you think I chose this particular luncheon to park it on display?"

"I—I don't know."

He smiled. "Look across the street, Julie."

I squinted into the afternoon sun and followed his gaze down to the row of luxury cars parked across the way. Behind the Benzes and the Bentleys lurked a swarm of photographers, lined up like soldiers and poised to shoot.

"Wow, that's—a lot. More than usual."

Chad grinned. "I made a few calls. Now, why do you suppose they're here?"

"Well, Chad, probably because Hollywood's most popular couple is enjoying a rare meal in the public eye. Those shots will be worth a ton. I wish you had told me, I would have brought lipstick."

"No, no, you look like Lolita in that Maybelline cherry shit you wear. Besides, it's not the lunch they're excited about."

Sigh. I'm so tired of his little mind games. He needs another outlet, like a Rubik's Cube or a kid or something.

I took a long pull of my gin.

"Okay, Chad. Why are they excited?"

"Because Hollywood's most popular couple is breaking up today."

Say what?

"Excuse me?"

"Great location, huh? The trendiest new café in Holly-wood; full bar, stellar menu, and the lighting is fucking per-fect, no? We'll look great. Well, I'll look great. You're going to be crying and ranting and stuff."

Or weaving his shrimp lips shut with my cocktail fork.

"Would you like to offer me some sort of explanation?" Goddamnit, my eyes were brimming over. Why was I cry-ing? This is pretend, Julie. Pretend!

"Oh, dumpling, are you tearing up?" He rolled his eyes. "That's sweet. Do me a favor, just swivel to the left a little, okay? Actual streaming looks better from dead on."

"I'm serious, Chad. I mean, what the fuck? I've done nothing but plump up your image for the past two months, and this is the thanks I get? You're dumping me? And you invited the press?"

"First of all, I'm not *really* dumping you, because we were never *really* going out. Remember? Fantasyland? Hello? Secondly, it's the image that's the problem, turns out. The public does love you, that's for damned sure. Frankly, they love you a little too much. And after last night's fiasco—I mean, you're even making headlines when I'm not with you, which is a total fucking disaster. Jesus, Phil should never have sent you there by yourself. I knew this would get out of control. You've been trying to upstage me from the fucking beginning."

I get it.

"So . . . you're 'breaking up' with me because . . . I'm getting too much attention? Oh my God, you're jealous? Jealous . . . of me? Ahahahahahahahahaha!"

"Let's not get ridiculous."

"No," I stabbed my finger at his face, "you're ending this whole fucking facade because people like me more than they like you! *You're* an A-list superstar, and *I'm* a bottom-feeding waitress, and people like *me* more than they like *you*! I mean, this is priceless!"

"Well, I'm glad someone thinks it's funny."

"You just don't get it, do you?" I sniffed. "Have you learned nothing from this entire charade?"

Chad rolled his eyes and glanced at his watch. On the street below us I could hear the popping of flashbulbs and an excited chatter.

"What was I supposed to learn, Julie? That the underdog wins every time? Please. People don't want grit, they want glamour! They want style, they crave something superhuman."

"Well, apparently not."

"That's *exactly* what it is. Do you think people would be following you around in droves if you were just a waitress? Huh? Do you think people want your picture because you look cute in a fucking headband? It's because you get to go to premieres, Julie, wear fancy gowns, and be at the elbow of a superstar. Your life was totally ordinary, and now it's spectacular. You're one of them, and you get to mingle with us. That's why people can't get enough. It's because they wish they could do it, too. Get off work at five, breeze into exclusive parties by eight. Eat caviar, serve hamburgers. It's a beautiful balance of everyday and out of this world. People love you, they want to be you. And quite frankly, I'm sick of playing second fiddle to a dumpy broad who shouldn't even be in the orchestra pit."

Son of a bitch. *Son of a bitch!!*

"Well," I balled up my napkin and squeezed it with rage, "what can I possibly say to that? People like me for who I am? That's a new one. And here I am, trying my damnedest to become someone else."

I took a deep breath.

"You have this idea, Chad, this misconception, about how the world is and how people operate. But how can you possibly know? You have no idea what it's like to be anonymous, to spend your life feeling punished because you're not a fucking beauty queen. As far as you're concerned, 99.9 percent of the population exists to admire and pamper you, and the remaining point one percent are the other golden children, who laugh with you at the rest of us!"

He snorted, "You're being ridiculous."

"Am I?"

"Yes," he snapped, "because some people are meant to be leaders, Julie, and some are meant to be followers. What would you aspire to be, if it weren't for us? What would entertain you, what would be scandalous, how would you spend your miserable little day if you couldn't read about the stars, and fantasize, and envy? What would you dream about, Julie, if it weren't for celebrities?"

"I don't know, Chad, what do you dream about?"

"Huh?"

"Well, since I'm supposed to want to be 'one of you,' and since *you* already *are*, then what's the next step for you? What do you aspire to be, since you're already famous and have everything that the rest of us want?"

He looked away from me and lit a cigarette, puffing furiously.

Ah, I get it.

"You don't know," I said softly. "You feel just as anonymous as I do, because even though the whole entire world knows who you are, *you* don't."

His gaze snapped to me.

"Shut up," he said.

"You poor son of a bitch."

"*Shut up!* I am not hearing this. I am not hearing this! I didn't bring you here to preach or be insightful, or whatever it is that you think you're doing, Julie! I brought you here so that you can make your exit, the way you're supposed to—in front of the cameras, so we can have some public closure on this nonsense."

"*My* exit? But I thought you were dumping me?"

"That's right, *your* exit. Leaving me alone at the table, leaving the press with a lonely, broken man who will only garner sympathy from his audience. I don't need the press glorifying you into a fucking relationship martyr. I refuse to be upstaged again by a commoner."

"I see."

Kippy chose this moment to bring my appetizer: tawny, quivering duck liver paté lounging on a bed of seaweed. I stared.

"So, what you want me to do," I began slowly, "is to pick up this foie gras and shove it in your face. Make a scene, right? For your public?"

He looked around nervously. "Well, I don't know about in my face, Julie. I just had my lips done."

"Oh really? I couldn't tell. How about I pour my drink over your head?"

"Well, Veelan just did these highlights."

"I see."

"Maybe the foie gras . . . yeah, that's not a bad idea.

Shove it in my face like you're really mad, but do try to do it higher, you know, like near my eyes. Wait, let me make sure I have a napkin . . . okay, I'm ready. Now, don't forget, make a big scene, really redneck, you know? Make them use the telephoto."

"Sure thing. Ready?"

"Ready."

I picked up the platter of foie gras and pushed my bamboo throne back from the table. He looked so pathetic sitting there with his eyes squeezed shut, his lips like pastel garden slugs.

"Are they watching?"

I looked down at the crowd of photographers, no longer trying to hide their presence but instead clustered below the balcony like a pack of hyenas, waiting to scavenge the breakup carcass.

"Yup."

"Okay," he hissed, "now! Now!"

With one last glance at the hopeful paparazzi, I stepped over to Chad, stooped, and gave him a peck on the cheek.

"Hey, what the . . . no! *No*, what are you doing? You're supposed to . . . *Julie!!*"

I smiled and strode from the balcony, foie gras in hand. "Sorry, Chad, but I just can't help you out on this one. Made enough of a fool of myself in today's papers, don't you think?"

I could hear the hummingbird buzz of a thousand cameras whirring and clicking, Chad's face illuminated as though attacked by a swarm of fireflies. He was gritting his teeth, so mad that his eyes were percolating pissy tears.

"Look toward the cameras, Chad doll-baby," I called behind me as I charged from the balcony. "Actual streaming looks better from dead on. Oh, hey, Kippy, can I get this sucker to go?"

THE DAILY BEACON

BREAKING UP IS HARD TO DO

Looks like America's favorite duo is flying solo once again. Chad Downing and his special nobody, Julie Jorlamo, appear to have called it quits yesterday, after an unusually public luncheon at Tinseltown's newest fusion sensation, Asian Invasion. No word on who broke it off, but Downing was noticeably disturbed, out of character for the Prince of Poise. Here he is, shown mere seconds post-parting, face screwed up like a gassy toddler. Jorlamo made a remarkably smooth exit, proving once and for all that the tramp is indeed a lady.

 Twenty-one

My self-satisfaction didn't last long.

The next day started out pretty normally: Riley licked my feet until I woke up, I had coffee and orange juice (with a little gin to make up for months of pink wine), and an enormous bagel with half a block of cream cheese.

Then the phone calls began pouring in.

Aaaaaarg. Fuck it. I let the machine screen them all.

Beeeeeeep

"Julie, honey, it's Mom. Listen, sweetheart, I'm so sorry to see that you and Chad broke it off. Not to mention that I had to learn about it in the *papers*, but that's beside the point, I suppose. I'm making lasagna for dinner tomorrow, honey, why don't you come over and we'll talk about it, okay? Love you, bubbie."

Beeeeeeep

"*Omigod*, Jule, it's Billie. You'll never believe who just called me . . . Betsey fucking Johnson! Omigod, she wants me to come and work for her! She said I was fabulous! Omigod!! You'd better call me, bitch! Oh, and sorry about Chad, but what the fuck do you care? Ciao!"

Beeeeeeep

"Plumpkin, what have you done? I thought we were in

this together! That motherfucker Chad, if he orchestrated this—don't worry, I'll get to the bottom of this, my little éclair. Keep your weight up, dumpling, we'll have you back on track in no time."

Beeeeeeep

"Mith Jorlamo, thith ith your both, Thtuart. You were thcheduled to work thith morning, and you are late. Get your ath down here, *now*."

Oops.

I was so damned proud of myself when I waltzed from that restaurant yesterday. It was waltzing into another restaurant, however, that brought my ego crashing to the floor.

"Look who made it into work today!" Kylie sneered when I got to Junebugs this morning. "I'm surprised you're still in town, after your big, heart-wrenching drama yesterday. Do you need a hug? How about a drink? Oooh, no, you're a Hollywood has-been now; you'll probably spiral into rehab."

"Drop dead, bitch."

She drew herself up.

"Excuse me?"

My eyes narrowed as I launched into ice queen mode.

"Drop. Dead. Bitch."

Kylie looked like I'd jammed a sourball up her ass.

"Stuart! Stuart!"

The dwarf came running. Waddling, actually.

"What?"

"Stuuu-art, Julie called me a bitch! In front of customers!"

He looked me up and down, coolly.

"Watch it, Mith Jorlamo. Now that you're wathed up, I don't think the dithtrict manager will give a thit if I fire your lazy ath."

"Stuart, if you don't stop talking about my ass, I'm going to slap you with a sexual harassment complaint, you fucking porker. How do you think the *dithtrict* manager will feel about that?"

"You're *puthing* it, Julie!"

"Yeah, yeah, get out of my way. I have tables."

Kylie snorted.

"Right, like you're going to get tables after the rest of us starved for two months. Go roll some silverware."

"You can't refuse to seat me!"

"Oh yeah? Just watch us."

Arg. So now I'm stuck here with nothing but grunt work to do?

You know what? Fuck this.

I yanked off my apron resolutely and was storming out the front door when Dixie caught me by the elbow.

"Where do you think you're going? Walking out, or what?"

"Um, I guess."

"Well, Jeeze, at least watch the front for me first so I can have a smoke!"

"Uh . . . sure."

And she was gone. For a sixty-year-old woman, she sure can hoof it when she's got nicotine on the brain.

It's a vicious cycle, I tell you. I try to leave, and get sucked right back in.

I shuffled my feet for a few minutes.

Nobody was coming in. Quite a change from the other day, when they were lined up out the fucking door to see me. Ah, fame. It's a fickle thing.

I began to sift through the menus, just to pass the time. They were all mixed up; inside out and folded wrong, and covered in Junebugs crust. Ick.

The door jangled. Finally, something to do. I plastered a smile on my face and looked up, ready to greet and seat.

Or have a heart attack.

It was Tyler.

"Uh . . . uh . . ." I stammered, absolutely dumbfounded. He's here, he's here! Oh my God, he hates me. What should I say?

"Uh . . . hey. Hi! You're here! Uh, you're here . . . for lunch. Of course. Where do you want to sit? Kylie? In Kylie's? Kylie's section? Let me grab a menu . . . oops!"

In my haste to get him seated, I bumped into the hostess stand and knocked it over. The pile of menus plummeted into a tangled mess on the floor. Smooth move, Jule.

Tyler chuckled.

"Well, at least fame and fortune haven't spoiled your charm. I don't care where I sit, Julie. How about one of your tables, just for old times' sake. I see you're not running around like a chicken on speed today."

"Yeah, no. No one's even asked for me. I'm not that upset about it."

"About what? The customers? Or everything else?"

A-hem.

"Why don't I put you at table twelve? That's a great table. Right by the window. Come on."

I led him to a table in the far corner of the restaurant, hoping that Kylie didn't see me sneak Tyler in. I at least wanted to apologize before he was inundated with her breasts and Catholic school giggle.

He sat. We stared.

"So, um, can I get you a drink? Something cold? Or hot? Or . . . whatever?"

He looked uncomfortable, so I just kept rambling.

"We have root beer, lemon-lime, diet—you must know

this by now!—milk shakes, floats, frappes, malts, freezes, ices. Or, you know, tea, coffee, hot choc—"

"Julie?"

I stopped.

"Yeah?"

"Why didn't you tell me?"

Um.

"Tell you?"

"You know. About you. And him. And . . . you two."

"Tyler!!" a banshee warbled from behind me. "Oh my God! I didn't even see you come in! How did you end up all the way over here?"

Kylie. Fucking she-beast.

"Julie," she continued in her saccharine trill, nudging me out of the way while she plopped her elbows on Tyler's tiny table, "what did we talk about before? They need you in the kitchen!"

"I've got this one, Kylie."

She swiveled her head. I swear she could have made the entire 360 degrees if Tyler hadn't been watching.

"I said," she hissed through her teeth, "they *need* you in the *kitchen*."

"You know what, Kylie?" Tyler chimed in. "If you're going to be my waitress, that's fantastic. Because I sure could use a hot coffee right now. And a milk shake." He winked at me. "Could you grab those for me? I'm just parched."

Oooh, did she look pissed. "Sure, sweetie," she gritted, and waggled her ass all the way back to the kitchen.

"Did you want fries with that shake?" I joked halfheartedly when she had walked out of earshot.

"Not with *that* shake." He shuddered. "Has the girl heard of mouthwash?"

Ooh, score one for the girl who brushed her teeth today.

"Julie—" he began.

"No, Tyler, let me go first. I'm sorry. I'm really, really sorry. I should have—-I don't know. I shouldn't have even—I don't know."

"No, no, I overreacted. I mean, look at me, I've been acting like a fucking stalker! No wonder you didn't want anything to do with me. I show up at your work all the time, I sit in your section for hours, I keep you from making any money. I've been thinking about it, and I can't blame you for keeping stuff from me. It's really none of my business!"

"No, but the thing is, Tyler—"

"Here we go!" Kylie chirped in a singsong voice. "Piping hot coffee and a *strawberry* milk shake! Your favorite! Oh, Julie, *you're* still here. Didn't I tell you to go in the kitchen? Huh? Like, five minutes ago?"

"We're right in the middle of something here, Kylie."

"The only thing you should be in the middle of is dishes, Hollywood. Or do I need to grab Stuart again?"

"Hey, you can grab Stuart all you want. I mean, that's your business. But I'm trying to have a conversation here!"

The she-beast spewed forth a guttural moan, eyes flashing with wrath as her spite was transfigured to absolute, primal hatred.

"You goddamned, motherfucking cu—"

"Hey, Kylie," Tyler jumped in once again, "I'm starving. Could you order me a burger, please? Medium-well. You know how I like it, yeah?"

Oooh, thar she blows.

"Wowwww," Tyler whistled as Kylie stormed away toward the kitchen, "I didn't know the human complexion actually had the pigment to turn that color."

"Ha. Hahahahaha. Um, ha. Um, Tyler . . ."

Jesus, I was bad at this whole "talking to boys" thing.

Tongue-tied, I shuffled my feet and waited for a moment of brilliance.

And waited.

Yep, still waiting.

Oh, fuck it.

"Tyler, I'm really, really sorry. I really like you, and I should have been honest, but I don't even know what the truth is anymore." Deep breath. "And I thought you liked Kylie and I didn't care but then when I saw you at the pet store I got all confused and I didn't know what to say because you looked so *mad* and you *should* be mad, but you really shouldn't because it's not what you think and if I could just explain, then I think you'd get it, or maybe not but I just want a chance to at least tell you, so then you could decide if you want to believe me or not, but you *have*tobelievemebecauseI'm tellingthetruth even-thoughyoudon'tknowthatbecauseyoudon'treallyknow meand—"

"*Julie!*"

Gulp.

The livid roar came from somewhere below me, so I knew it was only Stuart. But still, his cry was so infuriated, so downright fucking visceral, that I actually stopped, mid-sentence, and spun around.

Or was spun around, to be more precise; the hobgoblin had clamped his fingers into the meaty chunk masking my bicep.

He was practically foaming at the mouth.

"Wow, when was your last rabies shot, Stuart?"

Oooh, not a good time for jokes.

"Julie. Kitchen. *now*," he spat.

I glanced down at Tyler out of the corner of my eye. I

wondered if he'd jump in and save me. After all, I was being pinched by a midget with a viselike grip.

Nope, he was just laughing. I wondered what was funnier: my swifty, airhead monologue, or this mildly abusive episode of physical comedy?

Eh, what the hell. I didn't move a muscle.

"Thith ith inthubordination! Thith ith inthurrection! Thith ith motherfucking mutiny! Get your ath in the kitchen *right now*!"

Ha ha, this was physical comedy, no doubt. He was hissing like a fucking rattlesnake.

"What did I tell you about my ass, Stuart?"

"Get in the fucking kitchen!"

"*Stuart!*" I gasped in mock horror. "There's a *customer* present!"

"Don't you thath me, mithy!"

"Don't what?"

"Thath me!"

"I'm sorry, one more time?"

"Tha—*don't you talk back to me!! I'm your both!!*"

Tyler was now convulsing with silent laughter.

"Stuart, I'm not going anywhere with you, so you might as well just *fuck off*."

His nostrils the size of dinner plates, Stuart drew himself up, clearly trying to assume a stance of authority.

"You. Are. *Fired*!"

Ha *ha*, fired, am I?

"Oh no. You can't fire *me*, Stuart! You can't fire me, because I haven't done anything!"

Ooh, what a setup!

And now the pièce de résistance . . . I yanked my arm away from Stuart's clutches and grabbed Tyler's milk shake from the table.

No hesitation.

It was spectacular; pink and coagulated, and just *oozing* down Stuart's face, right into his sweaty collar.

"There!!" I screamed. "There, *now* you can *fire* me!!"

FREEEEEEEEEEEEDOM!!!!

I *pranced* out of that hellhole like a prize-winning pony, leaving perplexed customers, sour waitresses, a pathetic patsy, and a fuming ex-superior in my regal dust.

I was lighting a celebratory cigarette and savoring the satisfying crunch of googly antennae underneath my ortho-pedic waitress shoes when . . .

"So just like that, you're going to spill your guts, cause a scene, and then take off?"

I looked up in surprise, my lungs filled with nicotine and my heart filled with . . . something else.

"Well," I said feebly, "it seems to be my style to make an ass of myself and leave you reeling with no explanation."

"I've noticed that."

I looked into his smiling eyes, and just breathed for a minute.

Finally . . .

"So . . . what took you so long to chase after me?"

He laughed. "Your boss was in such shock after you dumped that shake on him, he wouldn't even speak, just stood there and stammered like an idiot. I had to practically fork-lift him so I could get out here!"

"I could have been gone by now."

He took a step closer.

"But you're not."

And closer.

"Lucky for you."

His face was so close I could count his eyelashes.

"Lucky for me . . ."

Oh my, he smells good.

"So, um, Tyler, about that day in the pet store?"

"Uh-huh?"

"What were you going . . . Were you going to ask me out?"

"I was going to ask you to dinner."

"Oh. Well, um, did you, um, do you still want to go?"

"No."

What?

"Oh. Oh, well then—"

He traced a finger lightly down my cheek.

"I was thinking breakfast instead. You're busy tonight."

Oh, mm, um, oh boy.

THE DAILY BEACON

JOHN DOH!

Chad Downing is officially unemployed! His career has been left for dead by producers of the barely anticipated *John Dough*. Claiming "creative differences," Studio SlickFlicks released Downing from his $7 million contract on Wednesday. Apparently, the haggard heartthrob has been pulling some shady antics since his highly publicized breakup with the adorably incognito Julie Jorlamo, showing up late for set calls and picking catfights with his costars. It seems that director Sol Solstein finally had enough. Downing's only comment? "Solstein's a genius. Happy Easter!" This is only the latest in an ugly string of calamities for Downing, whose longtime publicist, Phil Goldbergsteinman, unexpectedly quit two weeks ago, calling his former boss "a snobby little prick." Meanwhile, the jilted Jorlamo seems to have recovered quite nicely. Here she's pictured smooching her newfound love, a fellow unknown (with a killer smile) named Tyler.

Want More?

Turn the page to enter
Avon's Little Black Book —

the dish, the scoop and the
cherry on top from
SARA FAITH ALTERMAN

Dish Duty:
An Insider's Guide to the
Restaurant Realm

Waiting tables should be a mandatory rite of passage for every single person coming of age in the modern world. Or, at least, everyone who lives in countries with restaurants.

Working in a food service environment teaches valuable life lessons that, really, can only be rivaled by the cool, gritty wisdom of a Kenny Rogers tune. When you wait on angry customers, squabble with angry coworkers, and explore the depths of your own personal anger on a daily basis, you get to thinking about human nature and how, naturally, we're angry.

Just what is everyone so pissed off about? I can't speak firsthand for the customers (though I suspect it has something to do with inflation. Have you noticed the sky high price of chicken fajitas?), but as for me, let me tell you: for two dollars an hour I get covered in food, written up for not having my shirt tucked in, and spend at least twenty minutes a night listening deadpan while an octogenarian with the pipes of a football coach screams at me about the temperature of his meat.

It has to be done, though. Waitressing can be some of the best money you'll ever make in your life, even though every minute that ticks by while you're clad head to toe in honey mustard and flair feels like an entire Oliver Stone special edition director's cut DVD. But if you bust your ass enough, you can make enough money in one week to cover your rent, half a car payment, and two trips to a nudie bar, if you're into that kind of thing. Which I'm not. I spend the extra dubs on the dollar menu at the drive-through burger joint near my apartment.

Waitresses
Coffee, Tea, or Misery?

I've begun to look at my job in the same way that I regard ex-boyfriends.

The parallels are endless and amazing.

I know I can do so much better than waiting tables.

I know that whenever I'm working at a restaurant, I'm just upset all the time, I don't really act like myself, I can never really relax.

I know it's not healthy, that there are other places I could work that would appreciate me for who I am, for my individuality and independence.

And yet, no matter the hardship, no matter the emotional roadblocks, I keep going back. It's just so hard to stay away. It's tough love, but it's accessible love. And there's something so gratifying about that.

Over the years, I've developed a working model, some coping mechanisms for dealing with the job that I hate to love, and hate to hate. Variations on basic Darwinism, really, but they've worked out for me. My occupational skin is tougher than the steak at a pancake house; I can't be rattled.

The primary guideline for working in a restaurant is apathy. Don't *hate* the people who bark at you about the amount of seasoning on their onion rings; just don't *care* about them. Hate leads to stress, which leads to ranting, which leads to a whole lot of drama over something that should never have even been an issue in the first place. When you get upset about whatever it is that a customer is upset about, you sink to their level. And you don't want to do that. I don't care what restaurant you're working for—it isn't paying you nearly enough to justify expending any extra energy devoted to a temper tantrum, and, certainly, the five percent tip on a twenty dollar check that you're going to pull in won't cover the cost of the shrink you're going to have to see after your nervous breakdown in the kitchen. The best thing you can possibly do for yourself is to train your brain to fight disdain. Shrug it off. So you forgot some dude's extra coleslaw; don't cry about it. Please, for God's sake, don't cry about it.

Secondly, and nearly equally important to apathy, is to take up smoking. Mostly, it's a terrific way to remind yourself that you don't care about customers, about anything, really. Why else would you purposely glaze your two most vital organs with a sticky layer of tar and cancer? Because you don't care, and that's badass.

More notably, though, smoking a cigarette is really the only excuse you have to take a break when you wait tables. You can always convince a manager that you need to run outside and have a quick cigarette. It helps if the manager is a smoker himself, or, perhaps, if you begin to shake visibly once it's been more than an hour since your last nic fix. But try asking your boss if you can just step outside for a moment of fresh air? Or if you could, perhaps, just sit down in the back of the kitchen for a minute or two? It won't fly. Take a break? No! Of course you can't take a break! You're on the clock! Don't think you can waste a single cent of the Guatemalan teenager's sweatshop wage that we pay you to sweat bullets and run circles around on obstacle course of high chairs and mass-manufactured folk art. What? Oh, you're smoking a *cigarette*. Okay, but make it quick.

Of course, the danger of smoking a cigarette extends far beyond corroding the fragile pink tissue of your respiratory chambers. It's rare that you find yourself taking a smoke break *alone* during a shift, which can lead to the greatest, most perilous habit you can adopt in the restaurant business.

The grapevine game is like a vortex of cattiness. It's a powerful, magnetic black hole of gossip, presumption, and judgment that simply must, *must,* be avoided. There's always a ridiculous amount of petty personal drama that powers the staff at a restaurant. Waitress A is dating Line Cook B, who stuck his tongue down the throat of underage Hostess C when they were drunk on Pabst Blue Ribbon after a shift one night. Waitress D hates Waitress A because they both wanted to take the party of twelve that came in last week and ended up tipping forty percent on an already enormous check, as Waitress A was happy to brag about for the rest of the night. Hostess A is always flirting with Manager A, so she gets all the good daytime shifts, while Hostesses B and C are forced to spend their Friday and Saturday nights dealing with angry parents of cranky children yelling about the fifteen minute wait for a table.

It can be a little like an Olympic event, trying to keep up with all the chaotic gossip that goes down in the social bowels of a restaurant. It takes a well-toned mind and limber tongue.

Everything about your personal life is up for discussion among your fellow food servers, unless you are careful enough to keep that shit to yourself. So you have a crush on the Brazilian prep cook? Don't tell anyone; you'll be branded a slut. You're having a little financial trouble and aren't sure if you can make your Citibank payment this month? Don't tell anyone; you'll be branded a slacker. You're pregnant with the love child of a cast member of the new *Real World,* who you met at a bar one night while his season was still being filmed? Don't tell anyone; you'll be branded a liar. And then when the episode finally airs in six months, you'll be branded a slut again.

And don't make eyes at, make out with, or sleep with anyone you work with. Anyone. If the dude is enough of a gentleman to keep it to himself (which he likely won't be), then you have to be prepared for public analysis of your skills, tattoos, and personal grooming habits. God forbid, if your fling becomes an actual relationship, it will be practically impossible to keep any of your romantic issues out of the mouths and ears of your coworkers. It's best to keep the kitchen staff french fry out of your company ketchup.

Customers
Here's a Tip: Tip

When I took my first waitressing job and was still learning the ropes, absorbing the unspoken rules of the trade, I observed a lot of nasty, nasty stuff. I don't want to gross you out, but if you visit a "family" restaurant as a customer, go prepared to keep mum about mistakes with your order, unless they are grossly unbearable. Not that I condone this, but restaurant staff have been known to avenge any customer comment that they've interpreted as a personal attack by doing unspeakable things to food. I've seen hamburgers wiped on aprons, chicken cutlets dropped on the floor and sandwiched between buns that just had mold scraped from their crust. I've seen cigarette ash sprinkled on pasta, I've seen spit, I've seen hair, I've seen other unmentionable last minute additions. It isn't pretty.

Nor is it right. Obviously, you, as a patron, should have the right to complain if someone clearly fucks up your dinner. But, honestly, when I tell you that we're out of the honey peppercorn salmon special, let's keep things in perspective, shall we? I didn't just tell you that you need to have your leg amputated. I didn't just break the news that your house was hit by a meteor shower, destroying everything under its roof except your tax returns and the family heirloom tea cozy knitted from steel wool by your eccentric great-grandmother Gwendolyn. We're out of salmon. Calm the hell down. It helps to keep in mind that if the kitchen *does* manage to serendipitously locate one last piece of salmon after you've reduced your server to tears in the walk-in freezer, that salmon probably wasn't an oversight, but rather, purposely taken out of the line-up for the evening, if you catch my drift. So pick your battles, valued customer. Otherwise, you may find yourself praying to the porcelain gods, paying homage to your belly full of rot.

Are you, as a paying customer, aware that the fresh-faced young lady (or is it a dude?) serving you up a steaming slice of sweetness is actually making less money than a legless Mexican immigrant would have two hundred years ago? It's true; because restaurant employees get tips, the management feels justified in paying out between two and three dollars an hour. Of course, most of that whopping official paycheck goes to taxes. I've actually received a check for six cents. Opening that up was like tearing into a gigantic present on Christmas morning, only to discover that inside the box is a picture of the kitty you always wanted. I mean, it's *almost* a present. Just like six cents is *almost* a paycheck.

So tips are a major part of a waitress's income. True, it's unfair that customers are expected to pay the salaries of the people who wait on them, but think about it: for five dollars, you have almost total control of the person who is designated to serve the table you sit at.

You want something to drink? It appears.

You don't like it? They bring you something else.

The restaurant is too cold? Too warm? Tell your waitress! They'll adjust the temperature for you.

You didn't like the steak dinner you just ate, even though you devoured every single morsel of it except that very last scrap by the T-bone that's a little too pink for your original specifications? Just communicate that to your waitress, and she'll act as your personal liaison so you can effectively communicate your dissatisfaction to the managerial person authorized to discount or completely comp your meal.

Isn't all that worth an extra dollar or two? I know you just spent $17.95 on two Cokes and a plate of fried clams that you shared with your special friend, but the poor minion that you made run all over the place refilling your drinks and procuring extra little paper cups of tartar sauce deserves more than the $1.75 in quarters that you're going to leave in a pile on your dirty plate.

CONCLUSION
Help Me Help You

Servers and customers can learn to coexist peacefully, as long as there's mutual compassion, or, at least, mutual tolerance for imperfection. After all, dining out should be a pleasant experience, and trying to do your work should never drive *anyone* to cry in a meat locker. So go ahead, quit that financial consultant job, trash that night manager's position at the Gap, get off your couch-shaped unemployed ass and head down to your local family restaurant for an ineffective paycheck and dose of smoky indifference. You'll be happy you did.

That's a lie.

But the next time you go to dinner, you'll be happy that you don't have to experience the same drama and hardship that the bitch who slams down your chicken finger basket endures on a daily basis. Because you understand each other now, you see.

And if *you're* the bitch slamming breaded chicken strips all over the place, calm down, honey. It ain't the end of the world if the schmuck sitting at table 30 needs three more ramekins of blue cheese dressing.

And hey, there's always the chance that Kenny Rogers Roasters is hiring. Perhaps you should mosey on down there, tie on an apron, and keep things real while Kenny offers his customers *and* staff a steaming finger-lickin' helping of country wisdom.

SARA FAITH ALTERMAN

Rebecca Girolamo

SARA FAITH ALTERMAN is a regular feature writer for *NewEnglandFilm.com,* and is the associate director of distribution of *BuyIndies.com,* an independent film catalog. Since studying film theory at the University of Rochester and comedy writing with Second City, Sara has written sketch comedy for ImprovBoston and has had her work featured in publications, including *The Independent, Carolina Woman* magazine, and the Discovery Network's *Great Chefs* magazine. Sara lives in Boston, is working on her next novel, and hates writing about herself in the third person.

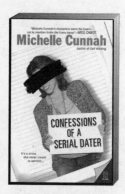